The Ridgway Women

The Ridgway Women

RICHARD NEELY

Thomas Y. Crowell Company
Established 1834　New York

Designed by Ingrid Beckman

Manufactured in the United States of America

Library of Congress Cataloging in Publication Data

Neely, Richard.
  The Ridgway women.

    I. Title.
PZ4.N375Ri [PS3564.E25]   813'.5'4   74-34347
ISBN 0-690-00748-5

    2   3   4   5   6   7   8   9   10

*To Lilyan and Harry
with love*

Books By Richard Neely

Death to My Beloved
While Love Lay Sleeping
The Plastic Nightmare
The Damned Innocents
The Walter Syndrome
The Smith Conspiracy
The Japanese Mistress
The Sexton Women
The Ridgway Women

Diane

ONE

THE FIRST WORD I ever heard Christopher Warren utter was spoken reverently inside an abandoned red-brick railroad station that had been converted into an art gallery.

"Magnificent," he said.

The word sang in my head like poetry.

"It *is* rather nice," I said, affecting a grudging tone.

He turned with a startled expression, apparently unaware that I had been standing behind him.

"Nice?" he said, mildly shocked.

I gave him what I thought was a cryptic smile. "Conventional," I said.

An exclamation point appeared between his heavy eyebrows. "The subject matter, perhaps. But not the artistry. Not by a long shot."

He pivoted away as though to deny my existence and resumed his admiration of the painting. It was an oil seascape done on a four-by-five-foot canvas. In the foreground, a towering wave had shattered into froth and spray against a huge offshore rock. In the background was a section of northern California's Mendocino coast—misted ocean, craggy cliffs, a somber headland under a pearly sky. The rock was the hero, its jagged, indomitable beauty heightened by deep blacks and grays and browns applied thickly with a palette knife. The scene had a brooding quality that matched the mood of the artist.

I knew. I had painted it, standing on the strip of beach below my house on a sullen afternoon. It had been hung only that morning to replace one that had been sold the day before.

The man stepped close to the painting and examined the price card. He was tall, erect, and square-shouldered, his hair dark and dense, short sideburns flecked with silver. The face he had turned to me was lean and tanned, and I had the impression of a long, strong-bridged nose. He wore brightly polished black loafers, dark slacks, and a brown suede jacket over a yellow sport shirt open at the throat. A Brooks Brothers' vision of today's country squire, I thought, and was suddenly conscious of my wrinkled blue jeans, drab gray sweater, and pony-tailed hair.

I watched as he strode to the table where Liz Proctor sat as that day's volunteer cashier. Her gnomelike face split in a delighted smile as he indicated the painting and whipped out a checkbook and wrote with rapid precision. No haggling, as was the custom with the weekend tourists, which made me wonder if he was a local resident.

In any case, the purchase had extended my record—three paintings sold in as many days, and each at the posted price. That was more than had been sold in the previous two months. I'd gladly have kissed the man.

The transaction completed, he returned to the painting and stood with hands on hips regarding it as he might a Wyeth. Liz Proctor followed and applied a SOLD sticker to the frame.

Turning, she noticed me standing off to the side. Her eyebrows rose in pleased surprise.

"Well," she said to the man, "how nice that you know the artist."

"I *don't* know him," he said. He had a deep, authoritative voice.

Liz looked puzzled, then grasped the coincidence and gave him an arch look. "It's not a him," she said. "It's a her."

I flapped a silencing hand. She ignored it, enjoying herself.

"D. Ridgway," he said. "I just assumed—"

"She's standing right over there," Liz said, nodding toward me, her small eyes twinkling.

He swung eagerly around, an anticipatory smile forming on his lips. It crumbled as he recognized me and a sheepish look crossed his face. Before he could speak, Liz's small, wiry frame sprang between us. She spread her arms with a little flourish and indicated each of us with a raised palm.

"Diane Ridgway," she said with mock ceremony, "may I present an admirer of yours—"

He grinned. "Christopher Warren," he said. "And I'm very much an admirer."

I murmured something polite, glad that it was Wednesday afternoon with only a few people in the gallery, and those at a distance.

He approached me, shaking a finger. "*Nice*," he said, mimicking my tone. "I felt you'd insulted my taste."

"You really do like it then?" I could never get over the fact that some people, a rare few, would actually pay money for something that gave me so much pleasure.

"I like it immensely."

"He *bought* it," said Liz. She closed one eye—her shrewd look. "I have his check for three hundred and fifty dollars."

I laughed. "You could have had it for less, Mr. Warren."

"I'd have paid more." He glanced at his wristwatch and said regretfully, "I'd hoped to bring it home today but I'm afraid it's too late."

"Too late?" Liz said. "All we have to do is take it off the wall."

"I didn't bring my car. In fact, I had no idea I'd be buying a painting today. I was out for a hike and just stopped by." He smiled at me. "Very glad I did."

The solution popped out of me without thinking: "I'd be glad to drive you. And *it*."

"Thank you, but that seems an imposition."

"Just securing the sale. No refunds once you get it home." He had a pleasant laugh.

We were sliding the canvas into the back of my Ford station wagon when I asked where he lived. He pointed inland, beyond a flowered meadow to a hillside forested with pine and redwoods.

"I'm back there in the woods. A house owned by people named Connors. I'm renting it."

I told him I knew the Connors slightly. They lived in San Francisco, where George Connors worked, and used the house for weekends and vacations, often renting it out. We got into the car.

"I gather you're just visiting," I said. He looked much too young to be retired. Mid-forties, I guessed.

"Yes. I took the house for a month." He turned his head to gaze wistfully out toward the sea. "I wish I could spend the rest of my life here."

I felt a sense of communion.

The feeling grew as we passed a ranch dotted with nibbling sheep and swung into a skinny road flanked by molting eucalyptus trees and split rail fences. He extolled the century-old Victorian houses, the rocky coves, the fragile sea life in the tide pools, the steelheading in the Gualala River, and—as we entered the forest approaching the Connors' house—the awesome majesty of the redwoods. I said little except to prompt, content to listen to such an eloquent spokesman for my own deep feelings about this land that had liberated me.

I eased the car into the rutted dirt driveway and parked behind a jeep (also rented, he said). The house was a smallish structure of unfinished redwood with a peaked roof. We both got out and I unlocked the tailgate and he gingerly slid out the painting. He held it at arm's length, smiled at it, and then at me.

"Look," he said, "why not stop in for a few minutes."

I imagined a wife inside, the explanations. "I really should get home."

"I hoped your husband was a patient man."

He was probing, knew that I knew it, and knew I approved. I stretched out a pause. Finally:

"I don't have a husband," I said.

He exhaled slowly. "You sure make a man hold his breath. All right, now ask me if my wife will mind."

"Will she?"

He grinned. "I don't have a wife."

I chided myself for feeling relief. I stared dubiously at the blue front door. "Well—"

"Come along. There are a couple of friends I'd like you to meet. In fact, I'm sure you know them."

"Friends of *mine?*"

"Yes. At least say hello."

He pushed on ahead, as if expecting me to follow. I did.

I stood inside the door while he took the painting and leaned it gently against a far wall. The downstairs was one big room with a counter separating the kitchen area. The furnishings were inexpensive—brightly slipcovered chairs and couches, throw rugs on a brown vinyl floor, a black metal corner fireplace, red curtains. Ladderlike stairs rose to a loft for sleeping.

No people. The room was half dark. I felt a stab of uneasiness. He came back, not pausing to switch on a lamp.

"Your friends seem to be out," I said. My hand crept up behind me and touched the doorknob.

"Oh no," he said. He sounded ominously casual. Gripping my elbow, he drew me into the room. I went warily, deriding my thoughts but unable to dismiss them.

"Stand there," he said as we reached the center of the room. It was a command. His eyes had an odd gleam.

Maybe he was crazy, I thought. Maybe he was wanted for passing worthless checks all over the county.

I stood rigidly as he released my elbow. He stepped back toward the front door. A switch snapped and the room lit up. I started to turn around, determined somehow to leave.

"Look straight ahead," he said.

Reluctantly I obeyed, peering at the painting he had rested against the wall. Two other canvases of about the same size stood beside it. Suddenly I was laughing, my palms pressed to my cheeks, my eyes watering.

"Our very dear friends," he said quietly.

The other two paintings were also mine—one of grebes patrolling the beach, the other of a rolling meadow bright with gorse and lupine. I owed my sudden success to one man.

"Why you—" I stopped before I said "wonderful man."

"I've become a collector of Ridgways."

"Oh, I'm so pleased." The words sounded fatuous. But there really was no way to tell him how delighted and moved I was. It was the most extravagant compliment I had ever been paid, unquestioned because of the tangible proof of its sincerity.

"Calls for a libation," he said.

We sipped sherry in front of the fire and he told me something about himself. He was a retired Colonel, United States Air Force, and for many years had been assigned to NATO, stationed most of the time in France and Germany. He had only recently returned to the States.

"And now?" I said.

"I don't know exactly. I've lived off Uncle for thirty years. It's time I found out how you civilians make it. When I leave this paradise, I'll go to San Francisco and settle down to something." He got up and poked at the fire. "I have no family."

"You never married?"

He kept his back to me. "My wife died more than a year ago." His voice sounded scarred. "What about you?" he said quickly, as if to protect himself against sympathy.

"I've been a widow for ten years."

He looked at me in surprise as he sat down. His gaze roved over my blond hair (I wished it was unlooped and falling to my shoulders), contemplated my eyes (eyeliner would have made them bluer), and seemed to study my soap-and-water complexion.

"Remarkable," he said. "You must have been a child bride."

"I'm thirty-eight," I said. It seemed important to dispel any illusions.

"No!"

"I've got a daughter who's twenty."

He shook his head in disbelief. "And I thought I was a young forty-eight."

He was and I told him so. I also told myself I'd better get out of there; the ingredients we were mixing could become combustible.

I got up to leave before he could suggest another sherry. He rose and looked at me regretfully but didn't protest. "Oh yes, your daughter."

"She doesn't live with me," I said. I didn't know where she lived.

"Married?"

"Not yet." She might be married; I had no way of knowing. The sense of loss, controlled when I was by myself, threatened to become visible under his questioning. I closed the subject by thanking him for a pleasant afternoon.

He followed me to the car and paid a final tribute to the paintings: He was glad he'd be able to bring some of this beautiful coast with him wherever he went. It was a charming little speech but not what I really wanted to hear. I wanted him to ask me where I lived. He didn't.

Driving away, I glanced into the rearview mirror and saw his hand raised in a half salute. I waved and rode my faithful Ford off into the sunset as The End printed itself on my mind.

My house as I approached it along the single-car lane stood in stark relief against the afterglow of the vanished sun. It was a fairly large, two-story structure of weathered shingles and gabled windows, landscaped by nature with Scotch broom, wild mustard, cow parsnip. On a city or suburban street, it would probably have looked hideous, but here—perched on a rocky bluff with the whole blue continent of the Pacific as a backdrop—it had, I thought, a sort of Gothic splendor.

I parked in the carport and entered through the side door that opened on the big square kitchen. The bottled-up depression that had been gathering since I left Christopher Warren was suddenly uncorked by the darkness. Quickly I flipped the wall switch, stood uncertainly for a moment in the fluorescent glare, then walked down the hall, leaving a trail of lights, and went into the living room. Never had the rafters seemed so high, the tweedy chairs and sofa so empty, the paintings crowding the paneled walls so impersonal. I poured a glass of sherry at the small bar and took it out to the deck.

The long pink-and-purple cloud on the horizon was a cliché. The stairs that descended to the beach, carved into rock and flanked by handholders of anchored steel, looked like they belonged in a medieval dungeon. The beach itself had been drowned by the tide. The waves lashed angrily at the base of the bluff. Nothing was beautiful.

I returned to the living room and started a fire in the cavernous fireplace—a symbolic act, I thought wryly, an attempt to rekindle the warmth I had reluctantly forsaken. Images of him darted about my mind. His erect posture. The humor in his eyes. The charming way he spoke. A strong hand pouring wine.

Oh, I was in a fine state. All because of a man I had known for an hour. But a man who had admired and bought my paintings, thereby demonstrating an appreciation of a lot more than sleek blond hair and oversized eyes and a tidy figure (though I hoped these hadn't gone unnoticed). To Christopher Warren, I was a person, an identity, a woman who need not depend on her sex alone to produce emotion.

Without calculation, he had stroked a yearning that had nagged at me since childhood.

My parents' notions of artists were based on stereotypes, half-truths and myths: all men painters were bearded libertines and anarchists; all women painters were promiscuous, rebellious and indifferent to personal hygiene.

I know that sounds prehistoric, but these were the kind of opinions that prevailed where I was born and raised. Picture a town so small that you could drive through it before you could say "What's that?" Plunk it down in the center of California's vast San Joaquin Valley, where the heat of the long summers shimmered like mirages above the black roads, where Mexicans and Portuguese stooped to labor in fields of artichokes and onions and sugar beets stretching flat for miles, where foliage and floors and faces were constantly coated with dust, where the young went jukin' on Saturday night and slopped white corn liquor from mason jars while the old folks drove to Merced and took in a Disney movie followed by a lemon phosphate. That was Justine in 1936, the year I was born. And that was just about Justine when I left.

My father owned a combination drugstore, ice cream parlor, and short-order restaurant. From the time I was ten I worked there summers and after school and was known as "the drugstore kid," just as others were called "the janitor kids," "the bakery kids," "the barber shop kids." My brother Jim, who was six years older than I, worked there too until he joined the army. A year later he was killed in Korea, which left me, at fifteen, an only child. I felt the loss of Jim terribly. He was the only one who encouraged me to "mess around with paint," as my parents described it, and urged me to get out of that town the moment I could.

I took over part of Jim's work as well as my own; willingly, because I could sense my father's disappointment in not having a son to carry on the business. But how I detested that store! I still feel an inner sting when I recall how the girls of my age (flirting with their boyfriends over a Coke) treated me like a dim-witted servant. And how the men diners—field hands, grease monkeys, truckers, their T-shirted underarms dark with sweat—would playfully slap my rump and make suggestive remarks as they sucked on their toothpicks. I complained once to my father but he nervously smiled it away, saying, "A man's got to act up a little now and then."

My father was not an unfeeling man. It was just that he, like his father before him, had been brought up in Justine and considered it a model of all that was right about America. He thought Cal Coolidge was our greatest president, until Eisenhower (I was in high school then), who he considered an almost supernatural figure sent by God to save us from the Communist atheists. He was also a staunch supporter of Senator Joe McCarthy, thought that San Francisco was Sodom and New York Gomorrah (the cities in between were branch offices), and that Chubby Checkers was corrupting the nation's youth with the Twist. Still, narrow as he was, I don't remember him ever saying a harsh word to me; but then I was an obedient child and kept my thoughts to myself.

My mother was a gentle, inarticulate woman who smelled of warm bread, pickles, and dish water. I don't think she ever read anything besides the Bible, and she rarely left the house except to attend church services or mourn at a funeral. The latter occurred fairly often because she didn't consider it necessary to have known the deceased. The image that sticks in my mind is of a thin, expressionless face, a lock of hair lying limp on her forehead, a smudge of flour on her cheek, a gingham apron tied around her protruding stomach. She was past forty when I was born—a "change-of-life baby," people said—and we couldn't have been more removed from each other if we'd lived on separate planets. Her whole life was dedicated to being a drudge—feeding the chickens, candling eggs, working the cream separator (we had two cows), putting up preserves, sewing and washing clothes, and catering to the appetites of a household that always included at least three boarders. We had a huge kitchen with a big iron stove, padded rocking chairs, and a long plank table covered with oilcloth, and it was there that everyone congregated. The living room ("parlor") was tacitly understood to be out of bounds, the drapes always drawn shut, except on those occasions when the church ladies, shrouded in purple and black, came to call.

I had never had a boy to the house. In fact, I had never had a boy, period. Not that my parents would have objected, though they'd have inspected him suspiciously and my father would have checked him out for three generations. It was simply that I had never met anyone who appealed to me. (They all tried to look like Sal Mineo, with pink shirts and tight black pants.) The desirable ones—the sons of packing company executives—were outside my circle, and the others—the sons of farmers and hole-in-the-wall merchants—were muscular in their attempts to make out, and vocal once they had. In my few encounters, I was more scared than offended, and turned them off by going stiff as a plank. So they labelled me a "cold fish." My, how wrong they were!

Generally, I suppose, adolescent girls express their unrequited yearnings in idolatry of movie stars and football heroes, in romantic fantasies and role playing. Mine were expressed in paint. It started with a seventh-grade class in art appreciation, progressed to dabblings in water colors, and then, with the encouragement of my teacher, burst forth boldly into oils. My parents were disdainful but protested only mildly when I announced that I was spending my hoarded allowance on tubes of paint, a palette, and brushes. In fact, my father permitted me to nail together an easel from scraps of wood in the hen house. He was somewhat grudging when I proposed setting up a "studio" in a corner of the small barn, but he went along, thinking, I'm sure, that it was no more than a passing fad. But as my interest grew with the years, he and my mother became gloomily resigned to my idiocy and never even spoke of it. When others did, they responded with embarrassed smiles, my father saying, "Better, I guess, than being boy-crazy."

I painted on every surface I could find or contrive—tautly stretched rags, pieces of wallboard, the bottoms of produce boxes, cut-up tarps. From my art teacher, Miss Cribbins, I borrowed books on the masters and on technique. Painting became a compulsion to reproduce in colorful abstractions everything I imagined and felt, but almost nothing of what I saw.

I was almost seventeen before I realized the basis of my obsession: a desperate need to escape from myself and my environment. I remembered my brother's advice to get out of that town.

In my senior year in high school I took a business course. For once, my mother's face showed a clear emotion: relief. My father bought me a portable typewriter; at last I had put away childish things and was embarked on something useful. I felt guilty accepting their approbation—the business course had been chosen merely to provide a respectable means of support for the day when I would abandon them to live in San Francisco.

A week after graduation, I quietly delivered my emancipation proclamation. It seemed a shame that anything so thoughtfully worded, so conscientiously rehearsed, should have been unnecessary. My father and mother simply looked at each other and nodded sadly. They had been expecting it for months.

Now, in retrospect, I was unpacking in the small room of the boarding house on San Francisco's Bush Street, enrolling in a night art class at Golden Gate College—when the phone rang.

"Hello. This is Christopher Warren."

"Why, *hello*."

"Forgive me for disturbing you but—"

"You're not disturbing me."

"Good. I seem to have misplaced my checkbook. I called the gallery but it's not there. They gave me your number. I wondered if I might have dropped it in your car."

"Hold on, I'll see."

I found it on the floor in the cargo space. Apparently it had slipped from his pocket when he had bent to slide out the painting.

"Not important, really," he said when I told him. "But I would like to know the figures. May I stop by tomorrow and pick it up?"

I said that would be fine and gave him directions.

"What time would be convenient?"

"About noon would be best," I said.

He must have guessed I was setting him up for lunch. His voice grew warmer:

"I'll look forward to seeing you," he said.

It was exciting to think that perhaps the checkbook had not been dropped by accident.

TWO

AND SO IT BEGAN.

He didn't stay for lunch but instead drove me in the station wagon up the coast to Mendocino City where we gorged ourselves on cracked crab washed down with cold Chablis. Afterward, we toured the village on foot, strolling along wooden sidewalks, browsing through false-front shops decorated with driftwood, peering at Victorian houses with their arched windows and gingerbread decorations and at plain New England salt boxes built by pioneer lumbermen.

"Reminds me of the Maine Coast," he said wistfully.

"Is that where you're from?"

"Yes. But I left there when I was ten. My parents were divorced and I went with my father." He smiled wryly. "And I mean *went*. He was constantly moving from one place to another. I didn't find my real home until I was eighteen."

"Where was that?"

"The army."

He must, I thought, have been as lonely as I. The rapport I felt for him quickened. Driving back, I found myself telling him about my own early years, my ambitions and frustrations. I had never confided so much to a man, not even to Fred, my husband.

"Do you see your parents often?" he asked.

"They're dead. They married late in life. Both were gone before I was thirty."

"You're an only child?"

I told him about Jim, killed in Korea. He gave me a startled look and for a few moments stared thoughtfully ahead. Finally he said, "Well, at least you have your daughter."

I nodded dumbly. I wasn't ready to go into that.

We saw each other almost every day. He shared my enthusiasm for riding and we rented horses to gallop along the beaches, roam ancient logging trails through giant redwood forests, canter across meadows aflame with April wildflowers. We hunted driftwood on deserted beaches, picnicked on the shady banks of the Gualala River, where he taught me to flycast. We wandered through the stunted pines and cypress of the pygmy forest, rode the rickety Skunk Railroad to Fort Bragg, drank steam beer in old wooden saloons. I threw a cocktail party and introduced him to all my friends, who in turn invited us to their homes. We became inseparable companions.

But no more than that. Not once had he sought to advance beyond a friendly goodnight kiss. At first I was flattered. I told myself that he respected me too much to initiate a casual affair. I reminded myself that he had lost his wife only a short while ago and was probably inhibited by a lingering loyalty. But after several chaste weeks I dismissed such pious explanations and decided that I wasn't sending out the right signals.

I started to rectify that one balmy afternoon on the beach below the house. I had set up my easel and was sketching in charcoal a group of sea lions cavorting beyond the breaking waves. Chris—it was Chris now—was stretched out on the beach a few yards behind me, smoking a cigarette and watching.

"You're really out there, aren't you?" he said.

"Out where?" I was concentrating on a line.

"Out in the ocean."

It was all the cue I needed. I dropped the charcoal and went to him, dropping down and moving my face close to his.

"You're wrong. I'm right here."

He looked at me for what seemed a long time, then tossed his cigarette aside and touched my cheek.

"You're a lovely woman, Diane."

I smiled. "Convince me."

He did. Kissing, stroking, our bodies fitting together. I knew he was as famished as I.

Then abruptly he pulled away. He stood up. I was too astonished even to feel rebuffed.

"There's something I must tell you," he said. He ran his fingers through his hair. His brown eyes appeared sunken, as though recoiling from some shocking sight.

"It sounds serious," I said.

"It is. Let's go up to the house."

Despite the sunshine, there was a chill in the house (at least it was inside me) and I lit a fire in the living room. We sat on a sofa and he stared morosely at the leaping flames for a long while.

"It's about my wife," he said finally.

Oh no, I thought, it can't be that he's bound to a ghost.

"I never told you about her," he said.

"Only that she died." I kept my voice matter-of-fact.

"Yes. You must have assumed it was from an illness."

"Wasn't it?"

"No." He hitched up on the cushion. "She was killed."

"Oh! Chris, I'm sorry." I was more startled than saddened. How strange that each of our marriages had ended in sudden death.

"*I* killed her."

I gaped at him.

"I don't mean *murdered* her. But killed her nonetheless."

It had happened on the outskirts of Paris when he had been assigned to NATO. A late party at the Officers' Club. He had drunk too much but felt capable of driving home. An abrupt curve in the road, traveled countless times. But this time cornered too fast and too sharply. A long screeching skid. A crash into a roadside stanchion. Her life had ended instantly.

He was standing when he finished, eyes fixed on the fire, hands knotted behind his back. I rushed to him and circled his waist with my arm. "Oh, my dear. It was an accident. You can't go on torturing yourself."

He just shook his head.

There was a long silence before I said, "Besides, it has nothing to do with us."

He drew away and said gently, "Somehow it does. Guilt, I guess. And apprehension. I have the feeling that a close relationship with a woman would lead to disaster. Call it a jinx complex." He waved a hand in deprecation. "I know that sounds absurd."

"No, Chris, it doesn't."

It was similar to the way I had felt for a long time after Fred's death: the thought of being intimate with another man had terrified me. But that fear had had nothing to do with superstition. Chris's notion that he was destined to cause suffering only made me determined to prove him wrong. I felt a compulsion to become an exorcist, ridding him once and for all of his demon. The method I had in mind was anything but occult. I had only to be brazen—but that took more courage than I then possessed.

"I think we should have a drink," I said.

He nodded, again gazing into the fire. It had settled into a steady glow.

I made double scotches, feeling the urgency of time running out: in less than a week his lease on the house would expire. The thought of him leaving seemed unbearable.

He accepted his glass without looking at me, still brooding over his thoughts. I sat on the sofa and in a minute he dropped down beside me. I reached for his hand and found a hard fist.

"That was the second death in the family," he said. "My son—"

"Oh, Chris!"

"Yes. In Vietnam. A grenade."

My God! Just like my brother Jim!

"Chris, I can't tell you how—"

"Don't. Please don't." He tossed off his drink. "Oh hell, I'm sorry. Why did I have to . . . I've spoiled your afternoon. What a way to end a wonderful day."

"It's only the beginning." I took his glass, draining mine, and went to the bar and made two more. Coming back, I took another big swallow. I handed him his drink and placed mine on the coffee table. I didn't sit down.

It was half dark now, only the fire casting a flickering light on the carpet. He seemed to be studying his drink, his head bowed. He didn't raise it until I whispered his name.

"Diane!"

It was not an exclamation of disapproval but of wonder and delight. At my feet lay my pink sweater. I wore nothing beneath it. He sat quite still until I unzipped my skirt. Then he came to me, his arms clutching as if in panic. We sank to the floor.

I was dimly aware that I was replaying an old scene, one buried for a decade in the pit of my mind, but this time performed freely and as a healing gift, for me as much as for him.

A thought darted into my mind: Later I must tell him about me. *Must.*

The thought was submerged by a great wave of rapture.

He stayed the night, a night of exhausted slumbers and tempestuous awakenings. The light was graying the bedroom curtains when I woke for the last time. He was resting on his elbow, smiling down at me. He kissed my eyelids and I became gloriously conscious.

"I love you," he said.

The whispered endearments of the night had not quite reached that far. My throat seemed to thicken, choking my voice: "Oh, and I love *you!*"

And once again we celebrated each other, slowly and fondly, with the confidence of knowing the best ways to please.

We showered together, dressed together, then walked the beach through a sun-struck mist that crafted miniature rainbows against the curling waves. Coming back, he insisted on cooking breakfast, a gargantuan affair that we gobbled up in front of a hissing fire.

Over coffee I said, "Now how's your jinx complex?"

He grinned. "It doesn't exist. Your therapy, Dr. Ridgway, is miraculous."

It was an opportune moment to release my own closeted skeletons but I let it go by, fearful that what we had created might still be too fragile to be tested. But I knew I couldn't postpone telling him much longer. If we were to go on together, he would eventually hear the story and justifiably feel deceived.

Were we to go on together?

"Chris, how long before you have to give up the house?"

His face turned solemn. "I have five more days."

"Couldn't you stay longer?"

"Negative. The Connors have rented it to some people. They move in the day after I move out."

I waited, hoping he would say he'd find another place. He was silent.

"You could move in here," I said.

He pretended to be shocked. "Horrors. What would the neighbors say?"

I snuggled against him. "There are no neighbors for a mile. Anyway, the people around here wouldn't think anything of it."

I felt him tense. He said seriously, "Maybe not, but I'm afraid I'm just a trifle old-fashioned."

The implication was clear. Oddly, I had not even thought of marriage, perhaps because I had considered myself self-sufficient for so many years. Now that it occurred to me, I was aware that, unconsciously perhaps, I had been wary of marriage lest it once again devour me.

But he didn't ask me.

Instead: "Besides, I can't go on being a bum. I've got to get a job. That means going to San Francisco. I couldn't commute from here. I'd be spending almost seven hours a day driving back and forth."

I thought of my house in Belvedere, a half hour's drive from San Francisco. The last I heard it had been rented to an executive of IBM who had a large family. I had kept it in the hope that Jennifer would some day return. Only then would I have found living there tolerable. It might be much more than tolerable with Chris. The presence of a man so obviously upright—a Colonel—might even reinstate me with the local gentry. I winced—*that* I could do without.

". . . be driving up weekends," he was saying. "We'll have from Friday night until early Monday morning."

"Let's talk about it later. Right now we'll just be happy."

But I wasn't happy. I was frightened. I imagined him loose in the city, saw him fawned over by nubile women, heard his voice on the phone regretting he couldn't make it that weekend, perhaps next—and then he might just fade away. No, if he was agreeable, I would go wherever he liked. It needn't be the Belvedere house.

"You've gone away," Chris said.

I gave my head a shake and drew back to look at him. Anxiety darkened his eyes.

"I'm right here, darling."

"I had the feeling you were thinking of someone else." He forced a smile. "Do I have a rival?"

"Impossible."

"It wouldn't surprise me. A lovely widow. Ten years is a long—" He stopped, his smile turning rueful. "All right, I'm fishing."

I kissed him quickly. "You don't have to. There were two men after Fred died. The first was more of a friend than anything else. The second"—I hesitated—"well, that ended long ago."

I told him briefly about Bryan Wilcox. A high-powered advertising man, twice divorced, with a sort of to-hell-with-it attitude toward life which suited my mood at the time. I omitted saying that he had filled a sensual need; that was implicit.

"I don't understand how it could have lasted so long, except that we were both lonely."

"Just as you and I are—or were." He had the look of a devil's advocate.

"Yes, but we like so many of the same things. Bryan and I

had almost nothing in common. He regarded my painting as just a bit of female foolishness—a ploy to appear creative. When I'd speak of it, his eyebrows would arch and he'd smile indulgently. Then he'd change the subject."

"Perhaps he was jealous of it."

I nodded. Just as Fred had been jealous of it, I thought. I recalled how I'd painted only when he was away.

"Some people can't help resenting what they can't dominate," Chris said.

I stared at him. "My husband was like that."

"Really? You mean he resented your *painting?*"

"Yes. Oh, not at first. Before we married he pretended to be very interested. Afterward, he acted like I was hooked on drugs."

That was a start, I thought, a natural transition into the rest of the story. I opened my mouth to speak, but Chris stood up, saying, "Well, I'm sure there were plenty of compensations. How about going to my place? I'd like to check the mail and change clothes. We can have lunch there or go out someplace."

He said little on the drive over, and I sensed he was wondering about my relationship with Fred. But soon after we arrived, he became loquacious. It was as though he wanted me to know everything about him in the hope that he would benefit by comparison with the previous men in my life.

He reminisced about his military career—combat in France, Korea and Vietnam, followed by staff duty in Japan and Western Europe. With my prompting, he led me to a closet where I admired his sharply creased uniform, shoulder eagles brightly polished, left breast festooned with multicolored ribbons. (Colonel Christopher Warren—how splendid to present him as my—as my *what?*) I read an official citation for valor signed by the President of the United States, and gazed fascinatedly at two souvenirs he had "liberated"—a menacing black German Luger and a short Japanese ceremonial sword. "For hara-kiri," he said.

I was delighted with his need to confide in me. He had all the ingenuous charm of a small boy bursting to recount his experiences at summer camp.

He was explaining the ritual use of the Japanese sword when he stopped abruptly, slapped his head, and said, "Good Lord, Diane, how can you stand me? I haven't stopped talking for an hour!"

"I'm glad." I studied his face, approving the candid brown eyes, the somewhat long patrician nose, the thick dark hair with glints of gray. Not really a handsome face, but strong and interesting and right now very dear. "I'm glad about what made it possible," I said. "Last night was wonderful."

He smiled roguishly. "Any reason to leave out this morning?"

I rose from my chair, bent down, and kissed him. "Even *better* this morning. We *knew* each other then."

I dropped to the floor, arms around his legs, cheek against his thigh. His fingers traced the line of my hair.

"Actually," he said, "there's so much about you I *don't* know."

I felt my body contract. "I told you about growing up."

"That awful town, yes. But nothing about after you left there, when you came to San Francisco."

That, of course, was the place to start—not, as I had planned, with the ghastly night that had taken one life and shattered two others.

THREE

"I LOOK FORWARD to seeing you at the meeting in Palm Springs on the 25th," said Mr. Ridgway.

I made a few shaky strokes on my pad. It was my fourth day in the stenotypist pool at Pacific Valley Foods and the first time I had been in the presence of Frederick Ridgway, vice-president of marketing. His personal secretary had left promptly at five and had recruited me for some after-hours dictation. "Don't let him scare you," she had said. So naturally I was scared.

He had not looked at me from the time I entered his office, just kept scowling down at a stack of letters on his desk and barking out replies. Once, during a long pause, he had muttered, "Stupid bitch," and my head had snapped up. The remark, thank goodness, referred to a correspondent.

He got up and stood at one of the plate-glass windows facing the bay. His back was toward me, the muscles just below his shoulders stretching the fabric of his dark suit. He was a big man but not at all lumbering; standing quietly, he seemed in rapid motion—jaws flexing, neck straining his collar, hands clenching and unclenching. Even his copper-colored hair, bristling from a slapdash combing, gave an impression of action. The total effect was of barely restrained power—an attitude, according to his awed subordinates, carried over from his days as an All-American tackle at Stanford. In fact, I learned later, it was due to a fanatical impatience to grasp the top rung of the corporate ladder. He was thirty-two years old.

He swung around from his contemplation of the view and finally looked at me. He started to speak, stopped, then simply stared. I riveted my eyes on the pad, shifted in the chair, and felt a flush rise from beneath the hem of my short skirt to the roots of my hair.

He said, "Cordially yours, now let's quit this nonsense and have a belt."

I had taken down every word before I gave a start. The pencil point broke. I looked up at him, feeling a pressure behind my eyes. He grinned, slid into his chair, and unlocked a lower desk drawer. His hand came up with a bottle of whiskey. I turned my head to gaze out the open door. Only a few lights were lit and I could almost hear the emptiness. When I turned back, he was regarding me with an amused smile. He shook his head and returned the bottle to the drawer.

"No," he said. "You deserve a lot better. We'll have it somewhere in style." His tone assumed I'd already accepted.

I shut my notepad and stood up. "There's one problem," I said.

He belittled it with a wave of his hand. "There are no problems, only opportunities. That's what I tell them in the board room. A damned lie, of course."

"I'm only eighteen," I said. "They won't serve me." I had an urge to be flippant. "You might ask me again when I'm twenty-one."

He eyed me all over. "By then you'll be married and tied down with kids." He got up. "Let's go. When you're with me, nobody'll ask you for an I.D. card."

Out on the sidewalk he took my arm and skipped me along with giant strides. He didn't speak. Glimpsing his face, I saw that it was thrust forward and set in grim lines. He struck me as the kind who approached any objective, even a drink, with a single-minded aggressiveness. I recalled overhearing someone say, "The Ridgway Principle—always look like you're rushing to meet the chairman of the board even if you're only going to the john."

He whisked me down an alley and across a street to a place called Gino's. There was a long bar on the right, red-padded booths in the center, and a dining room on the other side. The nearest bartender welcomed him warmly and asked, "The usual?" He nodded and looked at me. Unable to think, I said I'd have the same.

As soon as we slipped into a booth in the back, the drinks were delivered. The liquor was white—gin, I guessed—iced, and filled the stubby glasses to the brims. He made a toasting gesture before half draining his glass. Almost instantly his face relaxed and his eyes brightened. I tried for the same effect by taking a big gulp. My throat seemed to leap for my teeth. I choked, coughed, and my eyes watered. He reached around and slapped my back. "Should have warned you," he said. "These are doubles—straight vodka."

Once I'd recovered, I was cautious. But not Frederick Ridgway. No sooner did he rattle the ice than another drink appeared. He didn't suggest that I join him. By the time he'd downed three, I was finishing my first. I worried that I was going to be stuck with a drunk, and my boss at that.

But the drinks only made him more human. The second one helped to reveal that he had married at twenty-five and divorced a year later. ("She tried to dominate me with her money.") The third took us off on a couple of deep-sea fishing trips. After that, I forgot any correlation between intake and output. He just went on and on, mostly about business, words never slurring, thoughts never faltering, completely self-possessed.

Not once was I bored. Perhaps because I was flattered that a man of his standing and maturity should talk to me as an equal. But there was something more. He was so intensely absorbed in everything he said that I found myself drawn into sharing his feelings, even when I didn't quite understand what he was talking about. I became not just a captive audience, but his confidante, somehow a silent contributor to the inner vision he had of himself. I was too naïve then to realize that I was taking the first step toward surrender.

Several executives from the office stopped by and he introduced me in a forthright way. No embarrassment, no pretense that I was anybody but a girl who worked in the steno pool. Apparently he didn't care in the least if anyone suspected his intentions. And by not caring, he appeared to be above suspicion.

I offered only token resistance when he announced that I would join him for dinner. We walked the short distance to Ernie's, his stride as steady as when we had left the office. Inside the restaurant with its softly lit Victorian decor, he was greeted effusively by the maître d', who escorted us to a table with a RESERVED sign on it (quickly whisked away) and sat us against a pink-plush wall. There were more drinks—his two for my one—before he ordered dinner. Only then, while he attacked his châteaubriand, did he turn the conversation to me. I skimmed over the subject quickly—my hometown, where I was living, my art class—conscious of what a dull person I must sound. But he seemed interested in my painting and asked a lot of knowledgeable questions. I suspected he was merely being polite until he mentioned that he was a member of the San Francisco Art Commission. I was impressed. It didn't occur to me that this could hardly be a claim to artistic sensibility, the commission chiefly being concerned with civic ornamentation.

He had three after-dinner brandies at the bar, while I sipped a crème de menthe, then had a taxi called. Entering it, I felt a spurt of panic, half expecting him to say, "Your place or mine?" But he took me directly to my rooming house, not touching me on the way, his manner casually friendly. At the street door, he gazed at me admiringly for a few moments, gently patted my cheek, thanked me for a pleasant evening, and walked in a straight line to the waiting taxi. I felt like a little girl who had been taken to the zoo by a fond uncle.

For days after that, I would pass him in the halls (sometimes contriving it) only to be met with a brief smile and a nod, as though I were someone remembered only vaguely. Almost unconsciously, I started to hang around the office after the other girls had left, knowing he was still there. Once I peeked into his office from an angle and saw him take a drink from the whiskey bottle. I waited longer than usual that evening, pretending to type a letter, but when he finally emerged he walked right past me to the reception lobby to be greeted by a slim, dark woman who looked like a jet setter. That convinced me I was not to be Cinderella; midnight had long since struck and the glass slipper was not my size.

Then one Friday, at a few minutes past five, I was hurrying through the downstairs lobby when a hand gripped my elbow and a gruff voice said, "Well, I see you're going my way." I wasn't but I did, and we played the whole scene over again at Gino's and Ernie's. His goodnight was exactly as it had been before—but this time he asked me to go boating with him on Sunday morning.

I had imagined a small sailboat, a biting wind, cold spray on my cheeks, and had dressed accordingly: gray flannel slacks, yellow wool pullover, fleece-lined windbreaker.

The craft I boarded was a yacht—a forty-six-foot Chris Craft Constellation with wide decks fore-and-aft, two staterooms, two lavatories with showers, a main salon, a dinette and an all-electric galley. The floors were thickly carpeted and the orange-and-white furnishings sumptuous.

"You've got to be Greek," I said, after he'd given me the tour.

"This is the dinghy. Wait'll you see the ship." He plucked at my heavy windbreaker. "I'm afraid you misunderstood. It's *next* week that we go to the Pole."

I laughed and took it off, wishing I'd worn a cotton T-shirt underneath. The temperature must have been in the eighties; the sky was like an inverted blue bowl with a burning center. He wore white ducks, short-sleeved blue shirt, and a black yachting cap.

I had pictured us as part of the white-winged flotilla circling the bay around Alcatraz and Angel Island. Instead he headed out through the Golden Gate to the open sea. As soon as we cleared the great red bridge, he slid from the helmsman's seat and lifted me to it. Startled, I gripped the wheel as though preparing to ride out a storm.

"Relax, Diane. Swing to the right until we're near the shore. We'll follow it around to Bolinas."

I gazed at the towering promontories. "You're asking for a shipwreck."

"We could always radio the Coast Guard." He touched my shoulder. "Provided that's what we wanted to do."

It was the first time he had said anything the least bit suggestive. I smiled at him. Nervously. He dropped his hand.

We passed Stinson Beach, swarming with bathers. Rounding

the next headland, he took the wheel and brought us within half a mile offshore. We were off Bolinas, the beach looking like a thin spit of sand with only a scattering of people. He pressed something on the console and there was a ratcheting sound. I jumped.

"Anchor," he said. "This is a good place to swim."

I stared down at my clothes. "I didn't bring—"

"You'll find a lockerful of suits in the aft stateroom. Pick something pretty."

In the stateroom locker I found half a dozen bikinis stacked neatly on a shelf. Choosing a coral number, I stood between the twin beds and slowly undressed. How many women, I wondered, had shed their clothes in this room for purposes other than swimming? The thought ignited a spark of jealousy but no moral disapproval; Frederick Ridgway, a bachelor, worked hard and was entitled to whatever pleasures were offered him. Neither did I feel fright; obviously I was no more to him than a casual companion, perhaps amusing him with my innocence and eagerness to listen. Besides, it was unthinkable that a man in his position would risk seducing a girl of eighteen who pounded a typewriter right outside his office.

I found a pale-blue robe, wrapped myself in it, and went up on deck. He stood at the railing wearing black trunks, exposing a muscular body the color of the mahogany planking. The contrast with my own pale skin, as I gingerly disrobed, produced a pang of embarrassment. But he nodded in approval, took my hand to guide me under the railing, and we plunged over the side. The water was icy cold and I came up gasping and numb. I swam to the ladder, grabbed the bottom rung, and turned to watch him swimming away with a long powerful crawl. When he stopped, treading water, he waved for me to join him. I tried, taking a few leaden strokes, then gave it up and thrashed back to the ladder.

I was hanging on, strength drained, when he came churning back. I was shivering all over, my teeth were chattering, and I knew my lips were blue. He mounted the deck, reached back, grasped my wrists, and hauled me aboard.

"Are you all right?"

"It's nothing serious, unless dying is serious."

He grinned, swept me up, and carried me into the salon, stretching me out on a white lounge. He got a blanket and tucked it around me. "Don't move until I bring my magic remedy." He disappeared into the galley.

He came back with steaming mugs of some brown liquid. Soup, I thought, sitting up. But it was something else; I didn't care what, because the first swallow sent delicious warmth spreading all through me. I finished it, held out the mug like Oliver Twist and said, "More, please?"

I had downed the second one before asking what it was.

"Hot water, lemon juice, sugar, cinnamon."

"Mmmm."

"And a double slug of rum."

I laughed, feeling glorious. But standing up, dropping the blanket, my knees suddenly felt dizzy and I lurched against him. He held me close for a moment, then drew back. "That was Phase One. We'll now proceed to Phase Two."

Phase Two consisted of stretching out side by side on blue pads atop the deckhouse. Lying face down, I could smell the stain on the deck, feel the roll of the boat, while the sun warmed my skin beneath the drying strips of coral cloth. He was propped on an elbow and I could sense him looking at me and, no longer embarrassed, I felt proud of my figure and hoped that it pleased him. His hand, fingers spread, came to my hair and combed it down my back (I wore it long then) and he said, "It gets blonder as it dries. I like you blond."

His hand slid down and stroked along my spine. When it

moved lower, I forgot all the foolish notions I'd had about him while undressing in the stateroom. Right then he didn't care that I was eighteen and worked in his office and that I was supposed to be a casual companion who was a good listener.

The sun and the rum and the touch of his hand brought me arching toward him and before I knew who started it we were lavishing each other with kisses. It was still going on when he took me below.

His black trunks seemed vaguely reassuring when we lay on the bed beneath the curtained window in the master stateroom. I was too mesmerized to hear my bra unsnap, and hardly noticed when it drifted to the floor. The bottom strip seemed simply to evaporate, and except for a passing coolness, I was scarcely aware that I was naked.

Until, tilting my head as he kissed my throat, I saw my clothes heaped on the opposite bed. I sat up as though a reflex had been struck. There was no panic, only the hazy thought that I belonged in those clothes and that if I didn't get into them I'd turn into somebody else. But they were so far away. Everything was far away. Except Fred. And he was now sitting up, eyeing me strangely.

"What is it, Diane?"

"I don't know. I'm confused. And I guess a little drunk." Ambivalent, too—it must not stop; it *had* to stop.

"You're also a virgin," he said. It was a statement of fact, not an accusation.

"Yes." I'd rather have confessed I was a prostitute.

I expected a burst of anger or ridicule. But he smiled ironically and drew me gently back on the bed. "You're an endangered species." He sighed. "And I've just joined the conservationists."

If he had so much as hinted that he loved me, I'd have thrown myself at him. But we lay there without speaking until I felt his heart resume its normal rhythm. Then he got up, kissed me lightly, and left me to burden myself with clothes.

Going back, I stood close to him at the helm, noticing that the corner of his mouth was hooked into a small smile. I had the absurd impression that he was immensely pleased.

I didn't see him alone until more than a week later, when his secretary again assigned me to take after-hours dictation. It was almost six o'clock when he asked me into his office. As soon as I entered, he got up and closed the door, though everyone had left. I sat stiffly in my chair, notepad open, pencil poised, eyes fixed on the carpet. His shoes and the cuffed bottoms of his trousers came into sight. I could feel him staring down at me.

I raised my eyes slowly, trying to keep my face a blank. He was scowling; more at himself, I thought, than at me. The silence became intolerable. Then he reached down and tore away my notepad and flung it on the desk. The pencil spun to the floor. I couldn't move. But that didn't matter—I was practically yanked to my feet by his hands gripping my elbows. He kissed me almost as if he intended to inflict pain. But if there was any, I didn't notice. I only knew that some expanding weight inside me had suddenly dissolved. His fingertips were flicking at my cheeks before I realized there were tears.

He smiled then and the lines in his face smoothed out. "You've been reassigned," he said. "You are now vice-president in charge of paper cups."

I went a bit giddily to the water cooler and got four of them, two with water. Returning, it was I who closed the door. The bottle, half full, stood on the coffee table in front of the sofa. I knew that he'd already drunk from it; I recalled smelling whisky on his breath.

He sat me on the sofa, then dropped down a cushion away and poured the drinks. Watching him, I thought of all the times my mind had replayed the scene in the stateroom, each performance more glamorous than the last, until it had become a fantasy spun from gossamer. I waited for him to pick up where we had just left off.

"Did I ever tell you about my former wife?" he said.

I felt my mouth drop open. "Well . . . you said she had lots of money and tried to run your life."

"That's not the main reason I divorced her."

"Oh."

He drained his paper cup and poured himself another drink. "She was a tramp. By the time we'd been married six months, I learned that she'd slept with just about every man in her crowd. It was a large crowd and I'd become part of it."

I reached for his hand. "Oh Fred, I'm sorry."

"Don't be. I'm not. It made the divorce easier."

"Did she . . . after you were married?"

"I don't know. I didn't hang around to find out." He took a drink. "That's when I made a promise to myself." He put down his cup, sat back, and narrowed his eyes on me.

"What?" The subject was making me uneasy.

"I promised myself it would never happen again." He cocked an eyebrow, as if inviting some sort of confession.

It took a minute to register. "Fred! You don't think I lied to you!"

He capped the bottle. "I only think we'd better get out of here."

This time we didn't go to Gino's or Ernie's. Downstairs he hailed a taxi and gave the driver his address on Russian Hill. Going there, he seemed suddenly gripped by depression, replying to my nervous chatter with monosyllables.

But once inside his apartment his mood switched abruptly to merriment. He turned on the stereo, sang along with Frank Sinatra, then stood behind the red-leather bar and playfully lined up bottles as though preparing for a huge party. He downed a straight drink before mixing two with ice and a splash of water. Handing me one, he threw an arm around my waist and danced me across the white carpet to a window wall from where we could see Coit Tower and the two great bridges spanning the bay. "It's all mine," he said happily. "All of it." He sounded like he believed it.

I was delighted to attribute his euphoria to my inspiring presence.

"Take off your shoes," he said.

I kicked them off, reducing my height by two inches. Smiling almost maniacally, he gazed down at me, touched my lips, my throat, my breasts. He folded me against him, danced me around, waving his glass like a baton. His chest against my cheek felt like a slab of marble. We ended up at the bar, laughing crazily. He poured more whiskey, though our glasses were not empty. He reached to the wall and the lamps went out.

A blue glow filled the room. Blinking, I saw that it came from opaque glass panels bordering the ceiling. Our laughter had stopped.

"Now your dress," he said quietly.

I wished his tone had been less peremptory. But I reached back, slid down the zipper, and let the chartreuse shift slip from my shoulders. It was encircling my ankles when he picked me up and carried me to the bedroom.

It took a long time for him to change me from girl to woman. I was tense, apprehensive, my responses awkward. But he seemed not to mind. Once sure of my willingness, he was patient and gentle and perfectly controlled—until all thoughts of method or movement exploded from my mind and it was I, astonishingly, who became the aggressor.

We lay uncovered on the sheet. He snapped on the bed lamp

and looked at me. My face felt swollen, my limbs heavy, but there was an inner incandescence. He put an arm around me and rolled me against him. "You're wonderful," I said. Raising his head, he peered down to where I had lain. He sighed, as though in triumph. "You're my girl now," he said.

Later I discovered what his eyes had sought. On the sheet there was a small streak of blood.

Week nights we ended up in his apartment. Weekends were spent mostly on his boat, which sometimes never left the dock. He drank prodigiously but it didn't seem to impair his performance, either in the office or in bed. It pleased him to hold back from intercourse while in other ways bringing me to climax again and again, expending himself only when I was on the brink of exhaustion. It was certainly not something a passionate woman would object to (and I had found I was a passionate woman) but at times I felt a qualm that he should glory in my helplessness without really sharing it.

In the office he was properly reserved, but outside he didn't try to hide me. We still went to Gino's and Ernie's and to a lot of other places where we often ran into friends or business associates. He even took me to a cocktail party at the home of the chairman of the board and made a point of bringing us together. (Later, when they thought they were alone, I overheard the chairman say, "That's a lovely young lady, Fred," and Fred flushed with pleasure. So did I.) I didn't know where we were headed and didn't really think about it. I was too excited to think about anything except our next date.

I dropped out of art class, much to the disappointment of the instructor, Gordon Hathaway, who had given me a lot of special attention. Afterward, he called me a few times to invite me to dinner, but of course I had to put him off; regretfully because there had been a rapport between us. But that had been based on

our mutual interest in painting and I no longer had the time or
inclination to paint.

The week after Christmas I found out I was pregnant.

"I suppose you've considered an abortion," Fred said.

I had expected him to be as devastated as I was but he seemed
perfectly calm. He would have faced a business crisis in the
same way.

"Yes," I said.

"How do you feel about it?"

"It scares me. But—"

"Let's not try to solve it right now. Give it a couple of
days—get it in perspective."

By perspective I was sure he meant that if I brooded about it
for awhile, I'd see how ridiculous it was to hope for marriage.
After all, why should Frederick Ridgway risk a brilliant career
over a nobody from the boondocks? But I'd come to that
conclusion immediately. My only thought was to keep him for
as long as possible. And if that meant having an abortion, so be
it.

I wallowed in misery for two days before he asked me out. It
was a Friday, with the whole New Year's weekend before us.
We took a taxi and headed south, toward the Peninsula. I
started some small talk but was silenced by his look of grim
determination that I knew would remain fixed until we'd
reached whatever objective he had in mind. Suddenly I
suspected what it was: he was taking me to a doctor. And
without so much as asking my permission. I was too stunned to
speak.

Suspicion hardened into conviction when he directed the
driver to the airport and, arriving, showed me two tickets to
Reno. An out-of-state abortionist, I thought—to protect himself.

"We're going to a party," he said.

"But I have no clothes!"

"We'll buy some in Reno, tomorrow."

I went along with it, all through the hour-long convivial flight, all through the drinks at the Riverside Hotel bar, where he bought round after round for a dozen strangers. The doctor, I thought, would have a thoroughly anaesthetized patient. I was almost sick with suspense.

"Shouldn't we at least see our room, Fred?"

He handed me the key. "I'll have one more. You go up."

While he telephoned the doctor, I thought. I felt a surge of anger. Let him make his plans; I would not go through with it until we had a chance to talk—soberly. That meant waiting until tomorrow.

He had taken a suite—large living room and bedroom. I went through the bedroom into the bathroom, where I washed my face with cold water, applied fresh makeup, and combed my hair. Returning to the living room, I found Fred talking to a man who exactly matched my mental image of an abortionist—cadaverous, bald, gloomy looking, and wearing a rumpled black suit. Fred introduced him, but my head was pounding so with alcoholic fury that I didn't catch the name or acknowledge him.

"You've got to sign these," Fred said, taking some papers from the man.

I set my jaw. "No, I won't!" I relented slightly under his implacable gaze. "Not until we discuss it."

He surprised me with a smile. "You know," he said, "you may have a point." He rushed me into the bedroom.

He sat on the edge of the bed, pulling me down beside him. "Do you love me?" he asked.

I stared at him, then nodded stiffly.

"Then what's there to discuss? Unless you want to insist on a minister instead of a judge."

"What!"

"Judge Thompson's here to marry us."

"Oh my God!"

"The judge has agreed to mention Him."

He had planned every word and action, as though directing a play. Even the supporting players had been cast—the dozen or so people he had treated to drinks at the bar. They came storming in as I finished signing the papers. Two of them, a husband and wife, stood up for us. Barely stood, that is, because the husband kept swaying as though about to fall over and twice the wife lurched forward and had to be righted by the judge.

We were sealing the ceremony with a kiss when the door again burst open and white-jacketed waiters appeared bearing trays of champagne. A completely stocked bar was wheeled in and the room became bedlam. It was fine with me. I loved everyone.

The last guest didn't stagger out until after three AM. Alone in the bedroom, I undressed and stepped to the door to call Fred, who had lingered for a nightcap. He was at the bar drinking with the judge.

It didn't bother me that the marriage was not to be immediately consummated. There was joy enough in knowing that the "drugstore kid" had miraculously become the bride of Frederick Ridgway.

There was no public announcement. I quit my job and Fred simply dropped the word here and there, with the implication that we'd been married for some time. I don't think anyone thought to question him because he had a reputation for being a supreme individualist, scornful of convention. Jennifer's birth seven months later seemed to arouse no speculation.

Certainly the people who most influenced his career appeared to have no qualms. The reverse, in fact—six months after Jennifer's arrival the board of directors elected him president of the company. A year after that, he replaced the retired chairman of the board and became chief executive officer.

By then he had built the house in Belvedere, a mansion big enough to accommodate his ego and the demands of his new status. Immediately our whole life style changed. I can't recall a night when we were not entertaining or being entertained. On weekends the house was overrun with business associates of one sort or another—company men and their wives, chain store executives, distributors, food brokers, management consultants, admen, lawyers.

Fred's drinking got worse. Rarely was he sober after seven in the evening, and on weekends he stayed slightly drunk from the moment he woke up and downed his first Bloody Mary. But he had amazing stamina, as well as a rule that saved him from censure in his job—he never took a drop until the workday was finished. Socially, his capacity inspired only admiration—he was an iron man, a hard-driving leader who was immune to the penalties that alcohol exacts from lesser mortals.

The only time we could be alone together was late at night, and then only long enough for him to satisfy himself sexually. His tastes became bizarre. Once he took a lipstick and, laughing uproariously, scrawled obscene words on my body. Another time, he conceived a weird drama in which he was a pirate and I was a captive slave. It was just a game, he said, thus hushing my protests when he tied my hands to the headboard with a silk sash. I had the feeling of being raped, and though my body responded, I couldn't escape an aftermath of shame. I blamed that on my inhibited adolescence. After all, hadn't the sex books I'd read after our marriage endorsed the diversity of sex, including a degree of sadomasochism? Almost nothing was taboo if it produced erotic pleasure.

As the years passed, I began to understand why he had

married me. He had seen me as Galatea to his Pygmalion, virginal clay that he could mold to suit his fantasies. And he had been right—naïve, susceptible, awed by his eminence, I had eagerly sought to be and do everything he wished.

Despite that insight, I suppose I would have gone on being the completely pliable wife if I had not also come to suspect that he was using me as a scapegoat for the wife whose promiscuity had in effect made him a cuckold. "My beautiful whore," he would sometimes murmur against my cheek; or, "lovely bitch"—the words disguised as endearments so that neither he nor I would recognize that they were rooted in hate.

I was determined to do something that would return at least a part of me to myself.

"Fred, I've decided to go back to art school."

He put his coffee cup down carefully, wiped his mouth with a napkin, and regarded me without expression. It was a weekday, we had just finished breakfast, and he was about to leave for the office. I had timed the announcement for when I'd be sure he would be cold sober.

"I'm also signing up for an adult class in literature at the local college." I was determined to get it all out.

His lips curled into a disparaging smile. "My God, a dilettante."

"Maybe. But I feel that I should be doing something."

"Doing something? Hell, it seems to me you don't have an idle moment. Tennis, sailing, bridge."

"I know, but none of it's very satisfying. Besides, I'm never really comfortable with those women. I'm the wife of their husband's boss and they treat me that way."

"Glad to hear it." He studied his watch. "What about Jennifer?"

That was dangerous ground. If Jennifer's life was to be disturbed, he would thwart me. He adored her.

"She starts kindergarten next week. I can arrange my classes so that I'll be away when she is. Anyway, John and Anna can look after her if I run over a bit." John was the butler, Anna the maid.

His eyes seemed to measure me for a minute, then he shrugged. "Go ahead, it's your life." He got up. "Just make sure your culture kick doesn't interfere with us."

It was more than a warning. It was also an admission that he felt threatened. He left without saying goodbye.

So, as I had in Justine, I again sought release in painting. Working once more with Gordon Hathaway, I was surprised at how much I had missed him. He was a bachelor in his early thirties, a tall, thin man with light, wavy hair and a bony face set with pale-blue eyes as gentle as his manner. Never did he seek to impose his views on his students; always he encouraged us to work from the inside out.

"Think of the canvas as a mirror of your emotions," he said. "Make it reflect not just what you see, but also what's inside you."

"So I'll paint a can of worms," I said, smiling.

He smiled too, but gave me a thoughtful look. He knew, I guessed, that my return had been motivated by something more than a passion for art.

I attended his class three days a week for two-hour sessions. The literature class met on the remaining two weekdays, absorbing me almost as much as painting. I became the library's best customer, for the first time entering the strange worlds of Stendhal and Proust, Dostoevsky and Tolstoy, Wolfe and Faulkner, Shaw and Waugh. I discovered that Gordon Hathaway admired many of the same authors, and often after art class we would linger over coffee to discuss a book I was reading. A number of times I was late getting home, relieved to find Jennifer engrossed in some game that John had devised. Fortunately, Fred never heard about my tardiness.

Inevitably my outside activities were reflected at home. Coming up to the bedroom, anticipating a sexual encounter, Fred was apt to find me with my nose in a book. On weekends, the house thronged with guests, I would sometimes sneak off to paint in an upstairs room I had fixed up as a studio. He never commented on these defections, acting as though they were nonexistent. When I invited Gordon Hathaway to a cocktail party, he offered no objection. In fact, he astonished me by expressing a liking for him. After that, Gordon was a frequent visitor.

But all the while, Fred must have brooded about these challenges to his dominion. And, perhaps without quite understanding why, he retaliated.

First, through sex. Until then, his antics in bed had merely been childish. But as I became more preoccupied with other interests, he became brutal. Half drunk, he would strip me and maul me about the room, the blows more degrading than hurtful. He would bite me, squeeze my breath out, use force to engage me in acts that in earlier times I had joyously volunteered. When I protested, sometimes fiercely, he would withdraw into a sullen silence, then later, after I was asleep, penetrate me as though to inflict a wound.

A climax was reached one night when, enraged beyond words, he whipped off his belt and started toward me. I threw open the drawer to the night table and snatched out a pair of long, pointed scissors. Gripping them, my insides seemed to congeal into a block of ice.

"If you touch me with that, Fred, I'll stick this right through you."

That stopped him. He was sure I meant it, and maybe I did. I could see the fury drain out of him, replaced by a look of bitter disappointment. He turned on his heel and left the room. He didn't return to our bed that night and when I went downstairs the next morning he was gone. But not to the office (it was his first and only absence that I can recall). He apparently spent the day touring bars, where he would not meet anyone he knew. That night a bartender telephoned me from a town about ten miles north and asked me to pick him up. He had run out of money and credit and was passed out in a booth. I drove up, brought him home, and wrestled him into bed. The following day he left for the office without mentioning the incident.

I was sick with remorse. His invincible self-image, at least as it concerned me, had been shattered if not destroyed, and I, however justified, was responsible. I did what I could to patch it up—expressing penitence, vowing never again to lose my temper, suggesting a holiday together (he shook his head)—and we managed to achieve an uneasy truce. But the days of Pygmalion and Galatea were over and I could not or would not go back. Sexual intimacy didn't end but it became sporadic and covert—when the need grew urgent, we joined together wordlessly in predawn blackness and didn't speak of it afterward.

I'm sure we would have divorced if it had not been for Jennifer. Not because she was a catalyst uniting us—quite the contrary, as it turned out—but because I feared the trauma she might suffer if I took her from him. From the day she was born he regarded her with a sort of awed adoration. He loved to feed her, dress her, croon her to sleep, unabashedly announcing to his friends that he was competing for Mother of the Year. He showered her with gifts, including frilly clothes, took her boating, joined her in games. He delighted in showing her off and sometimes on Saturday mornings would drive her into town to parade her through the stores. (She *was* a lovely child—silky, copper-red hair, huge blue eyes, a friendly, outgoing disposition.) I still feel anxiety when I recall him, charged with Bloody Marys, roaring off with her while bellowing a song—"Give me the road, the white winding highwayyyy . . ."—as Jennifer squealed a giggling accompaniment.

(Yes, I had moments of jealousy, but these were more than offset by relief: I had worried that he would resent her as the little villain who had forced him into an unwanted marriage.)

Now, as our marriage faltered, Jennifer unwittingly became another instrument of reprisal. It was as though, unable any longer to possess me, he felt driven to possess the person closest to me. I doubt that he was incited by malice; he cared too much for his daughter to consciously exploit her. More likely, there was a vacuum in his life that demanded to be filled. But the fact remained, the attentions he paid Jennifer increased in frequency and ardor, the more so as I became immersed in my other interests. It was to him she ran with a skinned knee or a glowing report card or a tale to be shared. By the time I realized how wide the gap between Jennifer and me had become, Fred had moved in to occupy it.

But of course Jennifer was not enough to absorb his energies, nor could he be content to spend all his leisure with a wife who had seceded from his authority. The classic answer would have been a mistress or a series of affairs. Fred chose flight—he built a house on the Mendocino coast. It would be, he said, a refuge where we could get away from the constant round of parties and just fish and relax. The "we" turned out to be a group of his drinking-and-fishing cronies. They would sail up in the boat about every other week, leaving at noon on Friday and arriving home Sunday night, faces stubbled, eyes bloodshot, clothes reeking of fish. "Business junkets," he called them. "Deductible."

I tried on those weekends to reinstate myself with Jennifer, taking her to the zoo, the movies, the beach. She was always quietly agreeable, but I could sense her eagerness to return home where she found more pleasure in the company of John, who, relieved of attending to guests, was delighted to assume the role of surrogate father. (I felt no jealousy of John, probably because his wife, Anna, was unable to bear children.) Intuitively I knew that Jennifer blamed me for Fred's absences, but I saw no way to justify myself without depicting him as a monster.

Painting and reading occupied me for most of those husbandless, partyless days, and occasionally Gordon Hathaway would drive over for lunch and an afternoon of swimming in the pool. Jennifer had liked him from the first, but now she was standoffish, as though fearful that any display of warmth would be an act of disloyalty to her father. That thought might not have occurred to me if it hadn't been for a small but significant incident.

Gordon and I were sitting beside the pool, legs dangling in the water. Something I said made him laugh and he reached up and patted my head in approval. I turned to him, smiling, and from the corner of my eye caught a glimpse of Jennifer's face peering from her upstairs bedroom window. I thought nothing about it until a little later when I entered her room and found her sobbing. I held her close, feeling her stiffen in my arms. She would say nothing beyond: "I just don't *feel* good, that's all!"

I stopped inviting Gordon over, seeing him only at art class or for an occasional lunch in the city. No explanation was necessary; he was a very perceptive person.

That's about the way things stood until Fred's life ended.

I heard Chris light a cigarette. "What a rotten life for you," he said.

I looked up at him. "At least it taught me a lot about myself."

"Your husband must have been a fairly young man when he died."

"He was forty-three. Jennifer was only ten at the time."

"Was it sudden?"

"Yes." I thought of where to begin.

"I'm sorry," Chris said. "Just because I told you about my wife, you don't have to—"

"Yes, I have to."

FOUR

FRED SQUINTED at his watch in the light from the dash. "Chrisake, Di, it's only one-fifteen. Why'd we leave so early?"

It would have been useless to tell him that he had suggested it. Affronted, he would have demanded that we go back.

"I was afraid of the driving, Fred."

"Ha! You c'n *always* drive. Diane's Taxi Service. Sobriety guaranteed or double your life back." He gave a phlegmed laugh. He had not appeared drunk until he entered the car.

My hands tightened on the wheel as I peered through the dense ground fog. "I'm *not* sober, Fred."

"Well, then, not high enough. Maybe should fix that."

"Please, Fred, I'm exhausted."

We had left a dance at the Yacht Club. He had spent most of the night at the bar swapping yarns with his fishing cronies. But often, as I danced with other men, he had tracked me with his eyes, his expression becoming more sullen as the night wore on.

I knew that some time before dawn I could expect to be roughly awakened. We had not been intimate in weeks.

We reached the long driveway and I felt the familiar relief. I eased into the garage beside the Mercedes, suddenly dazzled by the bright headlights refracting from the white wall. Fred piled out, lurched to the door connecting to the kitchen. It wasn't big enough for his wobbling bulk; his head cracked against the frame. "Rub cold water on it," he muttered. I passed him as he turned on the tap in the sink. "I'll check on Jennifer," I said.

In the living room, Anna snapped off the TV and yawned off to bed. Upstairs, I looked in on Jennifer. She was sleeping as blissfully as her cat curled up on the other pillow. I bent down and smoothed a lock of red-gold hair, then picked up the cat, triggering a soft meow, and brought him down to the kitchen. Fred had gone up to our bedroom. I poured a saucer of milk and waited to watch the rough tongue flick it down. Waited, actually, for Fred to fall into a ponderous sleep.

But he was unnervingly conscious, propped up shirtless in a yellow chair gripping a water glass half filled with bourbon. A matching glass and the bottle were at his feet.

"The man you love," he said with a sardonic grin, "requests the pleasure of your company for a nightcap." He spoke clearly now; the whiskey in his hand and the proximity of more had swelled his confidence.

Refusal would only have provoked abuse. Silently I accepted a drink and perched on the edge of the bed, sipping slowly. By the time I had half finished, he had downed two more. He reached out, twisted away my glass, poured me another.

"A party, Di. Just the two of us."

"It's terribly late, Fred."

"Later than you think." His eyes slid over me. "It's been a long time. *Too* long."

I set my glass on the night table untouched. He looked at it, then at me. I could see his jaw flex.

"Stand up."

"Please, Fred."

His tone became reasonable. "I'm your husband, right, Di?"

I didn't answer. He repeated the question, quietly.

"Yes, Fred, you're my husband."

"Good. Glad we've settled that." He gulped at his drink. "And when your husband asks you to do a simple little thing like stand up, well, you do it, right?"

I stood up.

"It's nice to know we agree."

I stared at a point beyond his head. Something like a cold mist started to rise inside me. Fear.

"Now what else does a loving wife do for a husband who works his ass off to provide her with everything her little heart desires? Tell me that, Di."

I took a breath, held it, let it out slowly.

"I'll answer that for you, Di. She *entertains* him. That's the truth, believe it." He flourished an arm. "So, my gorgeous wife, *entertain* me."

I stared at the knuckled hand dwarfing the glass, at the heavy shoulders that could bring a huge frantic fish swiftly to gaff, at the mat of orange-white hair masking the deceptive layer of flab. And at the eyes, implacable as an executioner's, that had driven countless subordinates cowering into bars.

Numbly I undressed.

He put down his glass, extended his damp hand, and pawed my breasts, squeezed my thighs.

Like a farmer inspecting a heifer.

I recoiled, gasping with sudden rage. *"No! No, damn you, NO!"*

He drew back. His mouth wriggled into a smirk. "Once upon a time you were more obliging."

"We settled that."

He blinked at the reminder. "Yes, *you* settled it. With a pair of scissors." He gazed down at himself, then spit out: "You used those scissors to cut my balls off."

I felt a stab of pity. He had lost not only me, but himself as well. "I never intended that, Fred. But it's too late"—I meant the time of night—"to talk about it now."

He picked up the bottle and seemed to study the label. "Yeah, too late. Too goddamned late."

I gathered up my clothes, veered around him to the dressing room, and put on a nightgown. When I came back, he was still gazing at the bottle, his eyes accusing. He ignored me as I slipped into bed. Turning my back against the light of the floor lamp, I glimpsed him tilting the bottle. My eyes closed to the sound of a prolonged gurgle. I fell into a troubled sleep.

I was dreaming. Some amorphous creature was pinioning my arms above my head. Something bit into my flesh. My body thrashed and flailed but could not break away. Then a great weight descended on me. I struggled, wakened.

It was real. Fred was straddling my stomach, gripping my wrists, binding them with heavy cord. I could feel his heated breath gusting against my cheek.

"Good God, Fred! Stop it! Stop it!"

He paused, and in that instant I arched upward, dropped back down, rolled away and yanked hard on the encircling cords. My feet hit the floor opposite him. I straightened, backed away, ripped off the cords.

He heaved himself up slowly and I saw he was naked. His face was gaunt and frozen. His eyes bulged but appeared sightless, like those of a medium evoking the dead. *I* was the dead—the obedient bride of so long ago. I glanced at the bottle on the floor. It was empty.

I sprang toward the door but, with sudden swiftness, he swung around to block me. He grabbed my nightgown with both hands and ripped it off. I stood paralyzed as he waved the tattered chiffon like a red banner before letting it drop. He stepped sideways to the desk. I gave my head a hard shake and squeezed my eyes shut, trying to recover my wits. I heard a drawer slide open.

When I faced him, he was standing close. His hand was between his legs and he seemed to be fondling himself. Something glittered. He was slowly waving a long-bladed knife. He thrust it forward and I felt the chill of steel against my inner thigh.

He grimaced a smile. "Perhaps you should be enlarged."

Terror exploded into blind fury. "Fred, you're out-of-your-mind drunk! You're *crazy!*"

I should never have uttered the word. He glared at me as I backed off, then lunged forward, knife held low like a demonic phallus. I stifled a scream, fearful of rousing Jennifer and the servants. My legs struck the foot of the bed. He shoved me and I tumbled backwards on the bed, arms and legs sprawling. He stood poised to probe my pelvis. Then the scream burst out, piercing and distended, as though torn from the throat of a woman in labor.

He stiffened, shook himself, darted a hand toward my mouth to cap what had risen to an unearthly shriek. I twirled across the bed, sprang to my feet, and bolted for the door. He reached it first, whirled me around, and slapped me repeatedly with the side of the knife. Then, as I twisted away, he leaped at me.

I jumped aside and he crashed headlong to the floor. The knife spun from his hand, clattered against the baseboard. A single thought panicked through my mind: I was alone with a drunken madman determined to mutilate or kill me.

I grabbed the knife and turned toward him. He was on his feet, stumbling, rushing at me. Then he dived for me and . . . and the knife went through him, just below the chest. Even before I dropped it, I think I knew I'd killed him.

Turning from the torrent of blood, I saw at the open door the petrified figure of Jennifer, her pale child's face hideously contorted.

Behind her was John. He telephoned the police.

"Good God," Chris whispered.

My forehead rested on his knee. He rubbed my back to calm the trembling.

"It was unavoidable, Diane. Apparently the jury saw that."

"There was *no* jury trial. I couldn't subject Jennifer to that. It would have gone on for weeks, with every bit of Fred's ugliness publicly revealed. It would have been smeared across newspapers, broadcast on radio and television. She was only a child. I was afraid it would destroy her."

"I understand. Awful enough that she'd lost him."

"Yes. She never knew how heavily he drank. And she never knew of the sadistic abuse that had gone on in that bedroom. Her room was at the other end of the house."

"But how did you keep it from her? Weren't you prosecuted?"

"I was allowed to throw myself on the mercy of the court. There was only a judge involved. Most of the sordid details were given in the judge's chambers and were never released."

Quickly I finished the story. An autopsy disclosed that Fred's blood indeed contained a massive concentration of alcohol. Testimony of his Mendocino drinking companions elicited reluctant admissions of his bouts with the bottle, occasionally erupting into senseless rage. The picture that emerged was of a high-powered, hard-drinking business executive who could without warning swing from euphoria to truculence—symptomatically a manic depressive.

John and Anna testified they had been wakened by the screams and had heard sounds of violence. Jennifer had not been required to testify, both because of her age and because of a psychiatrist's deposition stating (I still remember the words): "The intolerably traumatic experience has resulted in psychogenic amnesia, forcing the material beneath the level of consciousness."

After a tearful plea to the judge, he acquitted me.

There was a long pause before Chris said, "Did your daughter acquit you?"

I stifled a moan. "No. She may even have believed I deliberately killed him."

"My God! Why would she think that?"

"I had the feeling she thought I was in love with Gordon Hathaway."

I saw no reason to reveal that, a year after Fred's death, Gordon had, in fact, become my lover. The affair survived for only a few months—long enough for both of us to reach the tacit understanding that his passion really belonged to art and mine was merely an erotic escape from loneliness. We drifted out as passively as we had drifted in and remained friends. He was now teaching at the Art Center in Los Angeles and we rarely saw each other.

Chris said, "Did she finally remember being at the door, seeing it happen?"

"She doesn't remember *anything*. Apparently it was erased permanently, thank goodness. She only knows what I told her, the partial truth reported in the press."

"You don't see her?"

"I haven't seen her since the day she turned eighteen. She wrote me a note saying only that she was going away. She was of legal age and there was nothing I could do. Since then, she's sent me three postcards, none with an address. I got the last one about two months ago. It was postmarked Honolulu."

"I'm sorry, Diane, deeply sorry. I see now why you've never talked about her."

Actually I had seen little of Jennifer since she was twelve. At her insistence, she had gone away to school; a good idea, I thought: perhaps her hostility toward me would diminish with absence, and also she would no longer be victimized by the taunts of her peers. I knew how demoralizing the latter could be. Not one of all the people I had known, excepting Gordon, had offered a word of compassion or sympathy. I know I should have expected that; all of them, husbands and wives, had been Fred's friends, not mine—sycophants really, bought and paid for by Fred's power to control their lives. But understanding had made me no less bitter. How righteous they must have felt in casting me out. Diane Ridgway, the notorious woman who had somehow managed to short-circuit justice.

But there had been more to it than moral outrage, I suspected. As a twenty-eight-year-old widow, I had suddenly become a threat to every wife in the community. After a few years of quarantine, thankfully relieved by Gordon, I was more than ready for a man like Bryan Wilcox, who didn't care if the so-called respectable people lived or died. But that had been no more than lust, acknowledged to myself but nevertheless defiantly pursued until finally extinguished by its own heat. I had then retreated gladly to a solitary, pastoral life in Mendocino, among people who asked no questions and made no demands. It had been enough—until now.

We sat in silence for a while, Chris smoking a cigarette. Then he got up, suggesting a cup of coffee. There was an air of reserve about him when he returned. Apparently he'd had more than enough of the Diane soap opera, the story of a tarnished woman.

I was sure I had lost him.

Jennifer

FIVE

As soon as I came down the ramp at San Francisco airport, I saw Paul Stafford in the concourse crowd. He stood out like a magnum of champagne in a gang of beer bottles. A beautiful man: razor-cut blond hair, medium long, eyes as blue as Waikiki water, taut skin still deeply tanned from the Hawaiian sun. He gave a high wave and I grinned and jiggled my head like an idiot. I'd been scared numb he wouldn't show.

I dropped my two flight bags when I was a yard from his chest and leaped the rest of the way. We hugged and kissed as though he was a returning war prisoner instead of the man who had left me only a week ago in Honolulu. A couple of guys started clapping and whistling, so we broke it up before things got too heavy.

"Let's see now, where were we?" he said, scooping up my bags.

"I was begging you not to leave. You were saying, oh, no, you'd fly on ahead and find us a neat place to live. I was saying

I'd walk out on my job and we'd find it together. You shut me up with your fascinating mouth."

"Now I remember."

"Did you?"

"Did I what?"

"Find us a place?"

"You'll see."

He'd probably managed to get my old pad back (I'd given him the address) but I decided to keep quiet and act surprised.

We skirted the rotunda and took an escalator down. I started for the bus loading station but he nudged me along and we clattered down some iron stairs to a dark garage. He strode ahead, past rows of cars, and stopped. I caught up and looked into the stall.

"Limousine service," he said.

"Great! I didn't know they rented VWs."

"Not rented, *bought*. It's a '63 but the engine's only two years old. The man said."

"It's beautiful. I'm paying half."

"Nope. It's a gift from me to you."

"Wow. Mr. Stafford, how can I ever thank you?"

"I'll come up with something."

"Now you're talking."

"Not here. We could get run over."

We got in the brown bug, worked up a little more excitement, then took off. We drove up Bayshore Highway to the city, then down Franklin to the Marina, where we took the long way around the edge of the bay. It was a bright, warm May afternoon with sailboats scudding across the flat water. In the distance, the arch of the Golden Gate Bridge was in purple shadow, the towers fiery red. Looking across to the opposite shore, I could see the wooded banks of Belvedere. With a telescope, I could probably have picked out the dock where my father had moored his boat, and above it, the big white house where I had lived and where he had died. I felt a stab of pain but the scar tissue held.

We rolled across the bridge, took the Sausalito cutoff, and twisted down the snaky road, soon passing the fancy view-apartments and old clapboard houses peeking through the trees. We leveled off on Bridgway, the main drag, where some bearded welfares were sunning themselves on the shoreline boulders. Ahead, cars were pulling off on the planked parking area fronting the white-and-blue Trident restaurant. Sea gulls swooped, water glinted, and a salted breeze blew gently through the open windows. Paul glanced at me and his lips moved into that ghost of a smile which was his maximum expression of pleasure.

"Why did I ever leave?" I said.

I saw his eyebrow arch.

"Okay," I said. "I know. But I was crazy then. I'm not crazy anymore. Except about you."

It wasn't really such a heavy subject but I was sorry I'd reminded him of it. Five months before, I'd left Sausalito for the Islands with a guy I'd met while helping out at Synanon, a halfway house for junkies. He'd turned clean, he said, and he knew he'd stay clean if he could just have me around. Well, he'd already had me, and not just around, so why not keep him company in paradise?

We went to Maui, bought a beat-up van, and lived in it on the beach near Lahaina. We'd get jobs, he'd said. I made it as a cocktail waitress. He made it as a thief, ripping off vacation homes of the rich near Kaanapali. He promised to quit that, and did until he ran into an old dealer buddy and started turning on with acid instead of with me. I finally split to Honolulu alone and took a one-room apartment three blocks from Waikiki's hotel strip. I didn't quite have the plane fare home, and besides, what the hell, why not see if the travel folders were telling it like it is.

I'd worked as a model and, with my long red hair and stacked figure, had no trouble getting jobs at fashion shows, business conventions (usually parading onstage in a sandwich sign), and in TV commercials, often working with crews sent out by mainland advertising agencies.

Men were strictly for laughs, both because it took a while to shuck the inner grime left by the acid head and because the guys, if married, were generally sneaky fanny-pinchers or, if single, were either champion bowlers, ace salesmen, or game-show contestants who had won an all-expense trip to Hilton's Hawaiian Village. Then late one morning I was sitting at the bar of the Captain's Room at the Surfrider having a mai tai and gazing out at the surfers when in walked the best looking guy I'd ever seen. He took a stool next to the wall, ordered a drink, and didn't glance my way. I tagged him for an actor involved in some location shooting.

I finished the mai tai and was about to split when a group of conventioneers stumbled in carrying tons of flowered leis. They'd just arrived and were really smashed, courtesy Western Airlines, and they thought it hilarious to shout "Aloha!" at me, kiss my cheeks, and smother me with leis. I played it cool but tried to cut out. I'd have made it if a fat clown with a wattled throat hadn't grabbed me in a bear hug and smeared my mouth with a big sloppy kiss. I was about to jab him with my elbow but was stopped by a low, lethal voice.

"I see you've met my wife."

Lover boy sprang back like he'd been goosed. Turning, I saw that my rescuer was the nifty loner at the bar. His eyes, then, had appeared wistful. Now they looked as hard as blue coral. The drunks all spluttered apologies, then skulked away.

The blond knight escorted me out, shrugging off my thanks

but saying nothing. I thought he was speechless with rage but, looking up, I saw a smile tugging at the corner of his mouth. He took me across to the courtyard of the Moana Hotel and sat me at a table under the huge banyan tree. He ordered a scotch for himself and another mai tai for me (so he must have noticed).

"Okay," I said, "if I'm your wife, what's my name?"

"Mrs. Paul Stafford."

"I like it. But you can call me Jennifer Ridgway."

He was a stockbroker, had been an account executive with a big Wall Street firm, but quit when he'd been aced out of a promotion in a political power play. Before returning to the corporate wars, he'd decided on a few weeks of hanging loose in the Islands. He'd arrived two days ago and was staying at the Royal Hawaiian.

"With the real Mrs. Paul Stafford?"

"I don't have a wife."

"Well, okay, with *somebody*."

"And I don't have a somebody."

I licked on a smile. "Maybe I could fix that."

He gave me a slow, roving look, starting with my long hair ("the color of marmalade," my father once said), shifting to my eyes (almost as blue as his but a little too large for my small nose and chin), then descending and lingering on the yellow strip of cloth cinching my breasts (my white beach robe had unaccidentally fallen open).

"I'm too old for you," he said. "Thirty-four. You look nineteen."

"I'm twenty. And I dig older men."

I said it facetiously but in a way it was true. I'd about had it with the childlike characters who hid their insecurity behind a manufactured cool, a layer of mysticism, and acres of hair. I'd been taking their trip ever since I left home—guzzled their wine, smoked their grass, shared their pads. I'd done it in

Mazatlan and Vancouver and Denver and Sausalito and in a commune on the Russian River, ending up on the recent bummer in Maui. I wasn't ready yet to abandon the hips—they were still my friends and I liked their gentleness and the way they shared—but I no longer felt a part of them. For a long time, something inside me had been yelling for more substantial fare, which maybe explained why I'd given time to Synanon and a home for runaways and day care for kids. That had helped but it was far from the answer. What I needed, I guess, was some groovy guy who had it all together and would do some of my thinking for me.

Paul Stafford turned out to be the guy. Three days later, in one of those big square rooms in the Royal Hawaiian, we took each other to bed. And afterward, we discovered we were alike in lots of ways. We had the same sense of humor, liked doing the same things, hated phonies, were wary of the establishment, and believed in making it on our own. The only gap between us was the *way* he wanted to make it: someday he wanted to own his own brokerage firm. I dug his independence but not the method; to me, the stock market was a jungle prowled by money grubbers who suffered from ulcers, headaches, and hemorrhoids. But the market was all he knew, and besides, I figured he was unique and therefore an exception. I'd never shot dope but I imagine it would hit me the way Paul did. I was completely freaked out.

I turned down jobs so that I could be with him all the time. He rented a pink jeep and we bucketed all over the island. We flew to Kauaii and to Kona on the Big Island. We snorkeled and surfed and sailed. But mostly we baked on the beach in front of the Royal, then had a drink on the terrace and went upstairs, showered together, and made love. Sometimes he came to my place, but generally it was the Royal, where it all seemed like some fantastic honeymoon.

In a few weeks I was broke. I called the model agency, said I was available, and lucked into an immediate assignment—a promotion film for the Visitors Bureau. Counting preproduction meetings, I'd be locked in for about ten days. I didn't tell Paul until I'd made the commitment, afraid he'd talk me into living on his money.

He gave me that wisp of a smile. "Quite a coincidence. We both hit the shorts at the same time."

"You? The way you've been spending it, I figured you were printing it."

"When I settle with the hotel, my net worth will be about a thousand dollars. Enough to fly back and carry me until I can line up a job."

Something squeezed my heart. "You sound like you're about to take off."

"In three days."

"Oh, no! Where will you go—back to New York?"

"Anyplace *but* New York. There's nothing there for me. And nothing *here* for me."

"Paul!"

"You won't be here. Not after you finish the movie."

"*Where* will I be?"

"Living with me. What's the name of that town—Sausalito?"

And here I was, rattling along Bridgway, passing the No Name Bar where a couple of leathered longhairs standing outside gave me a clenched-fist salute. We approached the apartment house where I used to live—a boxlike wooden building with peeling gray paint that sat on barnacled pilings. And we went right on by. I looked at him questioningly but he stared straight ahead.

About a mile outside of town he turned off on a dirt road that ran down to the water. He stopped in a rocky parking area facing a boardwalk that jutted into the bay. Getting out and

waving an arm, he said, "Your castle's over there someplace." I
shielded my eyes and gazed out along the boardwalk. My flash
impression was of a junkyard that had somehow been com-
pacted, flown high in the sky, and dropped in the mud.

"You moved the Royal Hawaiian," I said.

"Don't be hasty. Wait'll you see."

The house stood at the very end of the boardwalk. It was no
more than a cabinlike structure—peaked shingle roof, rough
batten siding, wood-railed deck—anchored on a mud flat. It
looked dismal as we approached but, once there, it suddenly
became something out of a fairy tale. On two sides there was a
sweeping panorama of the bay, now winged with sailboats
slanting around green-breasted islands, and beyond, the misted
city of San Francisco swooping up from the sea.

"Oh, Paul, it's too much!"

"The view's what sold me. But you'd better see the other
side."

We walked around the deck and got a close-up of the tangled
mess I'd seen from the road. Huddled together and joined by
narrow walkways was a weird collection of so-called houseboats:
mobile homes bolted to barges, converted steel landing craft,
tented platforms, splintered scows.

"Welcome to Hippy Haven," I said.

"Not really. I don't think there's a tenant under sixty."

They were senior dropouts, he explained—lowly pensioners,
the disenchanted, the nonaggressive. Perfect neighbors for
us—unobtrusive, unquestioning, and tolerant.

Inside the house, there was a small living room and a bedroom
separated by a galley and bathroom. Everything looked in need
of repair. The maroon paint was scratched and chipped around
the travel posters in the living room. There were worn spots on
the yellow sofa and cushioned chairs. The kitchen was sooted,

the refrigerator buzzed. The toilet sounded like it was having an asthma attack. All the carpeting was threadbare.

I must have looked a little out of shape because Paul said, "For one-fifty a month you don't get the solid-gold fixtures." He shrugged. "I know it's sort of ratty. But you wanted to be on the water and this was the only place vacant."

"It'll be a ball fixing it up. I'll start tomorrow. Paint, carpeting—vinyl would be okay—slipcovers—"

He shook his head. "Better not plow any money into it. We may be thrown out in a couple of weeks."

"Because we're not married? Ha."

"Nothing like that. It seems that our ecology-minded citizens have been having fits about the people here polluting the water. None of these places is tied into a sewer line. So all the wastes get dumped into the bay. Even the fish are hollering."

"So why not just tie into a sewer line?"

"Not that simple. There aren't enough sewers. They have to be built. In fact, they're being built right now. But it'll be months before they'll be in service. Meantime the local power structure demands that the residents get out. There's a big hassle about it. It should be decided in a week or so."

It seemed kind of dumb to take a place where we might be evicted even before we were settled. But I said, "Who cares. With you I'd live in a tree."

A smile dented his cheek. "There's one thing about this house I think you'll completely approve of."

"What's that?"

"The bed."

I smiled. "Prove it."

SIX

FROM THE DECK I watched Paul park the VW and walk to the stairs leading down to the boardwalk. His suit coat was slung over his shoulder, his tie was loosened, and he shambled like a man worried about a coronary. I recalled how up he'd been that morning ("today's the day!") and my heart took on weight.

He greeted me with a listless "Hi" and barely grazed my cheek with a kiss. Flopping into a canvas chair, he stared out at the water. I got him the local afternoon paper, still folded and tied.

"You relax," I said, "while I get us a drink. Tall, cold ones." It wasn't yet five o'clock, the day still warm.

He was turning a page when I came back with two vodka tonics and sat in the matching director chair. "Just what you need," I said, handing him a glass.

He let the paper fall to his lap. "What I need is a bull market."

"They said no?" I tried to speak as though it didn't matter.

"Not exactly. 'Don't call us, we'll call you.' Understandable. The indicators are all down. Every brokerage house in town is retrenching. Still, I thought with my credentials—"

"Weren't they impressed?"

"Impressed, sure. But my contacts are all in New York. If they were here, if I could bring clients along with me, that would be something else."

It had been his third job turndown in as many days, which made five counting the two brokers he'd applied to before I arrived.

"Something's bound to open up," I said. "Meanwhile I'll just put a little more water in the soup."

"Pretty soon there won't be any soup."

"Paul, why don't I—"

"I won't live off you, Jennifer." His voice was curt and final. "I'm not against your working. But what you make you'll keep."

I shut up. He'd made it clear before that he refused to be obligated, at least not to a woman. "A hangup I've had since I was a kid," he had said. "I was brought up by three women—my mother, her old-maid sister, and *their* mother. They made my life hell, and my father's too."

That same night, lying in the darkness, he had given me glimpses of that life. Afterwards, I'd put it together in a scenario . . .

Little things. Don't hang your head. Straighten your shoulders. Stop pulling at yourself. Said first by one, then the other two women chiming in.

Big things. His mother's voice rasping down the hall, penetrating his bedroom door:

"He will stay locked in his room, James, until I am satisfied he has learned his lesson."

"But Martha, the boy was only playing stickball."

"I had *forbidden* it. Ever since he hit a ball through Mrs. Sloan's window and she called the police."

"Paul paid for that window. He earned the money washing cars."

His mother's sister: "That was *his* story."

"Now look, Clara—"

His mother's mother: "Spare the rod and spoil the child."

Short silence. Then the sound of his father walking into the kitchen. Sneaking whiskey. Walking back.

"It's Saturday. I thought I'd take him to the ball game."

His mother: "To sit in that awful *press box?* With those *roughneck reporters?* Oh *no,* James."

His mother's mother: "No place for a boy."

His mother's sister: "Drinking and cursing. Disgusting."

"I'm sorry you fine people disapprove of my job. It doesn't seem to bother you that it supports you."

He must have taken a big drink. Why didn't he take another and another and then turn on them as he sometimes did?

His mother's mother: "Really, James!"

Or just leave, taking his son on one of their tramps in the woods. His father would laugh and tell funny stories and maybe make him a slingshot.

His mother: ". . . a *sports* writer. Always mingling with the worst type of people. Away from home half the time. Hardly a normal life!"

His mother's mother: "The Lord only knows what goes on."

His mother's sister: "The stories I've heard. Just terrible."

His mother: "And *you,* James, alone with your awful *weakness.*"

"My God. I'm going to work."

But stopping off in the kitchen first. The whiskey was kept in a mason jar hidden on the high shelf of the broom closet.

Then there was that hot day his father came home in mid-afternoon—not by train, as usual, but by taxi, all the way from Manhattan to Montclair, New Jersey. His voice from the street hoarse and angry, and so loud it brought Paul hopping to the front window.

His father was stumbling out of a cab, helped by the embarrassed driver, and he was flourishing an arm and shouting, "Look at yourselves, you goddam bloodless saints, you sanctimonious shits! Sitting there hoping to God something evil will happen so you can congratulate yourselves on your goddam piety!" Wow.

His audience was the three matriarchs and a few neighborhood ladies, all perched primly on camp chairs on the shady front lawn. They were looking away, pretending he wasn't there.

"Well, be happy! Something evil *has* happened. The drunken son of a bitch is home!"

He stuffed a wad of bills into the driver's hand and lurched across the sidewalk. Then, shirttail out, fly half open, he blistered them with every word that had ever been soaped from Paul's mouth and then some.

No sorrow for them, only for his father. And a strange pride, too.

Paul's mother didn't speak to his father for a week, and when she did—tearing him down and ordering him about—he answered meekly. Then he went off on a road trip with the Yankees and Paul was left alone with the three witches. Paul got a note from his father about every other day and autographs of the players. It was the only thing that made life bearable.

When he was sixteen, there had been a girl—Hope Drewes. But she had been pressured to break it off by her mother when his father had died of cirrhosis of the liver, leaving them almost penniless. Somewhere along the line he had married, but it had lasted less than a year. "She tried to mother me," was all he said.

I had wondered then why he had let so much of himself hang out. Now, I thought I knew. He was simply saying: Look, I refuse to be owned. I could understand that; I'd felt the same way. But not any more. Paul Stafford could do about anything he wanted with me, may women's lib forgive me.

I tried not to let him know that, scared that I'd remind him of certain women who had been his clients in New York. Widows and divorcees mostly, who flipped over him for the privilege of having him invest their money. I was sure he'd balled most of them because once he said, "I was a male whore, exchanging sweet talk and companionship for business." He didn't want to go back to that. Just the mention of it almost made me spit up.

He had set his glass on the deck and was staring at something in the paper. He groaned.

"Reading the obituaries?" I said.

"You could call it that. Anyway, a death sentence has just been handed down." He read: " 'Last night the Sausalito City Council, meeting in emergency session, voted to evict the residents of the controversial houseboat colony situated a mile north of the business district. The decision requires tenants to leave within two weeks, not to return until adequate sewage facilities have been installed. Estimates indicate this may take from six to eight months. A representative of the people affected stated that they will immediately appeal the decision to the County Board of Supervisors.' And so on."

"There goes our view." I wasn't too busted up. Plenty of other places we could go.

He picked up his drink and took a gulp. "At least we won't get tossed out for not paying the rent."

"Maybe this will change your luck." Little Miss Sunshine, like Shirley Temple in an old movie.

He threw the paper down. "I don't think you're getting the message. There's nothing here for me. I'm close to broke. I've got to make a decision."

I felt my stomach quiver. "Like what?"

"Like going back East."

"You mean New York?"

"Yes, Wall Street. I hate the idea but, dammit, I've got to start earning some money. Back there, I know I can get a decent job—perhaps pick and choose—despite the soft market."

"Well, okay, don't get mad. We'll split anytime you say." Big pause.

"Not *we*," he said quietly. "I'd go alone."

My glass clicked against my teeth. I blinked, feeling my lashes dampen. He spoke again quickly, his voice like a buzz in my head:

"Just until I got located. Then I'd send for you."

I tried to believe him but couldn't. He'd get caught up once more in that older sophisticated crowd and realize that the chick he remembered in cutoffs and T-shirt would only be a drag.

"Can't we think about it?" I said.

"Sure. No rush. I'll give it another week here. Maybe you're right—something might break."

We finished our drinks in silence. He went back to the paper as I went inside for a refill. I felt all unglued and helpless. It reminded me of when I had been away at school and would sometimes wake in the dark shaking with fright, believing I was lost and would never be found. Then I would see my father's face, almost as though he were alive, and the fright would go away. But not the pain.

When I came back on deck, his eyes were again narrowed on a news item. He took the drink without looking at me.

"Are you related to a Diane Ridgway?" he said.

I sat down slowly, hearing the ice jiggle. "My mother's name is Diane."

"Does she live near Mendocino?"

"Yes."

We had never discussed my parents. Once, to his question, I'd mentioned that my mother was a widow, that she lived up the coast, and that we couldn't make it together. He had settled for that, probably figuring me for just another generation-gap rebel. I had told him that my father had been killed ten years ago "in an accident," the word bitter in my mouth. If he assumed car accident, that was okay with me. Why spoil our fun by peeling off that ugly scab?

He said, "It must be her. Congratulations. You now have a new father."

I felt my mouth drop open. "My mother got *married?*"

"Sounds shocking, doesn't it? Anyway, the ceremony was performed last Sunday in her house near Mendocino. The happy groom is—" His eyes searched for the name.

"Don't tell me. I can guess."

He looked at me. "So you know him?"

The old resentment surfaced. "It's been going on for years. The last I heard, he lived in L.A. . . . Gordon Hathaway."

He squinted at the paper. "You're close. It seems that a Gordon Hathaway gave the bride away. So there couldn't have been much going on between them lately."

For a second I wondered if I could have been mistaken about my mother and Gordon. I remembered how often he came to the house and how they'd go off together and talk and sometimes closet themselves in her studio. And that day beside the pool, acting like lovers. Maybe I wouldn't have been so suspicious if, at the same time, she hadn't begun to cool it with my father. And then . . . no, not that!

"Okay," I said, "you've had your suspense."

"She married a Colonel, recently retired. His name is Christopher Warren."

"My, there's lots of news today. I don't know him."

"You will."

"I doubt it. I'm not about to take a three-hour drive just to give them my blessing."

"A fifteen-minute drive. It says here they're now living in your mother's house in Belvedere. That's only about a dozen miles away."

So she had come back to face her judges. Probably she thought that with a retired Colonel to front for her they'd grant her a pardon. And maybe they would. Most of them would suck up to anybody who smelled of status.

"You never told me your home was in Belvedere," he said. He had put down the paper and was looking at me curiously.

"I stopped thinking of it as my home a long time ago."

"Why? Because you and your mother didn't get along? Hell, you were a kid. Most kids hate their mothers, or think they do, at one time or another. They grow up and get over it."

"*You* didn't." My lips felt stiff.

"My mother despised the entire male sex, just as her mother did. I'm sure she wished I'd been a girl so I could have carried on the crusade. That doesn't sound like the woman who brought you up."

"My *father* brought me up." It was out before I could stop it.

He shifted his chair around to face me. "I guess I don't really know you, Jennifer."

"I've told you everything important." My mind fished around for a way to change the subject.

"That you went away to school? That you took off on your own when you were eighteen and hung out with hippies and ended up nursing a drug freak on Maui? Sure, you told me all that. But you've been strangely silent about anything that happened before."

"It wasn't interesting."

"Oh, I know. You just implied that your mother was having an affair with this Gordon Hathaway. That's pretty interesting."

"I shouldn't have said what I did. I'm not sure."

"I'll bet you were sure at the time you first thought it."

So he was laying the day's bad trip on me. I looked at my glass. It was empty. "I was only about ten at the time."

"About ten? Isn't that when you said your father died?"

"Yes. Paul, let's drop—"

"So that at the time your father died—killed in an accident, you said—you believed that your mother and Gordon Hathaway were lovers?"

I fidgeted. "You sound like a shrink. What *is* this?"

"It's an attempt to find out why you're so down on your mother."

"What difference does it make?"

"It could make a lot of difference to us. If you faced whatever it is that's bugging you, you might not be so uptight."

"I'm uptight?"

"Yes. Except in bed."

"Okay, let's go in and unwind." I tried to say it flippantly but my voice shook.

"First, tell me something. If your father had lived, would you still have hated your mother?"

I did some heavy breathing.

"Haven't you been placing some of the guilt for his death on your mother?"

"Goddamn it, Paul—" I started to cry.

He sat there, not touching me, until the tears stopped. Then he picked me up, carried me inside, and held me close to him on the sofa. My body went limp and I had the feeling I was caught in one of those time warp things, shooting me back to when I was a little kid.

"I think that was long overdue," he said. He kissed my wet cheek. "Want to talk abut it?"

Surprisingly, I did—if only to justify myself. I sat up, wiping my eyes with the back of my hand. "Okay. You asked if I've been blaming my mother for my father's death. The answer is, damned right I have."

"Good. You've admitted it."

"Because that's right where the blame belongs." I was cool now, almost detached. I said bluntly, "She stabbed him to death with a knife."

That zapped him. "Jennifer, for God sake!"

It had been dammed up inside me for ten years and now it came bursting out. As I spoke, blurry pictures formed in my mind. My mother defiantly declaring her love for Gordon Hathaway. My father, stunned, moving toward her, hands held out in protest. My mother grabbing the knife, leaping at him, plunging the blade through his heart.

When I finished I had a weird feeling that it didn't sound quite right. It seemed oversimplified, the way a child . . .

"You talk as though you were right there and saw it," Paul said. The horror in his voice was edged with doubt.

"I saw him after he was on the floor, dead."

"Jesus, what a thing to have to remember."

"But I *don't* remember. I heard about it from a psychiatrist. And it was in the papers." I told him how the shock had wiped out all recollection.

He was silent for a moment, then said gently, "What was your mother's version?"

"She said that *he* came after *her* with the knife. That he fell down, dropped the knife, and she picked it up—to defend herself, she said. And, get this, she said he just happened to run into it. An accident, she claimed. And, my God, the judge believed her and set her free!"

"But you still think it happened the way you just told it?"

. . . *the way a child might see it . . . a child who distrusted her mother and worshipped her father.*

"I don't know what I believe anymore," I said. "I only know that she admitted killing him."

The child's version had been sealed unquestioned in my mind, as though in a steel vault, and had not been brought out for inspection in ten years. Looking at that version now, I wondered about its value. I remembered my father's drinking, remembered sometimes being wakened by his voice shouting in their bedroom (she had goaded him to it, I had thought). Could I have been wrong about my mother and Gordon? Had she somehow been forced into what she'd done?

Paul seemed to read my mind: "You're a big girl now. Isn't it time you gave her the benefit of the doubt?"

I said sulkily, "What do you want me to do, throw my arms around her and beg forgiveness?"

"Nothing like that. But why not at least see her? It might be good for both of you."

I thought about it. What could we say to each other? She'd yak about her colonel and expect me to do the same about Paul and she'd think he was a bum when I said he was unemployed. . . . Hey!

A light had switched on in my head. My mother had tons of money. My *father's* money. And a big chunk of it should by rights be mine; if not now, then sometime in the future. I ought to have a say about it. Maybe that was the answer to Paul's job problem.

"Paul, I just thought of something terrific."

"What?"

No, not yet. I'd save the surprise until *after* I talked to my mother. For all I knew, she might tell me to go to hell and hang up.

"Let's make love."

I telephoned the next day. A woman with a slight accent answered: "Hello, this is the Warren residence." I told her who I was. "Ah, yes. I am Elga, the maid. One moment, please."

My mother's voice came on sounding breathless: "Jennifer! How wonderful!"

"How are you, mother?"

"I'm fine. Fine. I just can't believe—"

"I know. It's been a long time. I read that you'd gotten married. The least I can do is offer my best wishes. I hope you'll be very happy."

"Thank you, Jennifer. Where are you?"

"In Sausalito. I'm living here now."

"We're practically neighbors! Jennifer, I want to see you. I want you to meet Chris. Why don't you come and stay with us for awhile."

"Sorry, but no way. I'm living with a man."

"Oh?"

"I couldn't very well leave him."

"Of course not. Bring him over, I'd love to meet him."

"I'll tell Paul."

"Does he . . . is he . . ."

"You're probably wondering if he sells beads and pottery on the street."

"There's nothing wrong with—"

"He's a stockbroker. And very good at it."

"Wonderful! Please tell him how welcome he'll be. And Jennifer—"

"Yes?"

"I . . . I just want you to know how much I've regretted our . . . estrangement. I should have been more understanding. But perhaps now we can—"

"I've done a lot of growing up, mother."

"Oh, Jennifer, if you'll just give me the chance, I'll—"

"I understand, mother. I'll talk to Paul and call you again tomorrow."

I told Paul when he got back from the city (again no luck). "You go alone," he said. "Maybe spend an afternoon together. I'll meet her after you've signed the peace."

Then I told him that my father had been the chief executive officer of Pacific Valley Foods and had left my mother filthy rich.

His eyes popped, but all he said was, "Well, well, how nice for the Colonel."

I didn't mention that it could also be nice for Paul Stafford.

Standing beside the Volks, parked halfway up the long curving driveway, I gazed at the house where I had spent my childhood. It sat on a knoll, long and white, with fluted colonnades rising two stories from the brick veranda. Green shuttered windows, green entrance doors, an attached three-car garage (only a white T-Bird visible now). No lawn, no flowers, but the surroundings were lush with exotic plants and tall pines.

Everything about the place reminded me of another era, from the square stone chimney to the fancy locks with their wrought-iron keys. I pictured the big entrance hall with the roof for its ceiling, the broad staircase, the plate-glass lanai overlooking the pool, and beyond it, the slope leading down to the dock where my father's power cruiser had been moored.

I recalled those Saturday mornings when just the two of us would chug across the choppy bay, tie up at the Embarcadero, and devour a huge breakfast in a funky waterfront restaurant. He hadn't treated me as a child, but as an equal, sometimes swearing when he wanted to emphasize something. At the bar, old salts with stubbled jaws and worn black caps would turn and look at us with envy and admiration.

When we came back, we'd sit on the end of the dock and fish. I remembered the time I hooked a minnow and my father gaped at it. "We'll have it stuffed," he said. "We'll mount it on a Saltine." Laughing together.

To the right of the house, in a clearing, I saw the scuffed ground that marked where my swing had hung from a high limb. My father's words echoed through my mind: "Up! Wa-a-a-y up! Kick a hole in the sky!" Hands folding around my waist when I came flying back. Feeling secure.

Gone now. Gone for half the years I'd lived. As were the cat and the dog and the miniature horse named Ben who had pulled me in the undersized surrey. "You're Ben's Her," my father had said solemnly. I'd grinned proudly, not getting it until I saw the movie starring Charlton Heston.

How my father had spoiled me. More so than he ever had my mother. She had been more like an ornament, a glorified hostess who'd spent most of her time planning parties and jazzing around with the wives of the men who were always trying to make points with my father.

Father's dead.

Killed by the woman who now owned everything he'd worked so hard to get. I felt a sudden panic, an urge to blitz off and never come back. Then I thought of Paul.

I got back in the car and drove closer to the house.

At the door, I half expected my ring to be answered by John. John, with the red, jowled, kind mick face, who used to play games with me when my father was away.

But the person who greeted me was a young woman, the one who'd answered the phone, judging by the faint accent.

"You are Mrs. Warren's daughter?"

She had straight flaxen hair pulled back into a bun, a pink fraulein complexion, and wore a light-blue maid's outfit that fit loosely over breasts flattened by a tight bra.

"Yes, I'm Jennifer *Ridgway*." It seemed important that she knew whose daughter I was.

She smiled shyly, lowered her eyes, and motioned for me to follow her. Crossing the reception hall, I had the eerie feeling that I was being led backwards through time.

Diane

SEVEN

On the first Friday after Chris left, he phoned from his San Francisco hotel to say he wouldn't be coming up that weekend. He had run into some former military friends who he hoped might provide him with business contacts. I said I understood— sure in my heart that it was a maneuver of disengagement. I felt forlorn and frustrated, but not bitter. After all, it had been I who had instigated the affair.

Back I went to my painting, attacking canvases as though they were hostile objects that must be violently subdued. The next Friday came and went with no phone call. I had declined invitations to two cocktail parties—(still hoping, though deny- ing it to myself) but finally, in desperation, went to both of them.

On Saturday I woke at seven to a bright day and a dark mood, gathered up my art materials and a thermos of coffee and fled to the beach. By eleven o'clock, I had messed up one canvas and was starting on a second when, from behind me, I heard:

"Would you really rather be doing that?"

I spun around and froze. Chris stood there, smiling whimsically, hands thrust into his jacket pockets. I wanted to kick him, hug him, run him off the property, take him to my bed. But I didn't move or speak.

"I called you last night," he said. "And early this morning." He moved toward me.

"I was—"

A kiss interrupted me. It was a wild, graceless reunion. Standing there in the soft sand, we swayed, grappled, clung— each of us seemingly trying to smother the other. We were unbalanced mentally and physically; my hip struck the easel and it toppled over.

"Leave it," I said.

"Yes. I can't leave *you*."

We went up to the house, not breaking stride until we reached my room. We undressed silently, made love silently, doing all the things we had done before and adding undone things that our minds had had time to fantasize.

"No more being separated," he said afterwards. "I haven't the stamina."

"I haven't either. I'll move to San Francisco, take an apartment. We can be together every day. We'll come up here weekends."

"The first thing we'll do," he said, "is get married."

I was no longer wary of it. "Is that an order?"

"It is."

The wedding was like a festival. People came from miles around bearing food and wine and guitars. The day before the ceremony, Gordon Hathaway called; he just happened to be in San Francisco. He was genuinely delighted by my happiness and saw nothing improper about giving away the bride (nor did I; he seemed the only family I had). The celebration went on

for two days, followed by three days of honeymoon, Chris and I
not once leaving the house.

On the sixth day, over fireside coffee, we started to reacquaint
ourselves with reality. It was time, Chris said, that we thought
about moving to San Francisco where he could line up a job.
The idea of cooping ourselves up in an apartment seemed
dismal. I wondered about the house in Belvedere: would we feel
haunted by the reminders of Fred? The question evoked no
uneasiness and I concluded that love had immunized us against
past sorrows. Why not live there, at least temporarily? That
decided, I called the rental agent and asked when the house
could be made available. Immediately—the tenants had moved
out ten days before, the husband having been transferred East. It
seemed a good omen.

"Great!" Chris said when I told him. "Every man should
marry a woman who has two houses."

I had never mentioned the extent of my wealth, though it had
been on my mind for some time. The omission was due, I guess,
to a nagging qualm that such affluence might cause him to feel at
a disadvantage. It would be better to get it over with now before
he was shocked into awareness by the opulence of the Belvedere
house.

"Chris, I don't know why it's never come up, but I think you
should know that I'm quite well off."

He smiled, his eyes roving about the large room. "I didn't
consider you a poverty case."

"My husband left me a considerable amount of money."

"Fine. I didn't do too badly myself."

"He left me more than five million dollars."

He almost lost his mouthful of coffee. Setting his cup down
carefully, he stared at me, as though I had suddenly turned into
somebody else. "I hardly know what to say."

"Say you love me anyway."

"Well, of course, but . . ." He shook his head. "Give me time to get used to the idea."

I sensed him brooding about it for the rest of the day. He didn't mention it until that evening when we were having cocktails. Then he spoke in the manner of a military officer who has reached a fateful policy decision. Obviously, he said, our marriage had elevated him to a far better financial position than he could have expected if he had remained single. But his conscience demanded that the profitability be limited.

"It would be senseless, Diane, to insist that we live solely on my income. That would be unfair to you. And it would be unfair to me because I'd constantly be aware that I was depriving you."

"Oh, Chris, it wouldn't be as though I was giving you money to go out on your own and splurge. We'll use it for things we both want, for things we care about doing together."

He thought about it. Then, grudgingly: "All right, but it's not going to be one-sided. There'll be a strict limit to what I'll accept from you."

"Yes, Colonel. Sir."

Thank goodness that was settled.

But it wasn't settled. There was more brooding. Then, after we were in bed and had turned off the lights, he snapped his back on and said:

"There's another thing that should be decided, Diane. It sounds harsh, but I'm going to say it. If someday we should decide to separate—God forbid—I want it clearly understood that I will receive no money from you."

"Chris! Why worry about that now?"

He gazed resolutely at the ceiling. "I want you to feel secure. I want you to know that the only thing I want from you is you yourself."

I felt my eyes fill up.

"And we'll put that in writing," he said.

I protested but he was adamant. The day after we arrived in Belvedere he took me to a lawyer in San Francisco, where an agreement was drawn up, signed and witnessed by a notary.

"That leaves your will," he said in the taxi.

"My will?"

"Yes. I suggest we don't discuss my place in it for at least five years. Even then, I doubt if I'd agree to a share in it. The government is providing me with all the money I'll need until the day I die."

I squeezed his hand. "Chris?"

"Yes?"

"Your retirement was a terrible loss to the country."

He grinned, finally.

At the time, I was disturbed by the cold-bloodedness of the agreement. But that was quickly dissolved by my admiration for his independence and integrity. And, though I hated to confess it, I *did* feel more secure in his love.

Seeing him as a proud and sensitive man, I resolved that he must never feel diminished because of my money. Thus it was for me to suggest and for him to decide. New car? Fine. But one should be sufficient for the time being. Servants? A sleep-in maid should be enough, he thought, with outside help for the heavier work. It seemed to give him pleasure to trade in my Ford station wagon for a white T-Bird, to phone the employment agency and interview prospective maids, to arrange for professionals to come in once a week and clean the house and pool. Little things, of course—particularly for a man accustomed to supervising complex projects—but necessary if he was not to feel subordinate to a rich wife.

As for me, I was delighted to have a man handling things after all the years of going it alone. I felt wanted, pampered, protected. There was only one thing left to wish for.

And then that wish was answered. Jennifer called.

Physically, Jennifer had not changed at all in the two years since I had seen her so briefly. The same lava-spill of golden hair, the same delicate features that reminded me of a cameo on a Victorian brooch, the same swift, graceful movements, even the same faded-blue denims, now topped by a pink T-shirt.

Nevertheless there was a change. I had seen it when she first entered the lanai, her small feet sliding familiarly across the green-matted floor. It was apparent in her carriage—the listless droop was gone. And then I saw it in her expression—the sulkiness had been replaced by a sort of inner radiance that surfaced brilliantly in her eyes and her smile. That look had been turned on me but I knew that I was not the cause of it. Obviously, a man was. She was spectacularly in love.

As though by mutual consent, we had avoided the awkwardness of an embrace. I had simply clasped her hands in mine and said how pleased I was to see her and she had said the same. Then she had dropped down on the white sofa, her back to the pool, and I had sat facing her in the fan-backed bamboo chair. I felt overdressed and formal in my yellow-silk pants suit, a feeling heightened when Elga brought in coffee on a silver service and ceremoniously poured.

"Chris will join us soon," I said. "He's down at the pier."

A shadow seemed to cross her face. The pier, I guessed, had reminded her of her father. She nodded and sipped her coffee.

I went on: "I want to hear all about your young man. But first about you. We've got a lot of catching up to do."

What she had to say seemed rehearsed and artificial. She'd traveled around a lot (with girls), held a number of jobs (no details), had a few passing romances (not worth talking about), now lived on a houseboat with the bay for a front yard. She didn't mention Paul.

"Now about you, mother." Her tone seemed to say, Let's make this fast.

I did, until I came to Chris. Then, wanting, needing her approval, I became eloquent. Thinking back, I must have made it seem that Colonel Christopher Warren deserved to be immortalized in granite on Mount Rushmore. So solid, so kind, so understanding, so considerate, so . . .

"No chicken shit?"

I stared at her, then burst out laughing. She joined in.

"No, Jennifer, not a speck."

The strain between us eased.

"Now tell me about your young man," I said.

She smiled wryly. "That's twice you've said 'young man.' Paul is thirty-four, fourteen years older than I am."

I felt a slight shock. "Well—fine." I thought about it and found myself nodding in approval. Emphatically I said, "*Fine.* Jennifer, I think that for someone with your intelligence and, well, worldliness, a mature man would be very right."

"He is. Otherwise I wouldn't be living with him."

"Yes, you mentioned that on the phone."

"You disapprove?"

"Of course I don't disapprove. Especially if you really care about each other. Still—"

"Still you wish we were married."

"Oh, I'd prefer it, but—"

"Well, so would I. But he's got a hangup. He thinks a man should be able to support his wife."

"But you said—"

"I said he was a stockbroker. But right now he's out of a job and no one's hiring." Anguish clouded her eyes. "If something doesn't open up pretty quick, he's splitting for New York." She explained that he'd had an important job with a major Wall

Street brokerage house but had quit to live and work on the Coast. "His timing was off. The market's dying."

"Then wouldn't he have the same problem back there?"

"No. He's got clients in New York. His old firm would jump to get him back."

"I see." A sadness crept through me. "He'd take you with him, of course."

The radiance had vanished from her face. "He says he'd send for me. I know he means it now, but I think he'd change his mind after he got there. I'd be a drag." Her lips trembled slightly. "I'm afraid I'm going to lose him."

I recalled how crushed I had been when I thought I had lost Chris. I got up and sat beside her. "You mustn't worry," I said. "Perhaps I can help."

"Thank you, mother. But if you're thinking of a donation to tide him over, please forget it. Paul won't touch a dime that he hasn't earned. I think that's neat but—" She made a face.

"Has he said when he might be leaving?"

"Maybe in a few days, a week. We're being thrown out of our house, so I suppose that would be as good a time as any for him to cut out."

"Thrown out! Why?"

She told me about the sewage problem. I remembered seeing something about it in the paper but had paid it little notice.

"You *are* in a fix," I said. Impulsively I reached over and gripped her knee. "Dearest, let me think about this. I'm sure something can be done that won't offend Paul."

"You don't owe me anything, mother."

"It has nothing to do with *owe*. I want us to be friends. There's so much I hope to make you understand."

Her eyes seemed to search my face. "About father?"

I stifled a sigh. "Yes."

"Perhaps I'm beginning to understand."

"Oh, I hope that's true. Is that what you meant when you said you'd grown up?"

"Partly. Anyway, we needn't talk about father ever again." She mustered a bright look. "Instead we'll talk about your new husband."

A deep voice said, "Great! Let's talk about him now."

Chris, dressed in slacks and sport coat, stood erectly in the wide doorway, three tall drinks grouped in his hands. He beat me to the introductions with: "Hi, Jennifer. Welcome home. Calls for a libation."

She murmured something polite, regarding him with an odd look—quizzical, faintly suspicious—as though she had half expected a stern martinet. But as he distributed the drinks I saw the look melt away. By the time he had seated himself in the fan-backed chair and raised his glass in a smiling toast, she appeared totally disarmed. Welcome home. How ironical if it had come from me; how gracious when he said it.

"I've been looking forward to meeting you, Colonel."

"And I you, Jennifer. Call me Chris." He brushed self-mockingly at his broad lapels. "As you see, I'm a civilian now."

Jennifer smiled. "On you it looks good. You don't miss the Air Force?"

He gave me a warm glance. "I thought I did. Then I met your mother and found out what I was really missing." He grinned. "I understand you know something about that."

"I told Chris about you and Paul," I said.

Chris raised his glass. "All good wishes. I hope I'll meet him soon."

Jennifer gave a dry laugh. "The way it looks, it'll either be soon or never."

I explained Paul's difficulty in finding a suitable job and said that he might soon be forced to go back to New York.

"Rough," Chris said. He looked sympathetically at Jennifer.

"I can understand how he must feel about the job situation. I've been having a little trouble on that score myself. I'm either overqualified or it's something outside my experience." He swirled his drink, scowling at it. "A stockbroker. I wonder . . ." He stood up, rubbing at his chin.

"Wonder what?" I said.

"I wonder if he'd consider a small assignment from me. It wouldn't pay much, just a modest fee. But it should carry him for a few weeks, hopefully long enough for the situation out here to change. Call it a delaying action."

"I don't understand," Jennifer said.

"No, of course not. Here's the deal. For years while I was overseas, I invested in the stock market. I moved my account from broker to broker, depending on where I happened to be stationed—Paris, Frankfurt, Tokyo. I was fortunate. My investments about tripled in value. Some time before I retired and returned to the States, I decided to sell all my holdings. It was a lucky decision—pure luck, nothing else—I got out at the top of the market."

"Well," I said. "And I thought *I* was being secretive."

"No comparison. Anyway, every cent of that money, minus taxes, is now sitting in the bank, drawing only nominal interest. I've been intending to invest a good share of it but haven't gotten around to it. I might have if there was a broker I knew here, but there isn't. So what I need now is some good advice."

Jennifer said, "Forget the fee. Paul will be glad to recommend a broker."

"I want more than that. I want a complete analysis of my financial position. I want recommendations on specific stocks—in other words, a suggested portfolio. I may accept it or reject it, partially or wholly. The least I'd get would be an intensive briefing on what's going on in today's financial world. That could be advantageous when I finally choose a broker. Believe me, Jennifer, it would be worth a fee. Probably a bigger one than I'm willing to offer."

Jennifer thanked him but looked dubious. "I'll talk to Paul, but I think I know what he'll say. He'll suggest you discuss it with mother's broker. Keep it all in the family."

"Actually," I said, "I don't have a broker. Everything I have is handled by the bank's Trust Department. When I was first . . . alone . . . I was approached by every kind of money manager. All they did was confuse me. Now I only talk to one, a Mr. Chisholm. He's very conservative—thinks maybe I'm overinvested. He wrote me last week and suggested a meeting. I know he thinks I should put more into savings."

"Sure," Chris said, smiling. "That's how bankers make their money. But he could be right. Lately, the market's been pretty erratic. That's why I want expert advice, from someone with no ax to grind." He looked at Jennifer. "Why not bring Paul over tomorrow? Even if he turns down the assignment, I'll enjoy meeting him."

"Come for lunch," I said.

She hesitated. "Well . . ."

"It's settled," Chris said. "Now how about a swim?"

I kissed my fingertips and brushed them across Chris's lips. "What's that for?"

"For being so noble."

We were sitting on the pool coping, legs dangling in the water, the sun prickling our backs. Jennifer had just left.

"Noble? Not me."

"Oh, yes. You don't really need Paul's advice. You did that for me, so he won't take Jennifer away." I had not mentioned Jennifer's fear of abandonment, nor would I lest he think Paul was merely trifling with her. Was he?

"Well, you're partly right. It seemed rotten that you and

Jennifer should be estranged all this time, then have her whisked away just when you're about to make it up. I saw her looking at you. There was no hate there."

"Ambivalence, I'd say. I think she still blames me, but she's trying hard to forgive. Your helping Paul will help *us*." I stroked his thigh. "But you knew that. So, Colonel Warren, you are a noble man."

He gave my cheek a pat. "I said you were *partly* right. The fact is, I *do* need a financial consultant. I've been out of touch for some months now. The market was something of a hobby of mine. I'd begun to think I knew more about it than the brokers."

"They must have thought so too. Did you really triple your money?"

"Just about. All told, over the years, I invested about fifty-five thousand dollars. I came out with a hundred and fifty thousand. Of course, there was a tax bite. Still, I was left with enough to make me think I was a relatively rich man." He smiled teasingly. "Until I married you, that is. Now it seems like piggy bank money."

I said seriously, "It doesn't bother you, does it?"

He shook his head. "Not as long as I'm my own man."

"Oh, you *are*. I like having you make the decisions." I arched back and threw him a mock salute. "You, sir, are the commanding officer. I am a troop."

He laughed. "It's against regulations for an officer to fraternize with his troops. But in this case . . ." His arms went around me and he gave me a long, exploring kiss.

As he drew back, I said breathlessly, "I await your orders, Colonel."

"Good. You will proceed immediately to the bridal chamber. When I arrive, you will be out of uniform. Repeat—*out* of uniform."

Later, the mission gloriously accomplished, I told him that Jennifer and Paul were about to be evicted from their houseboat, explaining why. He sat up in bed, lit a cigarette, and gazed thoughtfully at a spiral of smoke.

"What would you think if I suggested they stay here for awhile?" he said. "Just until they can work something out."

"I'd think you'd read my mind."

"Then why not? This big house could use two more happy souls."

I had only one misgiving. "What if Paul is awful?"

"Well, we'll meet him tomorrow. We can decide then." He snorted. "Awful? How could anyone as fine as Jennifer love a man who was awful? Nonsense."

I moved to him, my eyes dampening his chest. "I love you, Chris."

EIGHT

CHRIS PUSHED BACK HIS CHAIR, lit a cigarette, and said, "Paul, I assume Jennifer told you I can use financial advice."

"Yes." Paul put down his coffee cup and glanced across the dining room table at Jennifer. "And I told her I had a plan that will save you a lot of money." He smiled at Chris. "Two words. Stay out."

"Stay out of the market?"

"Well, at least be cautious, and selective. Right now it's too unpredictable. Like a yo-yo, up and down."

"The Dow was up sixteen points yesterday."

"And down twelve the day before. It's shown a net loss of more than forty points in the last three weeks. I think, though, that it may be about to stabilize."

"Somebody must be making money."

"The bears. And a few shrewd speculators. The big investors, the institutions, are pretty much standing on the sidelines. I'd take a cue from them, stay fairly liquid."

Chris looked slightly disconcerted. "Hmm. You're saying, keep my money in the bank?"

"Oh, no. You can do a lot better than ordinary bank interest. There are still some special situations. And of course certificates of deposit, treasury bills, bonds."

I eyed Jennifer beside me. She was gazing uncertainly at Paul, doubtless fearing, as I was, that he was preparing to decline Chris's offer.

"Why don't you two discuss it?" I said. "There's something I want to talk about to Jennifer."

The something was to invite her and Paul to move in. Any qualms I'd had about him had vanished the moment we met. He was soft-spoken, charming, deferential to Chris. And he was as good looking as the men in the posh vermouth ads. Dressed in dark slacks, pale-blue sport shirt, light-gray jacket, he was a movie image of the successful stockbroker on his day off. It seemed incredible that he was unemployed. Chris, passing close to me, had whispered, "Ask them."

They adjourned to the study while Jennifer and I went into the lanai.

"He's marvelous," I said as soon as we sat down.

"I think so." Her eyes blinked rapidly. "Dammit, I wish I didn't. He's leaving for New York in a few days."

"He's made up his mind? Even after you told him about Chris?"

"Mother, he saw through that right away. He knows Chris dreamed up the offer just so you and I won't be separated. Pride! But don't misunderstand. He appreciates Chris's good intentions."

"But it really is more than that." I explained Chris's genuine desire to get professional counsel. "I'm sure that if it isn't Paul, it will be somebody else."

"Well, maybe Chris can convince him he's leveling, but I still don't think Paul will take it. He wants to be where the action is. If not San Francisco, then New York."

"And he's sure there's nothing here?"

"Zero. Oh, he has an appointment tomorrow with a broker-age house he's talked to before. They just want to keep him warm, he says, in case things start looking up. He thinks that if he hung around, he'd still be on the back burner six months from now. If he didn't starve to death first."

"What are your plans after he's gone?"

"We have to move out in two days. I'll stay with a girl friend in Sausalito until he sends for me." She brushed at her eyes. "But something tells me that's one trip I won't be making."

"Jennifer, Chris and I have talked it over. We want you to move in here." She started to protest. "I don't mean perma-nently, but long enough to see what develops. Paul, of course, is included. That is, if Chris can induce him to stay on."

"You're very generous, mother."

"Generous to myself."

"Let me talk to Paul first. I'm still hoping he'll take me with him. Meaning I'm dumb."

Chris and Paul appeared a half hour later. Both were smiling, Paul somewhat ruefully.

"Diane," he said, "your husband is a very persuasive man."

Jennifer jumped up. "You're staying!"

"For a while anyway."

She flung her arms around his waist and forced him into a little dance. Chris flashed me a self-satisfied smile. I went to him and clasped his hand.

"Don't credit me," he said with pretended modesty. "Paul thought it was a put-up job until I explained my situation. I'm sure he accepted because he can't stand seeing anyone losing money unnecessarily."

"Also," Paul said, "I can't stand the idea of leaving Jennifer."

I grinned idiotically at Chris. "You're a hero, Colonel Warren."

"In more ways than one. I also asked them to be our house guests."

"Wonderful!" He *was* a hero!

Paul freed himself from Jennifer. "That I didn't accept. I'm grateful, but it's too much of an imposition."

"But it isn't," Jennifer said. "Mother's already spoken to me about it. It won't be for long. Just until things straighten out."

"Please, Paul," I said.

He gave me a searching look, glanced at Chris, then let his eyes linger on Jennifer's eager face. He threw up his hands in mock surrender. "Well, I guess I can't fight all of you."

Jennifer smiled happily, her eyes glazed with astonishment at this sudden reprieve. Affection for Paul welled up inside me. I was sure she had told him about our estrangement and the reason for it. Perhaps he, like Chris, had been influenced by a desire to bring us together.

They moved in the next morning, all of their worldly goods crammed into their Volkswagen. I gave them adjoining bedrooms facing the front of the house. Chris had suggested that arrangement, and though I had assumed they'd share the same room, I didn't disagree. If he was opposed to encouraging unlicensed sex (I recalled his insistence that we marry), why make him uncomfortable? Besides, it was a small hypocrisy, easily circumvented, a fact conveyed by Jennifer when she gave Paul a lascivious smile and said, "Tonight, your place or mine?" (Chris was downstairs.)

Half an hour later, Paul reported to Chris in the study and they spent the morning in consultation. They came out at noon, took a swim, and joined us for a sandwich lunch at the poolside umbrella table. Watching Elga move off with our empty dishes,

Jennifer said, "Well, Paul, you can't knock the working conditions."

"Not to mention the commute. Chris, I'm being overpaid."

(The agreement was for one hundred dollars a day, five days a week, for three weeks—fifteen hundred dollars. "The way they live," Chris had said to me, "that could last them for a few months. I'm betting he'll have a job before then.")

"You'll earn every dime," Chris said. "Meanwhile I'll line up a broker. Tell me, do you know anything about Harrison and Weeks?"

"I ought to. I've called on them enough." Paul glanced at his watch. "In fact, I've got an appointment with one of their vice-presidents in exactly an hour and a half." He held up a hand. "Don't think I'm quitting you. They're just seeing me as a courtesy. I wish it was more than that. I think they're the best house in San Francisco."

"Harrison and Weeks," I said. The name had a familiar ring. Only Jennifer seemed to notice that I'd spoken. She looked at me curiously.

"Are you thinking of going with them?" she said to Chris. Her face had taken on a bold look.

Chris tweaked his nose and seemed to regard her appraisingly. "That would depend. I'd have to feel a sense of confidence in whoever was assigned to my account."

"Suppose—" Jennifer began.

Paul, frowning, cut her off. "Suppose I get moving. I don't want to be late."

It was obvious to all what Jennifer had been about to suggest. But it was naïve to think that a brokerage house of any stature would consider Chris's small account sufficient incentive to hire Paul. Of course, if . . . A thought startled my mind, darted away, then rushed back.

It stayed there, expanding but remaining unexpressed until Chris and I were in our bedroom getting dressed.

"Chris," I said, "I suddenly remembered something. Harrison and Weeks were Fred's brokers. How's that for a coincidence?"

He shrugged. "Not a remarkable one. They must have more clients out here than Merrill Lynch. Do you know anyone there?"

"I don't think so. Fred never discussed it with me. After the estate was settled, I had everything transferred to the bank's Trust Department. Somehow it seemed safer there."

"Well, you can be sure they know who *you* are."

"That occurred to me." I looked at him in the vanity mirror. "I've been thinking. Suppose I assigned at least a part of my holdings to Harrison and Weeks, on condition that Paul handle the account. Do you think they'd resent that?"

"I think they'd jump at the chance. But I'd hold off. It's no decision to be made on impulse."

"You mean you're not sure Paul's qualified?"

"Oh, I think he's qualified. Just from our conversation this morning I'm pretty much convinced that he really knows the market." He finished buttoning his shirt. "Also there'd be unique advantages to having him as your broker. And mine too."

"At least we'd be sure of personal attention."

"Yes, that's one thing. But there's more. I don't think we'd ever have to worry about him investing in something because he was hungry for the commission. That happens. And because of his relationship to us, through Jennifer, I think he'd handle our money as if it were his own."

"Well, then, why so hesitant?"

"Simple caution. There's still one thing that has to be checked out."

"What?"

"His character." He put his hands on my shoulders and gazed at me in the mirror. "Don't let this upset you, but the fact is that neither you nor I, nor probably Jennifer, knows a damned thing about him."

I felt a twitch of alarm. "I know. I've thought of that. But I couldn't bring myself to mention it to Jennifer."

"Why should you? She can afford to take him on faith because she has nothing tangible to lose. We have. We've got to know that he's one hundred percent honest."

I got up, nervously smoothing my green skirt. As gently as I could I said, "You didn't seem too concerned about that when you hired him as a consultant."

"That's different. As a consultant, he'd never actually handle my money. As my broker, he would."

"Yes, of course. And you're right to be careful. What sort of things do you think we should know?"

"Why he left New York. What his employers back there think of him. What others, outside of business, have to say."

"I'm sure he can provide you with references."

"References can be rigged. I'd rather make some inquiries of my own. I've found that the only sensible way to make a judgment of a man is to talk directly to former associates. Let me handle it."

"Certainly. I just wouldn't want Paul or Jennifer thinking we were suspicious of him."

"They won't know about it until it's done. If it works out as I hope and expect, they'll be glad I got the information. I may even take it personally to Harrison and Weeks, together with your recommendation and mine."

Paul returned in late afternoon, his manner somewhat bemused. "I can't figure it one way or the other," he said over cocktails. "I talked to several people, including Weeks, the president. There was no offer, just that they'd be in touch. The old story—don't call us, we'll call you."

When the Friday morning mail arrived, Elga brought it to me in the lanai, where Chris and I were having after-breakfast coffee.

I looked at the top envelope. It was addressed to Colonel Christopher Warren, bore a Washington, D.C., postmark, and had a United States Air Force return address with the name of a major typed above.

"Letter for you, Chris." I started to pass it to him when I saw that the one beneath was also for him. Postmark: New York City. Return address: Heller and Heller on Broad Street. My heart gave a thump. Paul Stafford's former employer! "*Two* letters." I riffled through the rest of the pile. Junk.

"You'll be interested in this," Chris said, after he'd opened the first letter. "It's from the president of the New York brokerage house where Paul was employed." He read:

" 'Dear Colonel Warren: This is to confirm our telephone conversation of this morning. As I informed you then, Paul Stafford is a man of high principle and sound judgement. His grasp of those influences which affect market conditions for good or ill is exceptional. While with us, he performed brilliantly for the clients he served. His resignation, occasioned by a desire to pursue his career on the Coast, was a deep loss both to the firm which I head and to me personally. I can assure you that whoever employs him will have made a wise decision. Very truly yours, Stanley Heller, President.' "

"Chris! That's wonderful! I'm so pleased for Jennifer!"

He nodded in satisfaction, then opened the other letter. "Now let's see what the Pentagon has to say, if anything."

"The Pentagon!"

"Yes, a former aide of mine—I see he's a major now—is

stationed there, in Personnel. At some time, Paul must have been in the service. It seemed wise to check his record."

I was slightly taken aback. "Well, you certainly are thorough."

"If you'd run into as many rogues as I have, you'd be just as thorough. Now, from the major." He read:

" 'Dear Colonel: In reply to your telephone inquiry of 24 June, I know you are aware that policy forbids me to send you verbatim extracts from Paul Stafford's service records. However, I think it proper to advise you that Stafford's conduct while in the service of his country was exemplary. His performances during combat in Vietnam, and later while serving as a staff aide in various overseas theaters, were both certified as Superior. His citations include the Vietnamese cross of gallantry, two silver stars, two commendation medals, one purple heart. He was honorably discharged with the rank of Master Sergeant. It was indeed a pleasure to hear from you, Colonel, and I trust . . .' Et cetera, et cetera. It's signed William E. Cathcart, Major, USAF."

I felt a surge of pride mixed with a sense of irony. My daughter, who for so long had scorned conventional values, was engaged—if that was the word—to a man who had distinguished himself both as a businessman and as a soldier; in fact, was a military hero.

"Well, now," I said, about to enthuse. But I was interrupted by a flash of annoyance. "I hope this is sufficient for you, Chris."

He gave me an injured look. "I'm sorry if you think I've gone overboard on this, Diane. I felt it my duty to do everything I could to protect ourselves." He paused, then added, "And that includes Jennifer."

I was instantly contrite. "I'm sorry, dear. I guess I've been feeling guilty about investigating Paul. But it was the right thing to do. Really, I'm grateful."

He came over and kissed me. "We all can be grateful." He fanned the letters. "Now excuse me while I show these to Paul."

"Do you think you should? He might resent having his past poked into."

"He'll understand when I tell him why. Strictly business—after all, we're giving him our accounts. He can take them to Harrison and Weeks or any other reputable broker, provided he's part of the package."

"You do agree now that it's a wise decision? No more qualms?"

"None. I think you'll do a lot better than with the bank. And you can forget about Jennifer's moving to New York."

"That in itself is a good enough reason. How much do you think I should switch?"

"I can't answer that. Why not have Paul look over your portfolio and make a recommendation? After he's got the job, that is."

"But if I'm to help him get it, they've got to know my intentions in advance."

"Good point. I could tell them, but it would be better coming from you. They'll know who you are and that your husband was a client of theirs—a very profitable one, I imagine."

I considered it. "Didn't Paul say he talked to Mr. Weeks?"

"Yes, the president."

"I'll call him today and tell him. But I'd rather Paul didn't know. I'm sure Mr. Weeks will cooperate. Just tell Paul that I want him to handle a portion of my investments along with yours. He can take it from there."

I telephoned Mr. Weeks later in the morning. Yes, he

remembered Fred Ridgway very well; for a time he had personally serviced his account.

"I'm Mrs. Christopher Warren now."

"Why, yes. I read about it in the papers. My best wishes to you."

"Thank you. My husband and I would like to make some investments. Would you be interested?"

"Very much so. I'd be glad to assign you one of our senior executives."

I explained about Paul, crossing my fingers when I said he was engaged to my daughter.

"Paul Stafford?" There was a pause and then Mr. Weeks cleared his throat. "Well, we were most impressed by him. Ask him to give me a call. I'm sure we can work something out."

"Would you mind calling *him*, Mr. Weeks? I'd prefer he didn't know I interceded."

He laughed softly. "Masculine pride. I understand. You can count on my discretion. I'll phone him today."

I said defensively, "He's an exceptionally able man, Mr. Weeks. I think any firm should be happy to get him, even if he didn't have my husband and me as clients."

"I'm pleased you feel that way. Confidence in your broker is essential."

"There's a good basis for it. My husband has received excellent references from people he's worked with."

"Fine. But your recommendation is good enough for us, Mrs. Warren. Especially when he's practically a member of the family."

The next morning, Paul Stafford became an account executive with Harrison and Weeks. When he came home with the news, Jennifer laughed and wept and the champagne flowed.

NINE

"YOUR MR. CHISHOLM IS RIGHT," Paul said. "You *are* overinvested in stocks, especially in this volatile market. You've got some twenty different issues. Offhand I'd say you should sell more than half. The Research Department agrees."

Chris and I were sitting in his office at Harrison and Weeks, where he was starting his fourth day. It was a small room, tastefully furnished with deep-green carpeting, beige drapes, walnut furniture. He had already given us the office tour and we had met several of the principals, including Mr. Weeks, who had welcomed us like visiting royalty.

I glanced down at the typewritten list of my holdings prepared by the bank. Only a few of the corporate names were familiar. (Fred's company, Pacific Valley Foods, stood out; a heavy investment there.) I remembered Mr. Chisholm discussing some of the others with me but I had only half listened, not being very interested.

"All of them seem to have shown good gains," I said.

"It appears that way—they've gained in points since they were bought. But a lot of them have actually lost ground in terms of true value."

"Inflation," Chris said. "The devalued dollar."

"Besides," Paul said, "every one has dropped in the past few weeks, some sharply. I'm sure a good many will bounce back in time. Others, I think, will continue to slide. Those are the ones that should be weeded out."

"I see. Then you agree with Mr. Chisholm that I should put more into savings?" Comparing him with Mr. Chisholm made me feel vaguely disappointed.

"No, I think I'd put some of the proceeds into income stocks—utilities, railroads. I'd want to study that further. But there's one investment that all of us here can recommend right now—bonds."

Chris leaned forward, frowning. "Income stocks? Bonds? That's just about the reverse of what you're suggesting for me, Paul."

"Your situations are entirely different. Diane has a large fortune to protect. Her primary concern should be safety and yield. Bonds will give her that—corporate and government bonds, tax-free municipals. Your objective, Chris, is growth. And from what you've told me, you're prepared to take calculated risks to get it. To me, the best answer is common stocks. And not just the blue chips. I'd be looking for underpriced issues that investors have either ignored or given up on."

"You're right. I'm willing to speculate."

"Why not? If it happens that you don't get rich, you've still got a lifetime retirement income that's guaranteed. On the other hand, Diane has no reason to build more capital. But she has every reason to preserve what capital she has and make sure it earns enough for her to live as she chooses. Is that a fair statement, Diane?"

"Yes, it is."

"I agree," Chris said.

"Paul," I said, "have you thought of how much we might realize from the stocks we'd sell?"

He looked at a pad on his desk. "I've worked up some rough figures, nothing final. I'd say around a million dollars." He smiled as my eyebrows rose. "Naturally, I don't expect to handle all of that. Chris tells me you were thinking of running about three hundred thousand through us, the rest through the bank."

"Well, something like that. I don't want to put an exact ceiling on it."

"No need to decide now. I won't be selling the stocks all at once; I'll hold off on those I think haven't yet peaked. Let's say that when I've converted about three hundred thousand dollars worth, we'll discuss it again. At that time, I'll recommend what to do with the rest and you can discuss it with Mr. Chisholm at the bank."

"Fine. It doesn't seem right, though, that the bank should profit from your work."

"Happens all the time. They may disagree with my recommendation and make one of their own. Then you'll have a choice."

I laughed. "That would be like asking a blind man to pick a color."

Driving home, I said to Chris, "The more I think about it the more ridiculous it seems to split the stocks between Paul and the bank. It will only lead to confusion, and possibly arguments."

"The same thought crossed my mind when we were talking. Still, I'd think twice about turning them all over to Paul. I'd like to see how he performs first. After all, you're talking about something like two million dollars."

"No, I'm talking only about the stocks he thinks should be sold—a million dollars worth. The bank could hang on to the others."

"That sounds sensible. But let's think about it."

A few days later Paul gave us a written report on the stocks he believed should be converted to other securities. His face flushed with pleasure when I announced that he was to handle the transactions for all of them. The next morning I went to the bank and arranged for their transfer to Harrison and Weeks. Mr. Chisholm appeared slightly wounded but graciously conceded, "You've selected a fine firm. I recall they did a splendid job for Mr. Ridgway."

Walking out, I felt surrounded by an all-male wall of security—Mr. Chisholm, Harrison and Weeks, Paul, Chris.

The next afternoon, that wall started to crumble under the impact of an innocent phone call.

I hung up the phone and sat perfectly still, hand gripping the receiver, my eyes as unseeing as those glittering from the mounted fish on the library walls. I had the vague feeling that something was terribly wrong.

I reconstructed the phone conversation. The caller had been Elliott Davidson. He was a vice-president (marketing?) of Pacific Valley Foods. He offered best wishes on my marriage (I began then dimly to recall him; Fred had brought him to the house a few times) and asked to speak to Colonel Warren. Sorry, my husband was not in. (He had gone into town to discuss a possible job; I'd forgotten the name of the firm.)

So far, nothing out of the ordinary. Then, simply to be courteous:

"Are you a friend of my husband, Mr. Davidson? I mean Colonel Warren, of course."

"Not a friend exactly. I used to do business with him in Europe some years ago. I was in charge of the company's overseas operations."

"Oh, I see."

"In fact, Fred met him several times."

I momentarily lost my voice.

"Recently," he went on, "I was moved to domestic sales. I thought it might be helpful for my replacement if he had a talk with the Colonel."

I looked at my watch. Three o'clock. "He should be here in a half hour or so."

"Fine. I'll call back."

So Chris had known Fred. Coincidental, but not in itself astonishing—Fred had frequently visited Europe on business; once, I recalled, as an adviser to a governmental committee investigating the needs of NATO.

But surely Chris would have remembered meeting a man as prominent as Frederick Ridgway.

My mind fished about for some reasonable explanation. Perhaps he had not at first associated the name Ridgway with the man he had met in Europe. Why should he?—Ridgway was not an uncommon name. But later, after I had told him of Fred's position, naming his company, recognition that I was his widow should have been immediate.

Assuming that, why would Chris have hidden the knowledge? To avoid talking about Fred after my painful revelation of his violent death? Possibly. But not probably. A brief mention that they had met would not have caused me any anguish. Deceit was the only word I could think of. Guiltily I pushed it away.

I was in the living room pretending to read a novel when he arrived home, impeccable in a dark suit. He came toward me smiling affectionately. Before he could kiss me, I said, "A man named Elliott Davidson phoned you. He said he'd call back."

He stopped and frowned slightly in puzzlement. Then his face cleared and he said, "Oh, Davidson, yes."

I closed my book. "I understand he's with the same company that employed Fred—Pacific Valley Foods."

He considered the statement by tucking in his chin and strumming his nose with his thumb. "Yes, that's so." He regarded me guilelessly. "Anyone want to say 'small world.'? I'm afraid it wouldn't apply here. I conducted business with a great many large corporations when I was in the service."

I was waiting for him to elaborate when the phone rang. It was picked up in another room. In a moment, Elga entered and announced that the call was for Colonel Warren. "A Mr. Davidson, sir."

He left to take it in the library. Why not right here, I thought, staring at the phone on the end table. I was tempted to eavesdrop but instantly rebuked myself. I was overreacting.

He was back in a few minutes, his face somber. He stood in the center of the long room, feet spread apart, arms folded. He looked at me as though assessing a new recruit. His voice was ominous:

"I understand from Elliott Davidson that you know I was acquainted with Fred Ridgway."

I tried to keep my tone even. "Yes. I'm surprised you never told me."

His jaw hardened. "You're not only surprised. You're furious."

"Not furious, Chris. Disappointed."

He scowled, paced the floor, halted in front of me, a towering figure. "Diane, I regret the necessity of having to explain this. I would have hoped that you would have understood immediately. But I see by your expression that you do *not* understand."

"Understand what exactly?" Why was *I* on the defensive?

"Understand why I felt it proper to withhold that information." A small wound colored his voice.

I said nothing.

He pivoted on his heel and dropped into a chair, facing me at an angle. "I didn't begin to wonder whether Frederick Ridgway was your husband until the day you told me of his death. I'm not sure it occurred to me even then. I was too absorbed in the tragedy itself."

"But if you knew him, you must somehow have learned of the way he died. Wouldn't you have remembered that?"

"I was thousands of miles away at the time. The news of how he had died never reached me in any detail. That, I needn't tell you, had occurred ten years before you and I met. Why would I connect the man you were speaking about with one I had known so many years before, who I'd met only a few times and then only briefly?"

My doubts began to fade. I revived them with: "But you knew before talking to Mr. Davidson that I was the widow of *that* Fred Ridgway. Isn't that true?"

He nodded slowly. "Yes."

"When did you know?"

He eyed me resentfully. "You mean did I know before we were married? The answer is negative. Several days after our wedding—that's when I realized it."

I stared at him uncomprehendingly.

"You told me that your husband had left you five million dollars. I recalled then hearing that Frederick Ridgway's death had made his wife a rich woman. Also, you said certain things that clearly identified him."

"Why didn't you speak up?"

He slapped the chair arm. "Because of fear."

"Fear?" It seemed an odd word coming from him.

"Fear that if you learned I had known Fred, you'd think I had *arranged* to meet you in that art gallery, that from the beginning I had callously planned to marry you in order to get your money."

The bald assertion, expressing what had been stirring in my own mind, left me confused and silent. He had managed to appropriate my disillusionment, reflecting it now in his tone:

"Why do you think I signed away all claims to your wealth? Not because I thought you didn't trust me. I believe you did. But I was afraid that somehow you would eventually learn what you have today. Then you would be bound to question my reasons for marrying you. I didn't want to risk having our marriage destroyed." Bitterness crept into his voice. "But it appears that my refusal to benefit from your money has made no difference. You still suspect me of ulterior motives."

His sincerity was unchallengeable. But I could not subdue a stubborn uncertainty. Despite his plausible explanation, the concealment coupled with the legal renouncement of my wealth seemed disproportionate to the possible consequences. Nevertheless, I must have misjudged him.

"I'm sorry, Chris. I had no right to doubt you. Please forgive me."

He accepted the apology magnanimously. "Of course I forgive you. I can understand your confidence being shaken. Now let's not even think about it again."

I guess I should have been grateful for his willingness to drop it so quickly—but I wasn't. Perhaps I should have talked further with Elliott Davidson. After all, I had inherited a large block of stock in the company, which entitled me to ask some pointed questions. Now I was reduced to: "Mr. Davidson said he hoped you could be of help to his overseas replacement. Can you?"

He stood up, as though at attention. "Negative. Davidson suggested that I might provide an entrée to certain influential officers in NATO. But the staff I commanded was all being reorganized when I left there. I don't know the people anymore."

"That reminds me. How did your meeting go today?"

He smiled blandly, as though happy to change the subject. "Excellent. I seem to have precisely the qualifications they've been looking for."

"You got the job?"

"Not yet. But the president as much as told me I could expect it in a few weeks."

"Well, I'm very pleased, Chris, if you are. What's the name of the company again?"

He hesitated, as if it had slipped his mind. "Transworld Oil, in San Francisco, head of purchasing. It's very hush-hush, so don't say a word to anyone. The man presently holding the job doesn't know he's being transferred."

It took an effort to believe him.

Jennifer

TEN

I scrunched up close to Paul in the bed and put my hand where it belonged. "Stay here all night," I said. "Then we can do it again."

"All right. I'll make it back to my room before the Colonel makes the morning bed check."

"What's that old line? Oh yes: Darling, we can't go on meeting like this. But I mean it. We've been here for three weeks and you still have to sneak into my pants."

He touched me. "What pants?"

"Mmm. But really, you've got a good job now. Why not be by ourselves?"

He snapped on the bed lamp, hiked up on the pillow, and lit two cigarettes. Handing me one, he said, "You're right. We should have left as soon as I started working."

"Well, *okay*. I'll look for a place tomorrow."

He pushed fingers through his tawny hair. "I have a feeling we should hang around a while longer."

"Why? To be glued to your clients?"

"Something like that."

"But now you've got an *office*—remember? Besides you've invested most of Chris's money and a lot of mother's. From now on, they can come to you."

He took a couple of drags. "I wasn't ready to say this but I will. I don't feel right about Chris."

I elbowed up next to him. "Hey! Lately he *has* been sort of weird. Like something's bugging him."

"I know. It started right after I got the job. At first I thought he was worried about risking his money. Now I'm not so sure."

"Why? Lay it all out."

He shifted uncomfortably. "All right. Ask yourself this. Why did he hire me as his financial consultant on the very first day we met?"

"Easy. He did it for mother. If he could keep you here, I'd stay too. Which is what mother wanted."

"Sure, that's the way it looked—an act of kindness to his new bride. Then what happened? He checked me out, got a terrific reference from Heller, my former boss, and from the Pentagon that was even better, better than I deserved, thanks to that Major being an old buddy. He got the references in *writing*, so they could be shown to Harrison and Weeks."

"Naturally. He was trying to nail down the job for you."

"Right. And he gave me his account for the same reason. But he knew that wasn't enough, so he talked your mother into giving me a slice of hers—about three hundred thousand dollars worth."

"I doubt if he had to twist her arm."

"Granted. He might even have worked it so that she was the one who suggested it. She trusts him. Why shouldn't she? He'd legally given up all claims to her money."

"Mother'd zap me if she knew I'd snitched. But keep talking."

He ditched his cigarette and lit another. "All that was more than enough to assure me the job, especially with a brokerage house where your mother was well known. But then he got her to raise the ante. Instead of three hundred thousand dollars, she assigned me stocks worth more than a million."

"Oh, Paul, you said yourself that made sense."

"It did and it does. She couldn't accept advice from two probably conflicting sources without ending up with a mishmash. Everything was neat and logical. I didn't question anything, except to wonder why I should be so lucky."

"But now you think it was more than luck?" My heart blipped. "My God, you don't think Chris is up to something!"

"I think I've got to consider it."

"Why not just believe that for once something worked out the way it should?"

"I might if it wasn't for the way Chris has been acting."

"So maybe he's nervous out of the service. He'll get over it."

"It's more than that. He's in my office practically every day wanting to know what I'm buying, how much I've invested, how much remains to be invested."

"I'd want to know too if it was my money."

"But it's not *his* money he's talking about. It's your mother's."

"Oh."

"He seems to think I'm not selling off her stocks fast enough. He can't wait to have that million dollars fully invested in bonds."

"Maybe he's scared the unsold stocks will take a dive before you sell."

"That's what he says. But the strange thing is he doesn't seem to take much interest in his *own* investments, only your mother's. He's even calling the shots. The other day, I showed him a recommendation, backed by the firm, to put about a third of the proceeds into a number of utilities and railroad stocks. He said absolutely not. Bonds, he wants, nothing but bonds. They're safer."

"Are they?"

"A bit. But the utilities and rails are almost as safe, the yields almost as high, and they offer one advantage that bonds don't—a chance for moderate growth. They'd be a small hedge against further inflation."

"What did mother say?"

"That gets us to the sticky part. Chris asked me—commanded would be closer—not to say a word about that recommendation to your mother. If I did, he said, he'd have to oppose it and there'd just be confusion and possibly bad feelings. He pointed out that your mother is already fairly heavily invested in stocks—the ones I suggested she hang on to and that the bank has retained. Besides, wasn't *I* the one who was so high on bonds? Then why not put *all* the money into bonds and forget about it? Well, there's nothing wrong with that kind of thinking, so I did it his way."

"What's wrong about it is that he's kibitzing but not telling my mother."

"And I'm not telling her either. What does that make me? An accomplice."

"Oh, come on. You make it sound like he's suckering you into a ripoff."

He twisted toward me and the sheet dropped to his narrow hips. "I can't avoid the feeling that I'm being used as a conduit, deliberately put in that job to convey your mother's money to him."

I stared at him.

"He could have had her down for a mark even before he met her."

"Fantastic!"

"Sure. I don't say I believe it; it's just speculation. I doubt if I'd have any suspicions if I hadn't seen how some con artists operate. All I'm suggesting is that we hang around a little longer and keep an eye on him."

"I guess we can't say anything to mother."

"No, not directly. But next time you're alone with her, probe around. Who knows, she might be aching to confide in you."

That meant having an old-fashioned heart-to-heart, which would have amounted to a revolution in my relationship with my mother. Not that we weren't friendly enough. We rapped together (about nothings), swam together, shopped together, just like those jazzy mother-daughter teams in the vitamin commercials. In fact, that about describes it—we were play acting. Beneath all the smiles and the sweet talk, there was a wariness about letting our feelings hang out. Thoughts were carefully formed into complete sentences before expressing them. Our reactions to each other seemed rehearsed. Silences were prickly. It was like we were both spooked by my father's ghost.

I tried but could never really wipe out the bitterness I'd felt for so many years. No matter how often I told myself that what she had done had been a crazy accident, one of those heat-of-passion things, I couldn't completely excuse her from guilt. The best I could do was treat her with a sort of cautious cheeriness, the way neighbors might treat a convict once he'd served his time.

That was my side of it. But of course there was hers. I hadn't even considered it in the past, but now I saw that she had as much reason as I to be bitter: a daughter who, since childhood, had shown her almost no affection, who for years had mentally

branded her a murderess, who had run off and left her to cope
with her misery alone.

It was a standoff, I guess, except that she was far more
determined than I to bridge the gap. I'd gone along mostly to
help Paul. But after that was taken care of, I'd begun to feel
dirty inside and wanted out.

Maybe Chris wanted us out, too, and mother was balking.
That could explain why they suddenly seemed turned off on
each other. True or not, it offered a starter for a probing
conversation.

"Mother, I have the feeling we're lousing up you and Chris."

She looked at me sharply. "What ever gave you that idea?"

It was mid-morning and we were in the lanai drinking coffee.
She was wearing a paint-splattered blue smock, having got up
early and spent a couple of hours in her upstairs studio. It was
the first time she'd picked up a brush since we'd arrived. Paul
was at the office and Chris had just left to keep a business
appointment.

"Well," I said, "lately you two have been acting like you'd
been mismatched by computer. I figure it's because you're
starting to trip over us freeloaders. After all, you're still
practically on your honeymoon."

"No," she said, "it's not you and Paul. It's not that at all." She
sipped her coffee, thinking hard. Then she got up, went to the
door to make sure Elga wasn't around, and came back to her seat
on the sofa. She looked into my eyes. "Jennifer, tell me
honestly, what do you think of Chris?"

"Why, he's fine. Great." My voice made the words sound
limp. I smiled brightly. "But of course I don't know him the
way you do."

Her mouth tightened. "I'm not sure I do know him."

"Hey! You sound—don't tell me you've found a skeleton in

his closet." Seeing her eyes flash, I added, "Just teasing, mother."

"I'm afraid I'm losing my sense of humor." She looked like she had.

"Want to tell me about it? Or is it too personal?"

"I *do* want to tell you, but—"

"Oh, forget it. Unless I can help."

"I think you can help. At least you can tell me whether or not I'm just being neurotic."

"Well, then . . ."

"But you mustn't say anything about it to Paul. Not yet, anyway. Is that asking too much?"

"Not if it doesn't concern him."

"It doesn't."

"Okay. Scout's honor."

Controlling her voice, she told me about the phone call from Elliott Davidson, the revelation that Chris had known my father in Europe but hadn't mentioned it, his reason being that he was afraid she'd think he was after her money.

The coincidence of that excuse with Paul's suspicions had my eyes bugging out and my mouth wide open ready to blurt. I blinked, clenched my jaw, and imagined the Colonel sprouting horns.

"I accepted the explanation," she said. "It seemed reasonable, and he was so sincere."

"But now you don't accept it?"

"Let's say I question it."

"Any reasons?"

"Nothing earthshaking." She wrinkled her small nose. "I hate even to mention them."

"Go ahead, mention them." I suddenly felt older than she.

"All right. The other day I was passing the study. Chris was inside with the door closed and he was talking on the phone. I overheard him say, 'I'm in a hurry now, so get rolling.' Then after a moment, he said, 'Fine. And you can forget the sir. This isn't tuslog.' "

"Tuslog?"

"That's what it sounded like. Military slang, probably. His tone was very officious and I assumed he was talking to someone who'd once served under his command."

"I'd say you're right. I'd also say he was placing an order for some gizmo that he could get cut rate from Uncle Sam. But why should that shake you up?"

"Because, on impulse, I knocked on the door, then opened it. He hung up fast and turned around and he had the strangest look on his face, as though he'd been caught doing something indecent. I apologized for interrupting and he said, oh, it wasn't important, he was just arranging an appointment. I asked if it was with the firm he hopes to work for. He grabbed at that and said yes, he'd been talking to the president."

"The *president!* He gives orders to a president he's hustling for a job? And what kind of president would call him sir?"

"Exactly. It seems obvious he wasn't telling the truth."

"Didn't you call him on it?"

"I was too stunned. All I could think of was that he must have a good reason for not wanting me to know. Perhaps a gift he was buying me."

"That's bullshit." I was beginning to get mad.

She smiled wanly. "Funny, I thought of the same word."

"Anything else?"

She flushed, causing her hair to look blonder. "Only what you've already noticed. We've suddenly become like strangers."

"No making out?"

She gave a dry laugh. "He stays on his side of the bed, I stay on mine. A number of times, when he thought I was asleep, he got up and went downstairs and stayed for quite awhile. He's restless, troubled about something, and I can't help thinking it's got nothing to do with our marriage." She breathed a sigh. "That's where I'm probably neurotic."

"You're not neurotic, mother."

"Well, I'll soon be a jibbering idiot if this isn't cleared up."

I said, knowing the answer, "Do you think it would help if Paul and I cut out?"

"*No!*" She exploded the word, startling us both. Her voice softened. "That's why I'm telling you all this, so you *won't* leave. What I've said is terribly disloyal to Chris and I feel awful about it. But that's better than being left here with nobody I can depend on." She banged the air in frustration. "If I could only prove my suspicions are groundless, I'd gladly eat crow for the rest of my life."

"What if you proved he was a crook?"

She closed her eyes as though meditating. When they opened, the pupils looked like cold-blue marble. "I've managed to overcome pain before," she said quietly.

Something melted inside me. It congealed when I glanced at her fisted right hand, the hand that had once gripped a thrusting knife. Instantly I shifted my thoughts back to the present problem, recalling what she'd said.

"What's this about Chris getting a job? You hadn't mentioned it before."

"I shouldn't have mentioned it now. Top secret, Chris said, because the man he may replace—the head of the purchasing department—doesn't know about it." She looked at her watch. "That's where he said he'd be this morning."

"Chewing out the president, no doubt."

She laughed nervously.

I said, "What's the name of this outfit, and who's the fearless leader?"

"Transworld Oil. I didn't think to ask the president's name."

That seemed as good a place as any to start my career as a private eye.

ELEVEN

THE SWITCHBOARD OPERATOR at Transworld Oil gave me the name of the president without my having to fake being a secretary who'd misplaced her notes. Mr. James Coyle. I thanked her and hung up.

The next step would be hairier. I went to my bedroom door, closed it, came back to the phone and dialed Transworld again. Another operator answered and I asked to speak to Mr. Coyle. I looked at the time. Almost noon.

"Hello, Mr. Coyle's office." A woman's voice, probably his secretary.

I apologized and said it was urgent that I speak to Colonel Christopher Warren, who I understood was meeting with Mr. Coyle. The Colonel, I said, was my stepfather. She asked me to hold on. Waiting, I started to sweat it, expecting the next voice to be Chris's. But it was the girl again, wondering if I hadn't made a mistake: "I've checked Mr. Coyle's schedule and have no record of a meeting with Colonel Warren."

"I'm sorry to be so much trouble, but I'm positive. And this is an *emergency*."

"Wel-l-l . . . one moment, please."

I held my breath.

"Hello, can I help you?" A man's voice, smooth. "This is Mr. Coyle."

I went through the whole bit again.

"I'm afraid that I don't know a Colonel Warren. Are you sure that—"

"He said he'd be discussing a position with you." My fingers bit into the receiver. "In Purchasing."

"Oh, I see. Then perhaps he's over there. Give me just a minute."

I lit a cigarette. Mr. Coyle was back in nine drags.

"Hello, I'm afraid there's been a mixup of some sort. I contacted both Purchasing and Personnel. Neither department has heard of a Colonel Warren and there's no opening in Purchasing."

"Oh, Mr. Coyle, I just found out I've made a really dumb mistake. I'm so sorry. The company I wanted was Transworld *Products*. They're listed just below you in the directory."

He laughed understandingly. "An easy error to make. But they have no connection with us."

Hanging up, I collapsed on the bed, conscious less of what I'd learned than of the relief I felt at not having to act out the whole scene. If Chris had answered, I'd have told him that mother had suddenly become ill and I thought he'd better rush right home. That would have been news to her, but I was sure she'd have been happy to fake leprosy if it proved he hadn't lied.

But he *had* lied, a senseless lie if the phone call she had overheard had been anything but sinister. (What had he said? "I'm in a hurry now, so get rolling . . . And forget the sir. This isn't . . ." I'd forgotten the word.) And he'd used the same lie as a cover-up for whatever it was that took him to San Francisco. It couldn't be to hide his meetings with Paul at his office; he'd always mentioned them openly, implying of course that they were discussing *his* investments.

I went down the hall to mother's studio. The door was open and I paused outside to watch her move a charcoal across an easeled canvas with quick strokes. She was facing away and over her shoulder I could see lines forming into a rough image of ocean, sky, and cliffs. The Mendocino coast, I thought, drawn from memory—a pathetic attempt at therapy through nostalgia. It was there that she belonged, not in this fancy too-big house that now seemed poisoned with bad vibes.

She sensed me standing there, turned her head, and smiled. "Hi. I thought you were in the pool."

I stepped inside, noticing the bareness of the room, canvases stacked against the wall, a single armchair beside the window. "No," I said, "I've been on the phone."

"To Paul?"

"To Transworld Oil. I talked to the president, Mr. James Coyle."

Her eyes widened. She put down the charcoal and wiped her hands with a cloth. She didn't ask why I'd called. She knew.

"Mr. Coyle never heard of Colonel Christopher Warren. And that goes for the personnel and purchasing departments."

Her face showed nothing. She moved to the window, staring out, one hand clutching the top of the chair. "I guess I'm not surprised." She swung around and instead of the sadness I expected, her eyes were cold with anger.

I told her the ploy I'd used and explained the scenario if Chris had answered. She shrugged, not really caring.

"I've dreaded even thinking about this," she said, "but now I see no other way. I've got to have him investigated."

I felt a squirming sensation, wanting to tell her what Paul had said. But first I'd better talk to him. Better still . . .

"Mother, I think it's a mistake to cut Paul out of this. He talks to Chris often, he knows your financial situation, and I'm sure he has some ideas about how you can be protected."

"I hate to burden him."

"Burden shmurden—he'll be glad you came to him. At least hear what he has to say before dragging in a shamus, although that's what he'll probably advise."

She slumped into the chair. "I'd have to get him alone. That won't be easy with Chris around."

"I'll tell him everything tonight. Then you can meet him someplace in town tomorrow. I'll arrange the time and pass you the word."

She agreed, the decision lifting her chin and straightening her shoulders. When I left, she was back at the easel sketching a soaring bird against a dark sky. But her eyes were glazed, as though her sight had been reversed.

I was coming in from a swim that afternoon, my foot on the stairs to go up, when I heard Chris's voice lash out from the kitchen:

"Get away from me, goddammit! You stupid woman! You're making it worse!"

He was answered by a shocked little cry. Not moving, I looked past the stairs and through the open kitchen door. Chris marched into view swabbing at his jacket with a dish towel. Mother had been in her room resting, so it must be . . .

"I am very sorry, Colonel Warren," Elga said. She sounded terrified.

"Sorry!" Chris's back was now toward me. He flung the dish towel away and clasped his hands behind him, fingers working. "There are a number of things you should be sorry about, Elga. The dust around here you don't seem to see. The ash trays you forget to empty. The not knowing where you are when you're needed. The—"

"I shall try to do better, Colonel Warren."

His voice stayed icy. "See that you do. I'm sure you're aware that there are any number of young women who would leap at the chance to enjoy the privileges afforded by this household."

Incredible, even from the man I now thought of as an aspiring monster.

Elga whimpered something.

He started to pivot on his heel, stopped. I skittered across the reception hall into the living room and half closed the door. His voice followed me, sounding like Big Brother:

"Very well, Elga. I'll say no more about it. But remember, you've been warned."

I waited until he'd stomped up the stairs, then went into the kitchen. I heard the whirring scream of the knife sharpener. Elga was at the sink counter, a carving knife jutting from her small fist. She was probably wishing she had stuck it through his gut.

"Hi, Elga."

She jumped and whirled around.

"Oh? Miss Ridgway." She nodded and forced her full lips into a smile.

"I heard the Colonel hassling you. What'd you do, throw acid in his face?"

My great wit was wasted: "Oh, no! I was serving him coffee and I spilled some on his suit. It was very careless of me."

"And for that he was about to drum you out of the corps? My God."

"He was right. I have not worked so good as I should." She wiped her eyes with her sleeve. "I do not want to lose my job."

"Relax, Elga. I'll see my mother and give you a standing ovation."

She looked puzzled, then smiled. "Thank you, Miss Ridgway."

I went to the refrigerator and got a Pepsi, thinking: Score one more against the Colonel; the pressure's blowing his brain.

Gulping from the bottle, I gazed at Elga, flaxen head bent, china-blue eyes squinting as she ran the carving knife back and forth through the screeching sharpener. About a dozen knives lay on the counter. I stared at them in fascination.

The blade had been long and thin. The handle was prickly, like the hide of a short-haired animal.

The sharpener went silent. I heard a door open upstairs and the sound of muffled voices. The voices stopped.

The handle had been locked in the fist, the blade pointing straight ahead. It glittered.

Elga raised the knife and, with her thumb, tested the edge. She put it aside and picked up another. She thrust it forward. The sharpener screeched, this time as if in agony.

The body had reeled toward it. The knife jerked forward. An inch, no more.

The screeching died. In all the house, there was only the sound of footsteps on the stairs.

The huge chest, meringued with orange hair, plunged into the knife blade.

The Pepsi seemed to harden in my throat, choking me. I put the bottle back in the refrigerator and hurried into the reception hall. My mother stood there.

"Jennifer, are you all right?"

Her voice seemed resurrected from some ancient time.

"I'm okay. Why?"

"Your eyes are glaring."

"They are?" I passed a hand across them. "How's that?"

"Better." She took my arm and moved me farther from the kitchen. "I was afraid you might have had a run-in with Chris. He came stalking into the bedroom muttering something about spilled coffee and people not knowing when they're well off." Her voice lowered. "I thought he was talking about Elga."

"It was about Elga." I told her what had happened.

Her reaction was the same as mine. "That's unlike Chris. Obviously he was distraught about something else and was taking it out on her."

I was about to vote Elga into sainthood when my ear again caught the screech of the knife sharpener. Then I realized why I'd been glaring at my mother. All the hate I had felt for her ten years ago had suddenly spurted through me.

It was gone now, or buried. But I couldn't talk to her.

I went up to my room, deciding to stay there until Paul came home.

TWELVE

As soon as Paul arrived, he went to his room to change into something loose. I followed, and while he unbuttoned and unzipped, I reported what I'd learned: Chris's mysterious phone call (including "tuslog," which I'd finally remembered), his and mother's turnoff and his occasional late-night prowlings, his lies about the Transworld connection (which placed him someplace else), even the nasty scene with Elga.

I ended with: "Now include his knowing my father in Europe and keeping it secret. Then add what you told me about how he's practically taking over my mother's investments. I'd say your con-man theory looks like fact."

He had interrupted me only once, when I said the word tuslog. "What the hell is tuslog?" I'd shrugged and thrown out my hands. Now he finished tucking in his red sport shirt and sat next to me on the bed.

"It's not yet fact," he said. "Everything you've got, and that

I've wondered about, is circumstantial. We have to be fair to the guy. He deserves to be presumed innocent—"

"I know, until proved guilty. Okay. Mother's decided to *get* the proof. She wants to hire a private eye."

Amusement tilted his mouth. "Why do that when she's got you? All right, take that look off your face. I know it's serious. But a private investigator—that seems like overreacting."

"I'm with you. So I got her to agree to talk to you first."

"Me?" He shook his head. "I don't know what I—" He stopped and tugged at his ear. "Maybe—" He let the word hang there.

"Maybe *what?*"

"Maybe there's a way I can get a line on him. Let me think about it. Anyway, I'll be glad to talk to her. If nothing else, it may give her some reassurance."

I suggested that she drive into town the next morning at about ten-thirty, call him at his office, and they'd arrange where to meet. Fine.

I passed the word to mother after dinner when Chris was in the john.

At breakfast, Chris announced that he would need the car that morning to drive into San Francisco.

"I'll drop you off," mother said, "then pick you up later. I've some shopping to do."

He hesitated. Then: "We'd better do it the other way around. My appointment is south of the city and the only way to get there is by car. I'll drop *you* off."

"Appointment? You didn't mention it."

He eyed her, patting his mouth with a napkin. "I thought I did."

"*South* of San Francisco," I said, smiling innocently. "That's where Candlestick Park is. I'll bet you're sneaking off to a ball game."

He smiled as though his lips were chapped. "The fact is, it concerns a job I'm interested in. At the moment, it's quite confidential. Except, of course, to your mother."

"I thought their offices were in the financial district," mother said.

His eyes narrowed on her, as if he suspected she was putting him on. "They are," he said shortly. He strummed his nose. "Their *executive* offices. This is one of their manufacturing plants. A guided tour has been scheduled. I was asked to attend. I'm due there at ten o'clock."

The elaboration of the lie plunged us into silence. Paul broke it by getting up and saying, "Well, I'm due at *nine* o'clock. I'll see you all later."

"I'll drive you to the ferry," I said.

As we left the room, I heard mother suggesting to Chris that he let her off at the St. Francis hotel and pick her up there on the way back.

"Now what's he up to?" I said to Paul when we were in the Volks.

"I'm thinking. Could you have been wrong about the job? The president—Coyle—might have had damned good reasons for pretending it didn't exist. Chris himself said it was supposed to be top secret."

"Okay, but then wouldn't Coyle have told him that his stepdaughter had called and lied about getting the wrong firm?"

"Maybe he did."

"You mean Chris would keep that to himself? Never! He'd hang me up by the thumbs. Right next to mother."

"I guess you're right. But maybe he'd already left Coyle's office and they haven't talked since. That was only yesterday, you know."

An idea hit me. My foot pushed down on the accelerator. We reached the boarding dock with five minutes to spare. I hopped out with Paul, asked him to wait as long as possible, and split for an outdoor phone booth. He must have guessed what was knocking at my mind because he didn't say anything.

It took me less than three minutes to find the number, place the call, and get the information. Paul was about to follow the last of the sleepy eyed commuters aboard the ferry when I rushed up to him.

"All of Transworld's plants are in the *East* Bay," I said. "They own nothing south of San Francisco. I got that from their chief phone operator. Who'd know better than the one who handles their calls?"

He groaned. "I was hoping you were wrong. But this about settles it. The man's a liar."

"And a crook."

"Not necessarily. That we've got to prove."

He kissed me quickly and took off.

I stood there seething with frustration as the ferry churned away. Paul of course was right. Proof. But waiting until something awful had happened was a dumb way to get it. We needed it now. Today . . .

A charge of adrenalin shot me back to the Volks. In about half an hour Chris would drive mother into town, drop her in front of the St. Francis hotel and continue on to—where?

The brown Volks looked no different than a zillion others. The odds were good that Chris wouldn't identify it with me if he happened to spot it in his rearview mirror.

I parked near the side entrance of the St. Francis, only a few yards from the crossing street that ran past the front of the hotel. I kept the motor running and through dark glasses watched for the T-Bird to reach the intersection.

I'd had no chance to get mother alone and report Chris's latest whopper. They'd left the house at quarter to nine, followed by me half a minute later. I'd caught sight of the white car on the highway, then again at the toll plaza, and finally when it began to skirt the bay in the Marina. There I'd turned off and taken a shortcut which I was sure put me ahead of them.

Now, at nine-thirty, the traffic had thinned out. Ahead I could see a section of Union Square Park, old folks sunning themselves on benches or feeding the pigeons, street kids sprawled on the grass or lugging portable stores to be set up on the sidewalks for the display of handcrafted jewelry, leather goods, pottery. A mime with a red-and-white painted face and dressed in a clown's costume was turning handsprings on a walkway.

The traffic light in front of me turned green. I glanced to the left and saw the white T-Bird stopped at the diagonal corner for the red light. The faces of mother and Chris were clearly visible. They both stared straight ahead, lips not moving.

They had passed through the intersection and were out of sight before I made the turn. Idling behind a cable car, I saw the T-Bird pull to the curb and mother step out. She paused until Chris rolled away, then walked off toward Magnin's, as slim and erect as one of their models. I jockeyed back into the mainstream traffic. The T-Bird was two cars away.

Chris drove around the square and headed back the way he had come, climbing the hill and going two blocks beyond Van Ness, where he turned left. When he took the on-ramp to the freeway, heading *south,* I began to wonder if the Transworld operator hadn't been mistaken; perhaps he was touring a plant owned by a company affiliate. But when he veered from the outside lane to the inner one, I knew—he was headed for San Francisco International Airport.

My God, was he skipping the country?

I hung far back as we rounded the overpass and drove along the level approach. He passed by the low overseas airline terminals until he came to the main building, then switched to the lane marked for valet service. He got out and waited for the attendant. I looked frantically around for a place to park. There was nothing except bus loading zones. So what the hell; it was worth a ticket or even a towaway. A bus edged out and I slid in, moving to the far end of the zone. As I slithered to the street, I saw Chris reach the sidewalk in front of the main building's glass doors. Two of them swung open automatically and he disappeared.

When I entered the huge rotunda I got a rear view of him standing at the PSA counter squinting at the lighted board that posted arrivals and departures. I knew that PSA ran flights every hour up and down the coast, mostly between San Francisco and Los Angeles. And San Diego. Hey! San Diego would place him right next to the Mexican border. But he didn't buy a ticket. Maybe he already had one.

He left the counter and marched down the concourse leading to the PSA boarding gate. I followed about twenty yards behind, half hidden by a group of GIs carrying rucksacks. He reached the fenced waiting area, went inside, and walked to the big window that looked down on the tarmac. From where I stood against a wall I could see only his back and a few taxiing planes far out on the runways. He turned and retraced his steps, coming right at me. I ducked behind two smiling old couples who were facing toward him. He stopped, and for a moment was hidden by the crowd that had begun to gather. Suddenly there was a burst of voices from ahead and people carrying hand luggage came streaming toward us. Then I got it—he wasn't flying out; he was meeting someone flying in.

That someone was short, fat, and swarthy, wearing a dark hat pulled down almost to his sharp little eyes. He carried a thin black attaché case, held close to his thigh. Bobbing my head, I saw him walk up to Chris, nod, and fall into step as Chris started back up the concourse. Neither one smiled, spoke, or offered his hand. They passed within ten feet of me, keeping in perfect step, as though demonstrating a drill.

I stalked them to the rotunda, where they crossed to the bar overlooking the field. When I reached the open glass door, they were seated at a small table next to the window and a waitress was taking their order. It was a big room, thronged with travelers. I sneaked inside and stood a few feet behind two men at the side of the bar farthest from the windows. Through breaks in the human wall, I could glimpse Chris and his companion.

They didn't appear to speak until the drinks were served, Chris's looking like scotch, the short man's a Coke. Then Chris said something, just a few words, and the other one took over. His lips moved rapidly but his face never showed expression. He talked for more than a minute, Chris listening silently, a couple of times jerking his head as though in approval. The man in front of me got up from the barstool and for a moment blocked my vision.

When I looked again, the short man was on his feet, his pudgy hand sliding a white envelope into his breast pocket. He faced Chris for a moment, seeming to stand at attention, then, without a word, turned on his heel and walked out.

I watched him go through the door, sensing that something about him had changed. Then I noticed that both his hands were swinging free. He had left the small attaché case behind.

Chris lingered at the table, sipping his drink slowly and gazing out the window. Finally he glanced casually around the room (I slunk behind a pair of bulky shoulders) and got up. Clutched in his right hand was the attaché case. I wondered vaguely how much money had been carried away in the white envelope by his accomplice. He must be the man mother had overheard Chris talking to on the phone.

I kept plenty of distance between us as I again trailed Chris across the rotunda toward the exit doors. From inside, I saw him cross the street to the valet service, where he handed his claim check to the attendant.

By the time I got back to the Volks, he had gone.

A parking ticket was under one of the windshield wipers. I left it there, went back into the terminal, and called Paul at his office.

"Christ Almighty," he said when I told him what had happened, "you could be setting yourself up for the morgue!"

"So you finally agree that the Colonel's a dangerous character."

"It's the other guy who sounds dangerous. But it looks for sure that Chris is into something crooked. He could be dealing in contraband goods—dope, jewels, laundered money."

"What's that got to do with mother?"

"Probably nothing. He might simply be using her as a respectable front."

"Then why's he poking around with her investments?"

"Maybe that's just to look protective—and busy. Or a diversion, a way to keep me from wondering what he's really up to. I've thought about it and I don't see how he could touch her there short of blowing the safe in her library. That's where she keeps her bond certificates."

"He may know the combination."

"Your mother told me that only she knows it. But even if Chris got it, he'd have to be crazy to steal those certificates. They're registered in your mother's name. Once they were reported missing—which would be immediately—they'd be listed as hot with every bank and financial institution in the country. He'd be collared the minute he tried to cash them in.

Whatever game he's playing, you can be damned sure it's a smarter one than trying to pass hot bonds. Look, I've got to go. I'll be late meeting your mother."

"Will you tell her about me following Chris?"

"Right now I don't want to talk to her about anything she doesn't already know. One more shock and she's liable to say something to Chris that will tip him off. We'll tell her after we've got it figured out."

"When I get back to town, I could check out a private detective."

"Wait until we've had a chance to talk. I may have a way to flush him out. And for God sake, don't you do any more snooping. Somebody's liable to remodel your beautiful face." His voice softened. "I've gotten pretty fond of it."

I'd have ignored the warning but I couldn't think of a new place to snoop.

Diane

THIRTEEN

As soon as Chris drove off from the St. Francis, I walked to a phone booth and called Paul. He suggested we meet at a coffee shop on Post Street at ten-thirty.

"Fine," I said. "I'm afraid I'm beginning to feel a little foolish about all this."

"You shouldn't, Diane. From what Jennifer told me, I think you have good reason for concern. I also think there could be an innocent explanation for these strange happenings. Anyway, try to be optimistic."

All through the night and on the silent drive in, I had been telling myself the same thing. But I was unable to shake the conviction that I was being manipulated by Chris for some sinister purpose. If only there were some way to get an insight into his true character . . .

Perhaps there was, I thought, as I returned to the street and contemplated a tall building rising two blocks ahead of me.

Behind that glass-and-aluminum façade were the offices of

Pacific Valley Foods. And in one of those offices sat the man who had inadvertently revealed Chris's first deception.

I looked at my watch. Almost an hour before my meeting with Paul. Time enough to see if I possessed any acting talent.

"You used to call me Elliott," said Elliott Davidson. He placed his elbows on his desk, cocked his head and affected a wounded expression.

I felt myself relax in the green leather chair. I tried a bantering look. "So I did," I said. "Just as you used to call me Diane."

I remembered him clearly now. He had been more than a casual visitor to our home. Fred had considered him one of his bright young men—about thirty at the time—poised and self-assured but not arrogant, deferential but never fawning. And candid—a burst of memory placed him as one of the men who had testified to Fred's occasional drunken rages. The thought bolstered my confidence.

"Well, Diane, I'm glad that's settled." He paused to give me an admiring glance. "You haven't changed," he went on lightly, "except to become even more attractive." He grinned. "I'd expand on that if you weren't a new bride."

"You've made the trip worthwhile, Elliott. I'm so pleased I stopped by."

He removed his black-rimmed glasses and rested his head on his hand, covering the receding hairline. He needn't have bothered; he was quite impressive as he was. Smooth round face, strong chin, good eyes, and in his dark, impeccably tailored suit, every inch the successful executive.

"You should have told me you were coming in," he said. "I'd have had the books doctored and declared a moratorium on three-hour lunches and chasing secretaries down the aisles.

Anything to keep a stockholder ignorant—especially a major one."

I laughed. "Whatever you've been doing, don't stop. I have no complaints." His breezy manner seemed to complement the role I had cast for myself—the knowing woman of the world, unembarrassed to discuss any subject. I said, "Actually, I was in town shopping and for no particular reason decided to stop in. This is the first time I've been here in ten years."

I caught a glimmer of sympathy in his eyes, quickly gone. "You look very happy," he said. He dropped the hand from his head. "That's a tribute to Colonel Warren." He paused, toying with a letter opener. "Had you known each other long?"

"No, we met only a few months ago, right after he retired from the service."

"Oh, I see. But naturally you'd heard about each other."

I evaded the truth. "I only know that he and Fred did business together. Now that I think of it, I never did know what it was all about. I must ask Chris."

"It was the same as *my* business with the Colonel, except that, as chief executive officer, Fred was brought in a few times when we needed a heavyweight. We had, still have, a contract with the government to provide food supplies for American troops abroad. As I'm sure you know, Colonel Warren was in charge of procurement."

"Yes, I know." I hadn't known. "Why would you need a . . . heavyweight? From all I've heard about you, you're extremely capable."

He thanked me with a smile. "Capable, perhaps, but I didn't have final authority when it came to certain big decisions. Fred, of course, did. It's a fiercely competitive situation over there." He laughed softly with genial cynicism. "Contracts don't always go to the companies making lowest bids."

Something Fred had often talked about came back to me. Airily I said, "You mean there had to be money under the table."

He arched an eyebrow. "I see you've been indoctrinated. Sure. That was s.o.p."

"S.o.p.?"

"Standard operating procedure. No honorarium, so to speak, no contract. Not in all cases, but often. We charge it off to promotion."

He hadn't actually said that Chris took bribes, but the fact seemed implicit. Was that so horrible? Here, the people who offered them in one form or another were respectfully called lobbyists. And those who received them? Was there a euphemism for crooks?

"Chris seems glad to be out of it," I said.

"I would think so. I suppose he told you that a year after he left NATO, all hell broke loose. In fact, you probably read about it in the press."

"I don't seem to recall . . ."

"It happened a few years ago. A congressional investigation. The committee probed into just about every product and service the armed forces bought. Ordnance, PX supplies, clubs, entertainment, and, of course, food. That's where we came in. Fortunately we suffered only a few minor shrapnel wounds. But a lot of people got busted for accepting or giving kickbacks, or for getting rich in the black market. As I say, that was a year after Colonel Warren was transferred. Too bad he couldn't have stayed. He'd at least have kept the thievery within tolerable limits."

A little thievery, fine; just don't be a hog. "You say he was transferred. Somehow I assumed he had been with NATO when he decided to retire. I guess because he was there so long and that's what he mostly talks about."

Elliott showed no surprise. "He was assigned to the U.S. Turkish Logistical Command in Istanbul. That's when I lost track of him. Oh, we did business with them but I didn't handle it. Small compared to the operation in Western Europe. There were less than seven thousand American troops in all of Turkey at the time."

I contrived a look of vague enlightenment. "Oh, I do remember him saying something—"

"U.S. Turkish Logistical Command—quite a mouthful. I shouldn't think you'd recall it. He probably called it by its shorthand name, TUSLOG."

It was as if my spinal cord had been plucked like a guitar string. The man Chris had talked to on the phone must have been a subordinate of his in Turkey. What service was he performing that had suddenly become so urgent? And why had Chris never so much as hinted that he'd been stationed in Turkey?

"Oh, yes, TUSLOG. That *is* the word Chris used." I stood up. "Elliott, I've taken up much too much of your time. I must get along."

"Drop in any time. Anything I can do for you, toot your horn."

Sitting at a corner table in the almost empty coffee shop, I poured it all out to Paul, unmindful that he had heard most of the story from Jennifer. He listened calmly, showing no reaction until I concluded with what I had just learned from Elliott Davidson. Then he stiffened and his eyebrows shot up.

I said: "The man I overheard Chris talking to on the phone must have served under him in Turkey—TUSLOG. That would explain why he called Chris sir."

Paul was silent, sipping his coffee.

"Don't you agree, Paul?

He looked at me as if trying to make a decision. "It's a reasonable assumption."

I thought back. "I recall Chris telling him that he was in a hurry. 'So get rolling,' he said. Apparently the man was performing some service for Chris that had suddenly become urgent."

He fiddled with his spoon, gazing down at the pink plastic table. I felt a surge of impatience.

"What are you thinking, Paul?"

He dropped the spoon and regarded me compassionately. "I was thinking how painful this must be for you." His jaw clenched. "I wasn't ready to mention this just yet—and I asked Jennifer to hold off—but now I think you'd better know."

He told me about Jennifer following Chris to the airport, meeting a man and exchanging an envelope, presumably containing cash, for an attaché case. My anxiety hardened into fear.

"It could have been the same man he talked to on the phone," I said.

"Yes, or a confederate of that man."

"It's all so cloak-and-dagger, as though he's involved in espionage."

He pulled reflectively at his lower lip. "Now that's a possibility I hadn't thought of." He mused over it: "A former Colonel taking early retirement . . . a clandestine transaction with someone he'd been associated with in Turkey, perhaps a CIA agent. You may be on to it, Diane."

"Perhaps. But why would he bother to deceive me about knowing Fred? Why pretend about a nonexistent job?"

"Well, he did explain about Fred—he kept quiet for fear you wouldn't trust him."

"Yes, he was very glib. And the job?"

"He might have invented it to account for seemingly doing

nothing, while actually accomplishing some secret mission for the government. Later, he could say the job fell through. Still a lie, but you couldn't knock it if it was for a good cause."

I burst out: "But I don't believe it's for a good cause. I can't, not when there's this hostility between us. Everything in me tells me he's into something criminal and that it's aimed at me. I thought about it walking over here and I've decided there's only one thing to do. Hire a detective."

As if to calm me, he held out a pack of cigarettes. I took one, seeing my fingers quiver as I brought it to my lips. Lighting it, he said gently, "What if you were wrong and Chris found out you'd had him investigated?"

"I thought of that too. It might finish us. I'm ready to take that risk." I took a few fast puffs. "Paul, would you be willing to handle it? I'm in no position to go scouting around for a private detective."

"I'll be glad to. But—"

"Today, if possible."

My free hand was knuckled white on the table. He reached over and covered it with his. "Look, Diane, first give me a couple of days. Let me see what I can find out. I have connections with some men in New York, former clients. Every day they're doing business with higher-ups in Washington. I'm sure they'll be glad to make some discreet inquiries. If there are skeletons in the Colonel's closet, they'll flush out every bone."

Gratitude flooded through me. I started to thank him.

"Save it until we see what I can get. I'll call New York as soon as I get back to the office."

Suddenly I gave a spastic shiver.

"Are you all right?"

"Yes. It was just the thought of meeting Chris, driving home with him."

And sharing the same bed.

The ride home was nerve-racking. Chris expressed surprise that I carried no packages and I told him that I'd had some things sent. I forced myself to ask him about his "guided tour" and he responded shortly: "Interesting but somewhat superficial. I learned very little." We then lapsed into a strained silence. The attaché case was not visible. Either it was in the trunk or he had dropped it off someplace. The thought of it had me bursting to talk to Jennifer.

The opportunity arose right after lunch. Jennifer suggested that the two of us relax in a shady spot beyond the deep end of the pool. Seeming glad to be rid of us, Chris said he had some notes to make and would be in the study.

As soon as we settled on divans, Jennifer said, "I spoke to Paul right after he got back from your meeting. So I know the whole bit."

We talked for a few minutes about what I'd learned from Elliott Davidson and what she had witnessed at the airport. Then I said, "I appreciate what Paul's doing, but I can't see how his friends back in New York can be of any help."

"It's worth a try." She thought a moment. "Who knows, they might turn up a former wife. Maybe he cheated on her, swindled her, and ran out on her."

I said gently, "His wife was killed in an automobile accident some years ago. It happened outside of Paris. They had been at a party where there had been a lot of drinking. Chris was driving and lost control. He blames himself terribly."

Jennifer said nothing. Her eyelids had lowered to veil her sight, as if insulating an intense inner concentration.

"He also lost a son," I said. "In Vietnam."

Jennifer stirred, her jaw clenched slightly, but her look of introspection remained unchanged. A minute passed in silence. Then she snapped bolt upright. "Holy shit!" she said. "It's a perfect fit!"

The attitude was more startling than the language. "*What* is a perfect fit?"

"I'll start back. The Colonel knew who you were before he ever walked into that art gallery. He leeches on to you, deals out the charm, does all the straight-arrow things that he figures will build him a lot of character. Isn't that how he played it?"

"I suppose so."

"Okay, that's step one. Step two—he needs some ploy that'll hook you emotionally. All right. How did your first husband die? By—" She took a breath and looked away.

"There's no need to go into that, dear. I understand."

She turned back, eyes dilated. "Ha, he says, why not tell you that *his* spouse was also killed violently—and by *his* hand. Wouldn't that synchronize your heartbeats?"

I nodded, recalling the empathy I had felt for him that day in front of the fire.

"So he's got you on the hook. All he needs is a gaff to land you. Step three—how about the death of a son?"

"You're saying there's a parallel between—"

"That's exactly what I'm saying! You'd lost a young daughter, hadn't you, or so you thought? He'd lost a young son. That made you soul mates. Fate had brought you together. Right?"

"I may have had that feeling. But there was really no necessity for such gruesome lies. I was attracted to him from the beginning and he knew it."

"Attracted! That's good enough for a shack-up but not for marriage. And marriage was what he wanted. So he had to make you feel needed." She looked at me curiously. "Tell me something, mother. Had he scored with you before he told you about his wife and son?"

"Scored. I guess I'm supposed to know what that means."

"You do. Had he?"

"No."

"So he was playing Mr. Clean. And after he told you. Then?"

I gave a shallow laugh. "A woman should have some secrets, even from her daughter."

"*Did* he make out?"

"Yes." In fact, Chris's revelation had so moved me that it was *I* who had seduced him!

"And right after that he proposed marriage?"

"Not right away. Frankly, I wasn't sure I wanted marriage. Then he—" I stopped. Suddenly I understood why he had left Mendocino, why for almost two weeks he had stayed in San Francisco while I brooded alone and painted furiously. He knew that when he finally did appear—that Saturday morning on the beach—I would be eager to do whatever he wished.

"Then he what?" Jennifer said.

"Convinced me we should marry. He got me when my defenses were down."

"And ready for the fleecing. And he's been sharpening the shears ever since."

"Jennifer, I think everything you've said may be true. What isn't clear is why he insisted on signing a legal document that denies him a penny of my money."

"So you'd trust him—trust him blindly. Then he could take you for a bundle without you getting on to him. Don't ask me how. Let's hope Paul comes up with some answers."

I looked up and saw Chris on the patio. He was in swim trunks and carried his white beach robe. Jennifer followed my gaze, then studied my face for a moment. It must have betrayed my revulsion because she said in a low voice, "There's no need to wait for proof, you know."

"You mean break with him now?"

"Sure. No explanation, except that it hasn't worked out—you

made a mistake. He'd have no choice but to split and you'd stay here. After all, the house is yours."

I watched Chris dive into the far end of the pool.

"Oh, Jennifer, I couldn't. I'd always wonder if I'd done him a terrible wrong."

After dinner, Paul took me aside and whispered that he had talked to the people in New York. They had agreed to telephone certain government officials in Washington and would get back to him through a spokesman.

"Did they say when?"

"Hopefully a day or so."

"This is Wednesday. What if they're delayed and want to reach you over the weekend?"

"I gave them this number. If Chris should answer, the caller will simply leave a name and ask me to call back."

I began to feel like I'd been blindfolded and was walking toward a precipice.

FOURTEEN

I SLEPT FITFULLY and so stayed in bed later than usual the next morning. When I came downstairs, Paul had already gone to his office and Jennifer and Chris were nowhere in sight.

The phone rang as I was sitting alone at the dining room table finishing my coffee. Elga entered from the kitchen and said the call was for me. I felt a flash of annoyance, thinking it was probably somebody with something to sell.

"Who would be calling me at this hour?"

"A Mr. Maguire, Madame."

"Maguire? I don't—"

"He says he used to work for you."

I pondered the name as I went to the phone in the living room. Maguire. It had a familiar ring but evoked no image.

"Hello, this is Mrs. Warren."

"This is John, Mrs. Warren."

That soft, melodious voice—I knew it instantly. He had

always been just plain John, never Mr. Maguire. Our beloved butler of so many years.

"John! How nice to hear from you!"

"I'm pleased you remember me, Mrs. Warren."

The name Warren was suddenly disconcerting. I had been accustomed to hearing him say Mrs. Ridgway, giving the "R" a slight roll. "Remember you! I shan't ever forget you, John. You helped make things so pleasant around here. Especially for Jennifer."

"How is Jennifer?"

"Fine. Wonderful. She's living with me now, for a while at least."

"She *is?*" His voice showed surprise. "Well, now, I'm surely glad to hear that."

"Yes, we've become quite good friends. How she'd love to see you!"

"And I'd love to see her." He paused. "The reason I called, Mrs. Warren: I heard you'd married and that you're not long back in your house. I thought, wondered, about employment."

"Employment?"

He gave his quiet laugh. "Yes. You used to consider me a pretty fair butler."

"You were much more than that, John. But now I understand. You and your wife are . . . available?"

"I'm available. Anna died just over a year ago."

I expressed my sympathy. Anna had been a strange, reclusive woman, her leisure hours spent closeted in her room. Perhaps that's why John had devoted so much of his time to Jennifer.

"I stayed on with the people we were working for, but recently they decided they wanted a couple. As they say in show business, I'm at liberty."

"Oh, John, how I wish . . ." I thought quickly. Why not?

Judging from Chris's outburst at Elga, she could use some assistance. And how wonderful for Jennifer to have John back!

"John, I think there's a good possibility it can be arranged. Why don't we discuss it. Let's see." Time was needed for Paul to get his information, time to settle whatever must be settled with Chris.

"I finish up here Saturday. I suppose Sunday would be inconvenient."

It was as good a day as any. "Sunday is fine. Can you make it about four o'clock?"

"I'll be there."

I rushed upstairs to tell Jennifer. But she was not in her room. Perhaps she was at the pool, although she usually waited until noon before taking a plunge.

Walking through the lanai to the terrace, passing no one, I saw that the pool area was deserted. Not even Chris. Maybe Elga would know Jennifer's whereabouts. I pushed into the kitchen and found no one there.

Stepping into the hall, I was struck by an odd uneasiness, as though the house had suddenly been abandoned. Then I heard a small blister of sound, like metal clicking against metal. It came from the study.

Instantly I was reminded of Chris's surreptitious phone call placed from that room. Now what? Feeling like one of those prying heroines in gothic novels, I crept down the hall and stood outside the study door. Again, the metallic sound, repeated. Without a speck of compunction, I kneeled and peeked through the keyhole.

I could see only Chris's left arm and hand and a part of the shoulder. Enough to know that he was seated at his desk, apparently leaning back. I thought of simply knocking, going in and asking if he had seen Jennifer, but some force restrained me.

My eye had begun to feel bonded to the keyhole when I heard a footstep in the entrance hall.

I snapped erect. But not before catching sight of Chris's right hand as it thrust forward and came to rest on the desk top. Gripped in it was a black pistol—the German Luger he had proudly displayed that day after I had so recklessly thrown myself at him.

The metallic noise must have been the clicking of the trigger. The gun, then, was empty. The knowledge failed to stem my rising apprehension.

"You are looking for Colonel Warren?"

It was Elga, facing me from the archway to the entrance hall. Had she seen me spying? Did it matter? "I thought he might know where Jennifer is. But I wanted to be sure I didn't interrupt him." Lame, lame, lame.

But she smiled understandingly, perhaps recalling his violent temper. "Your daughter is in the library."

I thanked her and brushed past. The library—what was Jennifer doing there? Never once since coming home had she entered it. The reason, I sensed, was because it had always been accepted as her father's room. "Your fish museum," she had once said to Fred, much to his delight.

I found her half curled up in the wing chair beside the barren fireplace. Her eyes were remote, swinging slowly around the walls to contemplate the mounted sea creatures that attested to her father's prowess.

Without any greeting, she said, "They look like idiots. Stuffed idiots."

I felt drawn to her mood. "Yes," I said, "but even idiots can feel. They can't."

"Once they could."

I sat in the chair opposite her. Absurd, I told myself—this

empathy for dead fish. Nevertheless, it was there, in my daughter, and transmitted to me.

"They were alive," she said. "Beautifully alive. Free. Maybe that's what he couldn't stand."

I felt a wave of shock. "It was just sport, Jennifer. That's all."

She looked at me. "Was that *all*? Why didn't he eat them then? Or throw them back? Why did he have to *own* them? Why did he have to stuff their skins and stick them up on the wall to show everybody he was their conqueror?"

"Oh, darling, they're just trophies." But my mind flashed back to Fred tying my hands to the bed.

"Maybe *we* were trophies, mother. And the servants, and everybody who worked for him. And this house and the cars. Everything."

This must stop, I thought. "You mustn't blame him. What you're suggesting is not at all uncommon."

The words released a pent-up fury. "That's what's so goddamned awful!" Suddenly she smiled. "Sorry, mother." She gave her shoulders a shake, stood up, and said in her normal voice, "I don't really blame him. It's the way he had to be." She seemed willing to close the subject.

I felt relieved. Ever since Fred's death I had been driven by a compulsion to protect the idealistic image she had of her father. Now, apparently she herself, without encouragement, had begun to perceive the cracks. She appeared ready to accept the reality. Perhaps she had at last grown up.

I said, smiling, "I'm sure you'll feel better once you've seen John."

"John?"

"Don't tell me you've forgotten him?"

Her mouth dropped open. "You mean . . . *John?*"

I told her about his phone call.

A light seemed to switch on in her eyes. Not simply the

warm glow of nostalgia. More like the purposeful gleam in the eyes of a religious celebrant.

"Fantastic!"

For me, that settled it.

When Paul came home I met him at the door. "Nothing yet from my contacts," he said. "The call could come tonight, but I doubt it. Most likely, I'll hear tomorrow, at the office."

"Paul, if they're unable to get sufficient information, I'll hire a detective immediately."

He nodded. "I guess that's the only thing left to do."

The next day, Friday, the call still had not come.

Arriving home, Paul just shook his head when I again met him at the front door. He handed me a manila envelope. "The last of the bonds. All your stocks have now been converted. Better put these right in the safe." He moved away as I started toward the library. But I was stopped by the sound of Chris's approaching footsteps. Without thinking, I took the envelope up to my room.

Shortly after nine—past midnight in New York—a growing dread threatened to crack the glassy surface I had so rigidly maintained. Quickly I excused myself. Chris glanced at me curiously but was silent.

Going upstairs, I heard him inviting Paul to a game of backgammon. Incredible that he could be so insensitive to the charged atmosphere.

But I was grateful for anything that would postpone his arrival in bed. Now the mere thought of his body next to mine released a shudder.

At 4:22 on Saturday afternoon the call rang through the house.

FIFTEEN

IN THE LANAI, I dropped the book I was reading and it slid from my lap to the floor. Chris, sitting nearby wrapped in his beach robe, rose and picked it up.

Somewhere, the phone was answered.

I waited an eternity of seconds before saying, "I've got my headache back. I think I'll lie down for awhile."

"Why don't you. I'll take another swim before cocktails. Perhaps you'll feel better by then."

I checked the living room and the library. No one was there. I looked in the kitchen. Elga was at the counter polishing serving dishes. She swung around and smiled. "The telephone? It was for Mr. Stafford. He took it upstairs."

I had to restrain myself from bounding up the staircase. Jennifer's door was closed. She opened it instantly when I called her name; she had posted herself there to guard Paul's conversation. I positioned myself tensely beside her. We stared toward the window.

Paul sat at Jennifer's small desk, pressing the phone receiver to his left ear. In front of him was a lined yellow pad. He was scribbling on it with a stubby pencil.

What few words Paul said were noncommittal. Just: "I see . . . When was that? . . . Give me that again . . . Hold it, let me get it down . . . Okay, go ahead . . ."

He was on the phone for a long while. When he hung up, he peered at his notes, seemingly oblivious of us.

Jennifer spoke first: "It's what you wanted?"

He didn't look up. "Yes."

A held breath tightened my voice: "Tell me, Paul, *tell* me."

He swiped impatiently at his light hair. "Give me a minute to put it together." He said to Jennifer, "See where Chris is."

Jennifer rushed out and was back in half a minute. She closed the door behind her. "He's floating belly-up in the pool."

Paul said to me, "I think we're safe here. But if I hear him coming up, I'll open the door and start some small talk."

I dropped into a straight-backed chair facing him. Jennifer perched on a corner of the bed.

"All right, here it is. I'll try to make it fast. I'm sorry, Diane, but I can't spare your feelings."

I looked at him levelly. "Please go ahead."

He consulted his notes. "Chris is everything you feared and a lot more. I'll start with his relationship with your first husband. As a procurement officer for NATO, he *was* suspected of taking kickbacks from Frederick Ridgway. But so were a few dozen others, from any number of U.S. suppliers. Somehow Chris managed to avoid court-martial and wangled a transfer to Turkey—the U.S. Turkish Logistical Command in Istanbul. TUSLOG—you heard about that."

"Yes. From Elliott Davidson."

"It's not at all strange your husband didn't mention it. At TUSLOG, he was again one of the high-ranking procurement officers. In fact, he was the kingpin of a huge black-market operation. He directed an organized ring of GIs and Turks. A lot of them made fortunes from the enormous premiums paid for American products. The premium was paid eagerly because American goods were banned from sale to Turkish nationals."

Paul explained that Colonel Warren had made the big connections: government officials who stole American goods at dockside or diverted them from supply depots. His crew of GI runners contacted cab drivers, shop owners, restaurant and hotel managers, landlords, striptease dancers, girl friends—anyone who was hungry for American products or knew someone who was.

"The Colonel ran it like a business—salesmen, delivery men, payoff men, accountants. The bigger operators drove expensive American cars, lived in plush apartments, kept girls. Some enlisted men netted more than three thousand dollars a month above their service pay. God only knows what the Colonel took in."

I said, "Then it's hard to believe he's now after money. He must have accumulated a fortune. Not to mention his retirement pay."

"No. They finally got onto him. The CID—criminal investigation. They were bound to sooner or later, the scale he was operating on. He faced a court-martial and knew he couldn't win. So he made them a proposition. He offered to pay back a huge sum and forfeit his retirement pay. In return, he demanded that all charges be dropped and he be granted an immediate honorable discharge. The brass bought it, except for the honorable discharge. That one stuck in their throats. So they compromised. He didn't get an honorable or a dishonorable—something in between."

"A deal," Jennifer said. "Just like in our free enterprise system."

"It saved everyone a lot of grief. The service was spared a scandal and he went free. But not *rich*-free, not for a man accustomed to his way of living. Apparently he held back something over a hundred thousand dollars, part of which he's investing through me."

I started to speak but Paul cut in: "Jennifer, would you check on the Colonel again?"

Paul and I sat in silence until she came back.

"He just ducked into a cabana to dress. We've got a few minutes."

I said, "The man he talked to on the phone and met at the airport—he must have been one of the black-market ring at TUSLOG."

"Probably. But he may now be out of this operation, considering the payoff at the airport. It looks like Chris isn't planning to share the jackpot with anyone."

"The jackpot being mother's money," Jennifer said.

"I think so, but there's no way to be absolutely sure."

"What else could it be? Everything he's done has been aimed at ripping her off."

"I guess Jennifer told you about the death of his wife and son," I said. "She thinks he used them to—"

"I've got some information on that." He looked again at his notes. "Colonel Warren's wife was *not* killed in a car accident. She divorced him five years ago in Paris and is still very much alive somewhere in Spain. And he had no son. He has a married daughter who lives in Atlanta, Georgia."

I was more dismayed than angry.

Jennifer said, "Now all we need is proof he's Jack the Ripper."

"The point is," Paul said, "it could be disastrous to wait for proof that he's after your money. You've got fair warning, based on hard facts, that he's a liar and a thief. So you're in a position to stop him cold *before* he makes his play."

I felt the muscles in my face congeal. "That's exactly what I intend to do. I'll face him with it."

"When?" Jennifer regarded me with a look of pleased surprise.

"Right now." I stood up.

"I'll go with you," Paul said. "He might get ugly."

"Thank you, but I think he'll cave in faster if we're alone. He'll know, of course, that you're close by. May I have those notes?"

"Sure. If he sees the handwriting, he'll know it's mine but that's all right with me."

"Paul, I'd rather you weren't involved. If he insists on knowing the source of the material, I'll say it came from a private detective. But I don't think he'll bother to ask. It's much too specific to be questioned. I think he'll be very happy to leave here quietly before I think up some charges to press. Considering the game he's in, I'm sure he doesn't want the sort of publicity a lawyer could provide."

"Where will you play the big scene, mother?"

"In the living room. I'll have drinks served, just so he won't suspect anything out of the ordinary. I'll say you'll be down shortly. I doubt if it will be more than a few minutes before Colonel Warren decides to make his exit."

Now that the detestable situation was resolved, I felt confident, a feeling reinforced by Jennifer: "Momma, you're a real take-charge chick."

A precautionary impulse took me down to the library to check on my bonds. It seemed only common sense to make sure they were accounted for before my confrontation with Chris.

Opening the safe, I recalled the certificates Paul had given me the night before. Thinking only of Paul's New York phone call,

I had taken them to my room, slipping them into the pocket of an old winter coat when I'd heard Chris coming up. I decided to leave them there in case he intercepted me on my way back to the library.

I wondered: Had he been waiting for *all* the bonds to be in my possession before making his move? I thought not; he would know that such an outright theft would almost guarantee his exposure. No, if my money was his target, he'd have contrived a plan he considered foolproof. But now he would be unable to put it into effect. I closed the safe and spun the dial.

Upstairs in my room, I called Elga on the intercom and arranged for drinks to be served in the living room. She was to tell Colonel Warren that I would be down in about twenty minutes.

I locked myself in the bathroom and went over Paul's notes again and again. Satisfied that I had memorized every fact, I folded the paper into a small square and stuffed it into an empty medicine bottle in the cabinet below the wash basin.

I washed my face and hands, applied makeup, combed my hair, and changed into a light-blue pants suit.

At precisely five-thirty, I descended the staircase.

SIXTEEN

I BEGAN in a quiet, matter-of-fact voice, facing him squarely, my eyes fixed on the bridge of his patrician nose. "Chris, I've learned certain things about you. If they're true, as they seem to be, it will be impossible for us to go on together."

I was prepared for an instant shocked reaction. Instead, he regarded me expressionlessly, as if I had made a banal comment on the weather. The only indication that he had heard was a slight hitching up in the dark-red easy chair, the removal of his feet from the ottoman, the careful setting down of his glass on the drum table.

His silence was so prolonged that I found myself squirming on the sofa cushion.

"You did hear me, Chris?"

"Yes, I heard you." His face remained stolid. "I'm waiting for you to go on."

He said it offhandedly, while adjusting his navy blue blazer and setting the crease in his gray slacks.

I mentioned the nonexistent job, not laboring it.

He offered neither defense nor explanation.

I skipped quickly over his relationship with Frederick Ridgway while at NATO in West Europe. "It was suspected that you accepted bribes for buying products made by Fred's company. But it wasn't proved."

His expression neither confirmed nor denied.

"Then you were transferred to Turkey, to an organization known as TUSLOG. Is that right?"

His nod was barely more than a blink of the eyes. Disconcerting. I took a sip of my drink. The next accusation would surely shake his complacency.

"There, I understand, you directed an enormous black-market operation."

He just looked at me, not even reaching for his drink to ease the blow. I felt my confidence waver, but steadied it with a deep breath.

Then everything that had been ballooning inside me, everything that Paul had reported, came bursting out. The connections. The price gouging. The enormous profits. The expensive cars and apartments. The girls.

He appeared unmoved, except to rub at his tanned, leathery cheek. My exasperation headed for fury. My voice rose.

"You were caught. You were to be court-martialed. But you bargained with them, bought them off. You paid back a lot of the stolen money. You forfeited your retirement pay. In return, they agreed not to prosecute, to let you go with some kind of questionable discharge."

He picked up his glass, swirled the ice with a finger, and slowly, meditatively, took a drink. Still he was silent.

"Good heavens, Chris, haven't you anything to *say?*"

His mouth thinned and tilted; almost, but not quite, a smile. He said softly, "On top of what I paid back, I was also fined ten thousand dollars. In addition, I was required to inform on some of my associates, Americans as well as Turks. Not *testify* against them—I refused to do that lest I be murdered—just inform." He said it as though confessing a boyhood prank.

"But you never told me."

"It's not something a person boasts about."

His manner—humble and somehow ingenuous—threatened to disarm me. He had not only admitted his guilt but blackened it.

"The omission is the same as lying. The fact is, you deceived me about something crucially important."

"Yes, I guess I did." He seemed not to care.

"You also deceived me about your wife and son. Your wife divorced you and is still alive. And your son is actually a daughter, also alive."

"True," he said. "I'd almost forgotten I had a daughter."

I heaved a frustrated sigh but pressed on. "The deceit, the lies could have had only one purpose; to create a false image that I'd find attractive enough to marry. But it had to be an image I could trust. So you signed away all claims to the very thing you were after—my money."

He smiled.

"I don't know how you planned to get it, and right now I don't care. The point is, you failed."

He finished his drink and said philosophically, "Not entirely. I've enjoyed your *hospitality*." He moved forward in his chair. "Which, I'm afraid, has suddenly ended."

It astonished me that he had yielded so easily. I had anticipated outrage, protests, bravado. I had girded myself for a lion and encountered a mouse. I felt suddenly deflated.

"Why did you decide to pick on *me?*"

He shrugged. "Simple. I was out of a job, had no prospects and not nearly enough money to suit me. I remembered hearing that Fred Ridgway had died and left millions to his widow. I looked you up and investigated. I got a fair amount of information from the back issues of the newspapers."

"Then you knew about—"

"I knew everything. That you'd killed Fred and got off. That you and your daughter were estranged. That your neighbors had turned against you. That you'd had an unsatisfactory love affair. I knew about your love of painting and that you lived alone on the Mendocino coast. I assumed you must have been very lonely, eager for male companionship. I figured out what kind of man might appeal to you. Temporarily, I became that man."

It was all unreal. So totally unreal that my emotions failed to respond to this unvarnished, almost proud recital of how callously I had been manipulated.

"You seem to have no feelings," I said dully. "You're like a . . . a psychopath."

I regretted the word immediately. His eyes became remote, opaque, as if to draw a shade over some telltale inner light. He grasped his glass, got up, and approached me, a melancholy smile playing about the corners of his mouth. He reached toward my half-empty glass—and smashed me across the jaw.

I reeled back, ears clamoring. My head was arched across the back of the sofa, eyes peering at a ceiling that undulated and whirled. All capacity for thought had been slammed from my brain.

His voice came to me as though filtered through an echo chamber: "That's for your high and mighty attitude lately."

I sucked in air, started to fling my head between my knees, when something with the solid stiffness of a block of wood blasted and deafened my ear.

"And that's for getting your daughter's boyfriend to check up on me."

My numbed cheek now pressed against the arm of the sofa. Blinking rapidly, I could see the fibers of the upholstery, as though through a spinning magnifying glass. I reached reflexively for my drink, gulped it down, let the glass drop to the floor.

In a moment, blood pulsed against my eardrums. My vision cleared. Tentatively I raised my head, to find that he had stepped back a pace. I darted a glance off to the left—the massive door opening from the entrance hall was closed. I hitched up on the cushion, still too astounded to feel even terror.

He stood with his legs stiffly apart, arms folded imperiously across his chest, face as hard as a fist. The gentle, good-humored companion had completed his metamorphosis into the brutal martinet.

"I heard it all. No, not quite. I missed the beginning. There's an extension phone in the study, you know. I was on it the minute you went upstairs. I listened right along with Stafford. When he hung up, I went for a swim. The way the three of you have been acting the past few days—as though the bomb was about to drop—I knew something was afoot."

Reason began to return. My concern with the evidence itself had blocked any thought of the phone extensions. And Chris had seemed so unaware. I reminded myself that Paul and Jennifer were waiting upstairs. If the monster in front of me struck again, I would scream. Instantly I felt more secure. I sat up straight and fixed him with a glare.

"If you're not out of here in half an hour, I'll call the police. I'll begin by charging you with assault."

Contempt twisted his mouth. "I'll leave when I'm ready. And I won't be ready for some time."

I knew he would bar me from the phone. But he couldn't if Paul was present. I stood up warily, knees almost buckling. He did not move.

I said, "I'll have you *thrown* out."

"Stafford?" He snorted. "Let him try."

I considered his figure. Its weight and height were a match for Paul's. But Paul, I was sure, was the stronger, and a dozen years younger.

I walked to the window wall, hidden by the closed heavy drapes. Reaching behind one, I found the small console and pressed a button. He eyed the action disdainfully but didn't protest.

The door from the entrance hall opened and Elga entered. Her ingenuous smile, under the circumstances, seemed ludicrous.

"Elga, will you please ask Mr. Stafford to come down." I prayed that Jennifer would remain upstairs.

"Yes, Madame. You wish more cocktails?"

"Not now. I'll let you know."

She started to turn, paused, and I saw her observe the glass on the carpet. Her face went blank and she hurried out.

Silence as we waited. Then the sound of feet descending the stairs. *Two* pairs. Ridiculous to think that Jennifer would stay put.

They stopped just inside the door. I felt Jennifer's inquiring look but kept my eyes on Paul. He gazed impassively from me to Chris, gauging the situation. I moved closer to him.

"He admits to everything," I said in a tight voice.

"Why not?" Chris said. "Your source sounded like he had all the facts."

"He listened on the extension in the study," I said.

Jennifer stepped forward, waving an arm. "Okay, so he admits it. So why doesn't he get lost?"

"He *refuses* to leave. I threatened to call the police."

"Did he try to stop you?" Paul said. Reaching back with his

foot, he kicked the door shut. He moved between me and Chris, who neither budged nor relinquished his arrogant posture.

I had hoped to withhold what had happened until Chris had gone. Now my hand went to my face and in a sudden rage I blurted: "My God, he nearly knocked my head off! *Twice!*"

"He *what!*" Eyes dilating, Paul stared closely at me. I dropped my hand from the puffed area below my ear. His whole body contracted as he whirled around to Chris. "Why you son of a bitch!"

Chris faced him coolly. Paul stalked toward the phone on the coffee table. Chris took a quick sideways step and blocked him. They stood jaw to jaw for a moment, then Paul shoved him aside.

Chris grabbed his elbow, yanked it, swung him around. Staring petrified at Paul's back, I saw him cock his right arm. The arm shot forward, propelling his fist into Chris's midsection. I heard a whoosh of air. Chris plummeted to the floor. He lay there, eyes rolling, hands clutching his abdomen. Paul strode to the phone and picked up the receiver.

"Stop! Right now you will stop!"

Paul froze. His jaw sagged as he turned around. Standing in the open door, the shy smile replaced by a malevolent grimace, was Elga. But not the homespun Elga we had known. Her face was vivid with makeup. Her yellow hair fell in waves to her shoulders. The loose-fitting maid's outfit had been replaced by a stunning beige suit that outlined her buxom figure. The cotton stockings had yielded to nylon, the flat shoes to spiked pumps. She was a page out of *Vogue.*

But startling as the transformation was, it was far less unnerving than what was gripped in her outthrust hand— Chris's black German Luger. It was pointed directly at Paul.

Slowly Paul replaced the receiver. Jennifer and I lined up beside him, stood there as though rooted.

Chris, cheeks flushed, labored to his feet, rubbing at his stomach. He forced a pained smile. "I'd have been more grateful, Elga, if you could have come about a minute sooner."

She moved to within a few yards of us, gun held level. "My apologies, darling."

He glanced scornfully at me. "You can see why I wasn't overly impressed by your indictment."

I looked from him to Elga, feeling the blood drain from my face.

"Have you forgotten, Diane? It was *I* who hired Elga."

"So she's part of the scheme."

He smiled benignly at the dazzling woman with the gun. "Elga is part of *all* my schemes, has been for quite a while."

"I am Colonel Warren's mistress," Elga said. "It is not an ugly word in Europe."

"I was afraid you might have begun to suspect our relationship," Chris said to me.

"The spilled coffee!" Jennifer said.

"Yes. It occurred to me, Diane, that you may have wondered about those midnight trips I took downstairs. It seemed wise to demonstrate that I found our maid offensive."

Paul said impatiently, "All right, you've got us. Now what?"

Chris considered him as if examining a bug. "A stupid question." He stepped next to Elga. She handed him the gun. He pointed it at me. "Into the library."

I moved forward on weighted feet. He halted me at the door and turned to the others. "See that they behave, Elga. If they make one false move, let me hear about it."

"How you'd love an excuse to hit her again," Jennifer said. "Big man."

"I won't touch her," he said. "I'll shoot her."

He marched me across the reception hall into the library. The safe was concealed by what appeared to be a wall cabinet. He stood close behind me as I opened the door. I jittered with the dial, missed the combination, then got it. I could hear his breath as I took out the bonds.

"Bring them to the living room."

Paul and Jennifer had not moved from their positions. Elga stood tensely in front of the drapes.

Chris indicated the chair where he had been sitting. "Put them on the seat."

I did so.

"Now, the three of you—on the sofa."

We sat down, Paul in the middle. Elga stepped next to Chris and he gave her back the gun. He picked up the bonds, sat down, and slowly riffled through them. Finishing, he inspected each one again, then squinted an eye at the ceiling. His gaze swung down to me.

"You're short, Diane. Short by about a quarter of a million dollars."

Mentally I saw my hand slip the bonds Paul had given me into the pocket of my coat. Instantly I erased the thought, absurdly fearful that he could read my mind. "Those are all the certificates I received."

He gave his nose a tug. "Oh, no. I was in Paul's office when he sold the last of the stocks." He drew a sheet of paper from his breast pocket and glanced at it. "That money was to be invested in bonds. Municipals. I have the list here."

"Nevertheless, I don't have the certificates." I supplicated Paul with my eyes. "Tell him I don't, Paul."

"You're both right," Paul said. "I did sell the stocks. But the transaction takes five days to clear. I got the proceeds yesterday and placed an order for the bonds. But I won't have the certificates for them until some time next week."

Chris eyed him skeptically. "You're lying."

Paul said harshly, "No. Settle for what you've got. Why be a pig?"

"Because he *is* a pig," Jennifer said.

He flushed. "That will be all from you, you little whore. Unless you want a print of that gun on your cheek." He glared at her. "If you hadn't been so damned nosy, none of you would be in this position."

Jennifer gave him a startled look. Leaning forward, she lit a cigarette with the table lighter. Her hand trembled.

Chris massaged his stomach, then got to his feet. He said to me, "Stand up."

I stood up.

"I'll take my souvenir, Elga."

She handed him the Luger and sidled off a few paces, toward the door. Chris placed the bond certificates on the chair arm. He moved back, closer to the drapes.

"Come over here, Diane," he said.

My legs felt like wooden stilts as I walked to within a few feet of him. He extended his arm full length and pointed the gun between my eyes.

"Now will you tell me where the certificates are?"

From the corner of my eye, I saw Paul push to the edge of the sofa. He said, "Chris, you've got better than three-quarters of a million dollars, a fortune. Are you crazy enough to take a murder rap for the rest? And not only you. Elga, too. She'll be just as guilty as if she'd fired the gun."

Elga's body jerked. "Chris—"

"The objective was one million dollars, Elga. I wasn't trained to accept partial victories."

In a voice dripping venom, Jennifer said, "I'll bet you were a real killer in combat. Women and children first. Colonel Coward—is that what they called you?"

She was trying to draw the heat from me to her. Successfully, apparently, because Chris lowered the gun and strode over to face her. Paul thrust forward slightly, body taut.

Chris looked at Jennifer with cold distaste, like a hunter at a caged hyena. He shifted the Luger to his left hand.

"I believe I owe you something, Jennifer." He stretched out his right arm and in a blur of speed whipped it down. *"This!"* His hand blistered across her jaw like a bullwhip.

The side of her face went dead white, then fiery red. Her mouth gaped and a moan grated from her throat. She swivelled away from Paul, so that she did not see him grasp the edge of the coffee table. His hands shot up, the table with them. Ash trays and lighter rattling to the floor, the table struck Chris as though hurled from a catapult.

He careened backward, the Luger dangling by its trigger guard from his forefinger. Paul leaped at him, hacked at his wrist. The gun dropped, bounced on the carpet. Paul lunged for it, stumbled, fell to his knees. Elga bounded in from the side, dived, skinned across the carpet, reached. But another hand got there first. Jennifer, galvanized by fury, had joined the battle.

Her fingers found the muzzle as Elga charged at her. My shin intervened and Elga sprawled forward on her face. Jennifer stood up, the grip of the gun firm in her hand.

But now it was Chris, shaking with rage, who started blindly toward her.

Paul extended his hand. "Give me the gun!"

I choked out: *"Jennifer!"*

Chris took another step.

She squeezed the trigger. A roar like artillery resounded through the closed room. She squeezed the trigger again.

Chris lurched, clutching at his chest. He spun away, whirled, sagged, eyes bulging in fixed dismay. He staggered to the heavy drapes, clawing for support. He crumpled, crashed to the floor, ripping the drape from the rod. A last-blood convulsion turned his face down. He lay still.

Paul stood frozen in astonishment as Elga darted past him and wrenched the gun from Jennifer's hand. Breathing heavily, forehead speckled with sweat, Elga leveled the Luger at us.

She backed off to the fallen body. Kneeling, she grasped his shoulder and turned him over. A crimson stream gushed down the shirt front, dripped on the carpet. Covering us with the gun, Elga reached a quivering finger to the pulse in Chris's neck, held it there. Slowly she withdrew her hand. Her lovely face contorted into ugliness.

"Good God," she said in an awed voice. "He is dead."

Jennifer

SEVENTEEN

I GUESS I'D HAVE GONE for that gun even if the Colonel hadn't tried to hash my face. From the second he pointed it at mother's head I felt this thing—compulsion, I guess you'd call it—rise in me like a bucket coming out of a dark well. The bucket was filled with a clouded memory of two people standing in about the same positions and wearing the same expressions—the woman white with terror, the man seething with rage.

The only difference was that, in the memory, the weapon was a knife. After I got clobbered and Paul knocked the gun to the floor, I seemed to see it as a glittering blade. I was aware of making a dive for it, and then I sort of blanked out. I wasn't conscious of squeezing the trigger and I heard the noise as though it came from far away. When the Colonel whammed to the floor, it seemed like the climax of a weird dream, acted out in slow motion. Not until I saw the blood pouring down the front of him did I realize that I had made it happen.

There was a terrible silence. It was broken by a small cry

from mother, who swayed to my side and lowered my arm, still half-raised in the firing position. With a quick, panicky movement, she swung me around and hugged me tightly. I could feel our hearts beating together, but that's all I felt. The rest of me was as rigid and unfeeling as a block of wood.

Mother drew back and stared into my face. Her eyes glistened with what seemed a sort of tortured recognition. Vaguely I sensed that she was recalling that night ten years ago when my father lay lifeless on the bedroom floor in a creeping stain of blood. Suddenly my knees sagged and I started to go down. Hands grasped my elbows. I turned my head and met Paul's agonized gaze. I gulped air, clenched my jaw, and straightened, nodding that I was all right. Paul stepped aside and we looked toward the woman crouched beside the Colonel's body.

She seemed to float to her feet, peering uncertainly at her gun hand, as if to verify that it held a weapon. She shook herself like an animal, hissed out a breath, glared at us defiantly.

In a low, guttural voice, without inflection, she said, "I am in charge now."

Paul stared thoughtfully at the body next to her feet. "Are you, Elga? I'm not so sure."

Her eyes spilled out hatred. Edging to the chair where the dead man had sat, she snatched up the bond certificates and shook them at us like a club. "These, they will not compensate, but I will take them."

"They're no good to you," Paul said. "Try to cash them and you'll be arrested."

"Oh?" Her mouth looked about to spit. "That is not what the Colonel told me. They are—what is the word—negotiable. As good as money. Anyone can cash them."

Paul shook his head. "This is Saturday. Every place they could be cashed is closed. By Monday those same places will

have been notified that they're stolen property. They'll blow up
in your face."

"Ah, you think so. There are other ways . . ." Her lips
fastened to her white teeth and for an instant her eyes wavered.

"Now I get it," Paul said. "The Colonel planned to fence
them, sell them at a discount." He turned to me. "There are
underground characters who trade in that sort of thing."

"The man he met at the airport," I said.

"You can believe it. He'd probably pay about half their face
value."

Elga's silence and a tremble of the gun seemed to say he'd hit
it. I shot a glance at mother. Her gaze was riveted on the body,
as though seeing it as another man's ghost.

"Elga," Paul said, "in your spot—without the Colonel—your
fence will probably grab the whole bundle and not even leave
you plane fare."

"Enough, Mr. Stafford. I will take my chances."

Paul chewed his lip. I could almost hear the wheels turning
inside his head. Mother was now staring at him as though
seeking salvation from a guru.

Finally he said, "Getting double-crossed is the least of your
problems, Elga."

She attempted a sneer but blew it. "What else?"

"The odds say you'll be arrested for murder."

Her head snapped back. "That is nonsense!"

"Is it? You're holding the gun—the Colonel's gun—that fired
the shots. Sure, you can get rid of it. But the bullets will show
that they came from a German Luger."

"But fired by Miss Ridgway. There is nothing that will
indicate otherwise."

"I'm afraid there is. The police will establish that the Colonel
was your lover, and therefore you were the one most likely to
have access to the gun. The police will also learn that he planted

you here as a maid. The disappearance of both you and the bonds will prove that you had to have stolen them. I think they'd logically surmise that you fought with the Colonel over the loot and shot him."

Her outstretched hand seemed to wilt.

"In fact, we'll swear to the police that you killed him. It would be your word—the word of an obvious thief—against the word of three respectable people. You'll be hounded wherever you go."

She made a sucking noise, as if she'd run out of saliva.

Paul gestured resignedly. "That leaves you only one way out, Elga."

She looked puzzled. "Which is?"

"Kill us all."

I heard mother gasp. But it was a mild reaction compared to Elga's. Her eyes popped with fear, her body seemed to shrink and visibly squirm.

"Go ahead," Paul said. "You're going to be nailed for one murder. Why not make it a massacre?"

She wiped a palm along her curved hip, glanced furtively at the body, shuddered, moved away. Her face was pinched with thought. Slowly it smoothed out and a crafty look made slits of her eyes. "What if I left the bonds?"

"You mean would that persuade us to drop the whole thing?"

"Yes."

"How can we drop it? We've got a dead man to account for. I'm not about to drag Jennifer into that. It will be a lot less trouble to hang it on you."

She breathed a sigh. "Very well then, Mr. Stafford. What if there was no dead man—nothing here for the police to find?"

"You mean dump the body?"

"Yes, bury him someplace. No one was close to him, except me."

"He has a *wife,* standing right here."

"Madame Warren, you should *care?* He was your enemy. Also, your daughter—she would be out of it."

I turned to mother. She was looking past me at Paul, her eyes appealing for guidance.

"I'm sorry, Diane, but I'm afraid the decision has to be yours. He was your husband."

Mother rubbed a hand across her eyes. "How would we explain his . . . absence?"

Paul said gently, "Considering his record, I don't think anyone he knew would ask for an explanation. But if it ever came up, you could simply say that the marriage was a mistake and he took off, you don't know where. That would be the end of it."

She peered into my face and the misery in hers told me what she was thinking: Must her daughter be dragged through another murder investigation, one that was bound to dredge up the nightmare of my father's death?

Gritting her teeth, she nodded to Paul.

"All right, Elga, you've got a deal. We keep the bonds, you take the body, and we all keep our mouths shut."

"Very good." She frowned. "But I will need transportation."

There was a heavy silence. Then mother snapped, "Take the T-Bird."

"You can hide him in the trunk," Paul said. "After you've buried him, you can leave the car someplace. Eventually we'll get it back."

Suspicion arched her penciled eyebrows. "What is to prevent you from calling the police as soon as I leave? They would recognize the car, the license plate. They would find the Colonel's body in the trunk and me with the gun that killed him."

"You'll have to take our word that we won't call them."

She tossed her pale-yellow hair. "In the circumstances, that is not good enough." She scanned us, one by one. "The only way I can feel safe is to take a hostage."

Paul's voice turned ugly. "Now look—"

"It must be someone with the strength to manage the body, the stamina to dig a deep pit. You, Mr. Stafford."

"No!" The word leaped out of me.

"You would prefer it was you, Miss Ridgway? I accept. You look like a strong girl."

"Jennifer, you mustn't!" Mother grasped my elbow, as if to hold me back. "You shot Chris. Elga might"—her voice caught—"might want revenge."

"I'll go," Paul said. We started to protest but he interrupted: "I'll be perfectly safe. She has nothing to gain and everything to lose by shooting me."

"Correct, Mr. Stafford."

"Let's get moving," he said.

Elga had been casting glances at the ripped brocade drape, now attached to the rod by a single rung. She backed up to it and fingered the edge. "We will wrap him in this. It will hold in the blood."

"Where will you take him?" mother said.

"It is better you do not know. But it will be someplace where no people go. He will be buried deep. He will never be found."

Elga gave the drape a yank and the thick burgundy-colored material fell in a heap to the floor, partially covering the body. She drew herself up and faced us, the Luger steady in her hand. "You, Mr. Stafford, and you, Miss Ridgway—you will do it. I must be sure there are no tricks."

"First the bonds," Paul said.

She glanced at them regretfully, then tossed them toward mother. They fell short and scattered on the floor. Mother made no move to pick them up.

Elga said, "That is my part of the bargain. Now yours."

Paul and I spread out the drape. He handled the corpse, rolling it to the center and enfolding it as though in a cocoon. Each taking an end, we hefted it. I half-staggered but said, "I'm with it."

Mother went with us, Elga guarding from the rear. We lugged the dead weight through the entrance hall, past the kitchen, and out the door that connected with the garage. We eased the body down on the oil-stained concrete behind the T-Bird and mother handed Paul the keys. He opened the trunk and stuffed the shrouded remains in beside the spare tire. He banged the lid shut.

"We will need a shovel," Elga said.

There were several in the corner. I went to them and picked one with a medium-sized handle. Elga told me to put it on the floor in back, which I did, leaving the passenger door open. She passed me as I rounded the car and stood beside mother, next to where Paul now sat behind the wheel.

With one foot inside, Elga paused and eyed us over the car top. "Perhaps you are wondering why I did not tie you up."

We said nothing.

"It seemed unnecessary. I am sure you know that if I detect any sign of police interference, I will kill Mr. Stafford."

She ducked inside and slammed the door.

Paul said, "This will take time. I'll call when I can."

Mother and I stood silently as the T-Bird backed out. We walked to the edge of the driveway and watched the car travel the half-circle, reach the road, and speed away in the gathering dusk.

I had a premonition that I'd never again see Paul alive.

EIGHTEEN

I FINISHED MY THIRD CUP of coffee, no longer tasting the lacing of brandy, and put down the cup. This time it didn't rattle in the saucer; my hand was steady. For the hundredth time I looked at my watch.

"Nine fifteen," I said. "He's been gone almost two hours."

"I know. We'll just have to be patient. It would take quite a while to"—mother hesitated and her voice thinned to a whisper—"do what he had to do."

We were sitting in the library facing each other next to a dying fire. We had stayed there after mother had scooped up the bonds and returned them to the safe, neither of us willing to enter what I now thought of as "the death room." Huge, heavy silences had been broken by bursts of jittery talk—about Paul, about all the freaky things that had led up to the shooting. The shooting itself was too ghastly even to be mentioned.

We were waiting for the phone to ring.

I tried to imagine where Elga would search for a gravesite.

Where no people went, she had said, and where Chris would be buried deep. Perhaps some cruddy strip of beach fronting the bay to make the digging quick and easy (elsewhere the ground had hardened under the constant sun). And not too far from the airport, I guessed, so she could make a fast getaway after she'd left Paul and ditched the car. For sure she *would* ditch the car in order to escape the police should Paul decide to call them.

My heart gave a big thump.

Suddenly I knew why I'd sensed that Paul was on a one-way trip. Elga couldn't afford to let him live. If she did, he could blow the whistle on her as soon as he was dropped off. She wouldn't have the dead man and she might not have the Luger, but what she would have was almost as incriminating—the stolen T-Bird. Once she was picked up in that, Paul could lead the police to the buried body, maybe even have a clue to where she'd chucked the gun, and she'd be nailed for murder. Even if he had no such intention, I couldn't see Elga chancing it. I stood up.

"Mother, I'm about to go up the wall. I think we'd better call the cops."

She started as if I'd again fired the gun. "We can't! You heard her—she'll kill him!"

"I'm afraid she'll kill him anyway." Quickly I told her what I'd been thinking.

She closed her eyes for a couple of seconds. When she opened them, they had a fierce glitter. "You may be right. But if she's caught, she'll naturally accuse you. Jennifer, I won't have you subjected to a police investigation."

"You're afraid I'll crack?"

"One of us might."

My mind made a small spin. "So what's the difference if we tell it like it was, including my shooting Chris. As Paul said, they won't sock it to me. I may even get a plaque. But they'll throw the book at Elga—attempted armed robbery, car theft, kidnapping, maybe even . . ." The word murder—this time Paul's murder—died on my lips.

She looked away. "I just can't stand the thought of the past being brought up again. And that's what would happen."

There it was again. The past she was talking about concerned her and my father, not really me. I dug why she wouldn't want that blasted again all over the media, but that wasn't reason enough to risk Paul getting his brains scrambled, assuming he was still alive. I felt a jolt of anger. The heat of it burned in my voice:

"What you're actually saying, mother, is that because you're afraid of some bad publicity about yourself, you're willing to stand by and let Paul get his head shot off!"

She jerked back as though I'd slapped her. Then she slumped, took a sighing breath and said, "Of course you're right. Jennifer, I'm sorry. Call the police."

Despite the apology, the old bitterness rose and lumped in my throat. I reminded myself of the nightmare she was going through, swallowed hard, and went to the phone. As I reached it, it rang.

"Paul!"

"Yes . . . I . . . Jennifer, I . . ." There was a slight bang, as though he'd bumped into a wall. ". . . need some help."

"Paul, what happened? What's *wrong?*" Mother now stood beside me.

"She . . . clobbered me senseless . . . Don't think . . . it's serious. I've been hiking for miles."

"Where are you? I'll leave right away."

"Not sure. A Chevron gas station . . . It's closed . . . I'm in the phone booth outside." Again I heard the bang. He was having trouble staying on his feet.

"*Where?*"

"Couldn't find a name on the road. North . . . about a twenty-five-mile drive from you . . . next to the water."

That seemed to place him somewhere above San Pablo Bay.

"About ten miles back . . . passed a sign . . . said China Camp."

I had him almost zeroed in. China Camp was a colony of dilapidated wooden buildings, now abandoned, that ran down into the water. It was a minor tourist attraction. A movie had been filmed there.

"I know almost exactly where you are. Don't move, I'm on my way."

Silence.

"Paul!"

"Sorry . . . knees started to go."

I thought of the drive back, Paul maybe lying unconscious on the back seat. "I'll bring mother. Hang in. We should be there in a half hour." Considering the curvy roads and the probability of fog along the bay, it would take all of that.

Mother ran upstairs for bandages and disinfectant while I went out and started the Volks. When she slammed in, I gunned the car around the driveway, only to be slowed by traffic on the main drag. We stopped for a red light and I noted that a foggy mist had speckled the windshield and slicked the pavement. I turned on the wipers.

Mother said, "Did he explain what happened, aside from being hit?"

"No. I couldn't get into that. He sounded punchy."

Her hand squeezed my shoulder. I felt it tense. "You were right about Elga," she said gently. "She *was* afraid Paul would call the police, so she knocked him unconscious."

"I was only partly right. Thank God she didn't kill him." I

raced the motor. "By now she's probably ditched the car. She may even be high in the sky flying back to wherever she's from."

The image of an airplane reminded me of the short, dark man Chris had met at the airport. Obviously he was either a fence for the bonds or a go-between. What had been in the attaché case? A down payment? I crossed that out; guys like that would be strictly C.O.D. (Besides, it had looked like Chris paid *him*.) Maybe phony papers—passport, visas, other credentials—to get them out of the country under assumed names.

The light changed and we moved ahead toward Highway 101. Reaching it, I turned north and joined the clog of Saturday night cars. Cutting off at San Rafael, we skirted a brightly lit shopping center, then passed a long stretch of residential developments. Beyond that it was all narrow black road rimming the shoreline. Soon there was only a sprinkling of cars, then none. Fog billowed overhead, dropping more moisture, as we reached a curve in the bay and started rolling through wooded hills. We flashed past a sign pointing to China Camp. I drove another eight or nine miles and . . .

"There he is!" mother said.

He was half lying down, propped on his elbows, under the canopy of the darkened gas station. I pulled in beside him as he swayed to his feet. Jumping out, I ran up and gingerly patted his shoulders, resisting a hug lest his ribs were cracked. Apparently not, because he pulled me close and held on for dear life. Just like the day I'd arrived from Hawaii.

"Thank God," I said. "I was afraid you were dying. The way you sounded—"

"I feel better now. All this fresh air." He touched his scalp and his fingertips came away smudged with blood. "Split the skin, that's all. But it put me out for a while. Then I had to hike a few miles to this gas station. I was still stunned when I called you."

Mother came over and placed a hand on his cheek. "I've got some first aid supplies, Paul. I'll drive while Jennifer fixes you up."

He thanked her and we got in the car and drove off, Paul and I in the cramped back seat. He used the disinfectant but not the Band-Aid; his hair on top was stiff with blood, which he'd wash out when we got home. He told us the story.

As I'd guessed, Elga had found a small isolated beach unfit for swimming, picnicking, or mooring a boat. While she held the gun on him, Paul had dug a trench and dropped in the body.

"All the time I was digging, she kept yakking at me to hurry. When I was a few feet down, she started to panic and told me to quit. I got on my knees and began pushing the sand in with my hands. That's when my head exploded. The shovel was behind me and I guess that's what she used. It was gone when I came to and Elga had pretty much filled in the trench."

"She was worried that we'd phone the police," mother said. "Jennifer was about to when you called."

His hand gripped mine, then left to strike a match. He looked at his watch. "She's had plenty of time to get lost. Elga we can forget."

"I'd like to kill her," I said. "Slowly."

"Don't be too hard on her. Sure, she's a thief, but maybe because it was the only way she could keep Chris. Once she was trapped, she did the only thing she could do to stay out of jail." He rested his head on my shoulder. "Anyway, she didn't get the bonds."

We passed a street light and I could see the blood crusted in his tawny hair. "No, but she got *you*."

"A small price to be rid of her. I think we'd be smart to write it all off and try to get it out of our minds."

The voice from the front seat was grim: "I agree."

Two against one. The hell with justice, I thought.

We got home a little before eleven. Paul went to an upstairs bathroom to wash out the wound. Mother joined me in the kitchen for a cup of coffee. We were both knocked out.

We wondered what to do about locating the T-Bird, not much caring. "Let's try to get some sleep, then decide," mother said. She got up quickly, leaving half her coffee.

Paul came in. He had soaped the wound and applied more disinfectant and a Band-Aid. "It's about an inch long," he said, "but not serious. The worst part will be ripping off the adhesive."

Still, I worried. "I'm as good as new," he said. But his eyes were glazed, his cheeks haggard.

I told him about waiting until morning before doing anything about the T-Bird.

"Might as well. But we'll have to tell the police that it was stolen. We can say we were out in the Volks when it happened."

That made me mad again. Not simply because Elga would escape punishment, but more because mother and Paul—mostly mother—were so willing to guarantee her safe passage. I suppose I was being unreasonable; their only thought was to avoid the agony that would accompany a homicide investigation. But would that be any worse than spending our days and nights sweating out whether the corpse would be discovered? Not for me it wouldn't. Already I could see Chris's eyes staring up at me accusingly from the sand pit. They started to turn into my father's eyes and I gave my head a hard shake and got it together.

Mother had gone to her room and Paul was rummaging around in the closet under the sink. He came up with a new dish rag and a can of something. "Cleaning fluid," he said. "For the living room carpet. We won't want to face *that* in the morning." I nodded dumbly. Chris's blood seemed to seep through my brain.

When he returned I heard mother coming down the stairs. There was the sound of the library door opening. Paul looked at me wonderingly. Then he smiled.

"Probably putting the bonds in the safe," he said. "The ones I gave her last night. They weren't with the others. Much to Chris's displeasure."

"Then she did have them, just like he said." In all the excitement she hadn't thought to mention it.

"Yes, worth a quarter of a million. With that gun pointing at her head, it took a lot of guts to deny she had them."

My mind replayed the scene. "Thank God you talked Chris out of it."

"I doubt if I was very convincing. But it didn't matter. That's when the action started."

Mother came in, saying, "Well, that's a relief. The bonds I lied about to Chris were where I put them, in the pocket of an old coat."

"You doubted it?" I said.

"While we were having coffee I suddenly had the awful thought that Elga might have stopped here. She may not have believed I didn't have them. I'm the world's worst liar."

"*I* believed it until Paul just clued me in. But I can't see Elga even taking the time out to go to the john. She was too frantic to get away."

"She's probably out of the country by now," Paul said.

"I'm sure you're right," mother said. "But she must be desperate for money. Anyway, all the bonds are now in the safe."

Desperate for money, I thought. Hell, yes. She probably had

been totally dependent on Chris for anything beyond walking-around money.

"Mother, when did you last pay Elga?"

"A week ago. She wasn't due again until next Saturday."

A tiny sacrifice compared to what she'd anticipated—a junior partner's share of at least three-quarters of a million dollars. Okay, half of that if Paul was right about fencing the bonds at a discount. That still should have put her cut somewhere in six figures. But it had been shot out of her hands by a German Luger.

It seemed a sure thing that she had nothing besides a plane ticket, bought in advance. Good for a one-way trip to Chris's connection, who I now figured operated in Mexico. After she'd told him they'd blown it, what then? He'd brush her off and she'd be stranded in a strange country without enough cash to buy an enchilada.

Or would she try to recruit the accomplice—maybe tossing in her gorgeous body as a bribe—to come back and recoup the loss?

I wouldn't have given odds that we'd seen the last of Elga.

NINETEEN

WHEN MOTHER AND I CAME DOWN in our robes the next morning we found Paul in the kitchen making coffee. He had already called the police about the car.

"Were you asked any difficult questions?" mother asked. Her eyes had a burning look, like someone with a high fever.

"No. Happens every day, the cop said. Usually teen-agers sometimes hopped up, just wanting to cruise. Ninety percent of the time, he said, the car turns up within a mile or two of where it was stolen."

"Too bad you couldn't tell him to check the airport," I said.

"I didn't have to. He said that all parking areas adjacent to transportation terminals would be notified. Routine."

We brought our coffee to the lanai and took turns questioning where we stood.

Would any of Chris's former associates seek to look him up and become suspicious? There might be inquiries, we decided, but we doubted the suspicions. Chris had left the military in disgrace, his crimes probably known to everyone who had served with him. What could be more natural than to assume he had tried and failed to get his wife's money and had gone on to easier marks?

His former wife? She was somewhere in Spain and probably never again wanted so much as to hear his name. His married daughter in Atlanta? Chris had as much as said that they never communicated.

"I can't see how there can be any repercussions," Paul said.

"There's still Elga," I said.

They were silent, looking at me.

I told them my theory—that Elga was broke, that she might know how to contact Chris's connection, that he might team up with her to steal the bonds, by force if necessary. Laying it out again, seeing their faces tighten, I began to feel I was right on. A million dollars! If they netted only half of that, they could take early retirement.

"It's something to consider," Paul said. He *was* considering it, his pale eyebrows almost joined.

Mother sighed in exasperation. "If only it wasn't Sunday! I'd take the bonds to the bank and lock them in my safe deposit box."

"You'd better do that first thing tomorrow," Paul said.

"Why didn't you do it from the beginning, mother?"

"I never really thought about it. The safe here is very secure, and your father always kept valuables in it. Besides, it never occurred to me that the bonds could be cashed by anyone." She thought a minute. "And perhaps I wasn't keen on running into Mr. Chisholm at the bank. He had looked so hurt when I took the stocks from him."

"Anyway," Paul said, "who'd have imagined Chris was into this kind of heist. The Mafia, sure, but not eagle colonels, even a busted one."

Thinking of him, I suddenly found it hard to breathe. "It doesn't seem real. None of it seems real."

"I know, dearest," mother said. "I feel that way too. It's just as well. The less real it seems, the quicker it will pass."

"To think I could do such a thing. Just stand there and kill him."

"Exterminate," Paul said. "He was vermin."

"Jennifer, there was nothing else you *could* do. You were protecting yourself. You were protecting *all* of us."

I had a strange, dreamy feeling. "He came charging straight at me. I don't even remember pulling the trigger."

"Don't! You've got to stop this!" Mother's voice trembled but there was a flinty look to her eyes.

"I'll go get dressed," I said. I had an almost panicky need to be alone.

In the reception hall, I hesitated outside the closed living room door. Last night Paul had cleaned up the blood. Had he got it all? Daylight would tell. I went in, drawn as much by morbid curiosity as by a sense of neatness.

The drape on the left side of the window was shut. On the bare right, slanting sunlight poured in, forming dark leaf patterns on the beige carpet. The area cleaned by Paul looked bleached and scruffy. I walked over, bent down, and took a close look at the nap. Not a trace.

I stepped back, not moving my eyes from the scrubbed patch of carpet. Again I saw Chris's final contortions as he wrestled with death. Before the gun exploded, there had been an odd gleam of surprise in his eyes, like that of a man strolling innocently along a street and suddenly being stabbed by a passerby. A chill crawled up my back. That look seemed to be connected with something locked deep inside me that for days had been struggling to burst out.

I went to my room and stretched out on the bed, my mind trying to shove its way into a huge void.

When I got up and started to dress I was shaking like a junkie trying to kick the habit cold turkey. I wasn't sure why.

After lunch, a cold pickup that nobody wanted, Paul changed to his trunks and went out to siesta beside the pool. Mother flaked out in her room and I went to mine for some more heavy thinking.

Lying on my back, one hand over my eyes, I mentally reenacted the scene that had been bugging me. But this time I cast the characters in different roles, changed motives, and introduced a new player. The drama was reaching its climax when my mind blanked out. I slipped into a troubled sleep.

Waking up was a real downer. Squinting at my watch, I saw it was three o'clock. I heard Paul come up and go into his room, probably to get dressed. I changed to a jade bikini, covered it with a short white robe, and went down to the pool. Apparently mother was still resting, or more likely in a deep, tranquilized sleep. At lunch she had looked ready to go over the edge. That made two of us.

I did twenty laps to get my gravy flowing.

As I was returning through the entrance hall, the door chimes sounded and I nearly left my skin. In that hushed house, it was like the crash of cymbals in a tomb. I went to the door, wrenched it open—and almost threw my arms around the man who stood there.

"*John!*"

He had aged only slightly. Same thick hair, grayer now. Same jowly red face with the laugh lines fanning out from the corners of soft blue eyes. And the same musical voice:

"Jennifer. It *is* Jennifer, isn't it?"

"The same one you used to throw off the pier." Depression had vanished.

"Well, it's only been two years but I barely saw you then. Now, you're sure a lovely young lady. Doesn't surprise me though. T'was all there in the beginning."

He stepped inside, a tall, heavy-shouldered figure in dark suit and tie and carrying a gray homburg. He could have passed for head mick at the Irish embassy.

He gazed around the hall, eyes shining reminiscently.

"Just the way you left it, John." Something made me add, "Nothing's changed since my father died."

He started slightly and a shadow seemed to cross his face. It was a look I'd seen before, a long time ago, as though in a fantasy. The scene I had been rehearsing while lying in bed sprang to life.

"Something wrong, Jennifer?"

Now, anguish only touched his face; back then, it had been stamped in deeply.

"No, I guess . . . I guess I swam too many laps."

The scene in my mind sharpened. I tensed against terror, but was surprised by a feeling of peace. An uneasy peace, but peace nonetheless. It only had to be ratified.

"Did your mother tell you? We had an appointment for four."

"Yes, she told me. She's upstairs. I'll get her—but after you and I have a talk."

I led him into the library, where we sat facing each other beside the fireplace. His eyes roamed the room, lingering on the finned corpses curving stiffly from their dark-wood mountings.

Yes, the fish had given some insight. And Elga's knives, and the look of the Colonel when he fell, and the blood spreading on the carpet—and, most of all, mother's desperate attempt to cover up the crime committed in her bedroom so long ago.

Amazing that I should be so calm.

"John, before you see mother there's something I've got to tell you."

He grinned. "With you, I must've been the world's champion listener."

"It's about my father."

His eyes dilated and he set his jaw.

"John, I know that *I* was the one who killed him."

I had not been absolutely sure until the truth of it flashed across his face.

Mother was rushing down the stairs when I stepped out of the library, and closed the door. I half-skipped to her, prepared to fling my arms around her, beg her forgiveness for all the years . . .

"Jennifer! Is John in there? I completely forgot our appointment."

I checked myself. Time enough later. "It's all right, mother. John and I had a lot to talk about."

She frowned. "I was going to ask him if he'd work for us again. But now . . . well, it seems out of the question."

"Why should it be?"

"I've decided to sell the house. The thought of staying here gives me the creeps. I may take an apartment or go back to Mendocino. I don't know."

"John could help show the place. Afterward, you could take him wherever you decide to live. With his wife gone, he'll probably jump at the chance."

"You know, that might be a good idea. I'll talk to him."

I gave her a quick squeeze. Her face colored with surprised pleasure.

The minute I closed myself in my room, without any warning a huge sob shuddered through me and my eyes began leaking rivers. It had nothing to do with sadness or happiness but was just some big ugly thing that had to destroy itself. It was gone as quickly as it had come.

I showered, slipped on a yellow shift, and went into mother's room. I was standing by the window when she came in.

"Oh, here you are." She smiled in self-approval. "John will be delighted to come back. In fact, he can't wait to start. Just as soon as . . ." She stopped. "Is something the matter, Jennifer?"

I had slumped into a chair and was massaging my throat, which had suddenly contracted. I shook my head and began lamely: "Seeing John made me remember something, I—"

"If you're worried about Chris, please don't. I told John he was off on a trip. Later I can say we've separated. John won't think to question it."

Her voice was steady, her head high. Apparently sleep and the meeting with John had recharged her. I borrowed some of her courage.

"It wasn't about Chris," I said. "It was about my father. Did John say anything about him?"

She eyed me warily. "No. Your father wasn't mentioned." Her face tightened. "Why? Did John say something to you?"

I got up. "No, I said it to him."

"Oh?" She turned half away, then back. "Jennifer, just what are you talking about?"

I took a long breath. "I told him . . . Mother, everything about that night has come back to me. You didn't kill father. *I* did."

There was a deafening silence. Then she burst out: "No, Jennifer, no! You've been imagining things! It's not true!"

But her chalky face, her stunned eyes were a confession.

"John admitted it, mother."

"Why would John say such a—"

"I tricked him. I said I knew I'd done it and let him assume you'd finally told me. I guess he thinks that's what brought us back together."

"John is mistaken!"

"John didn't say a word about what happened. But I know—most of it anyway. Let me tell you."

"No. *No!*"

"You've *got* to listen. It's the only way we can really understand each other."

She sagged down on the bed. I paced the floor and let it all spill out.

I'd been blasted awake by a scream coming from the other end of the house. At first I thought it was something heard in a dream. But I jumped out of bed and opened my door. I heard a rush of feet, slapping noises, angry grunts. Terrified, I streaked down the hall. Reaching my parents' closed door, I heard a crash, as though a body had slammed to the floor. I threw open the door and saw father lying near the bed, saw mother standing over him. Then the glitter of a knife, on the carpet next to the wall. My only thought was that mother had somehow knocked father down, that next she would snatch up the knife and stab him.

"I remember thinking, I've got to save Daddy, she's going to kill him. I whizzed into the room, grabbed the knife, and stepped between you. Daddy was just getting up. He staggered back a couple of steps and stared at me, then at the knife. I was holding it in my fist—I remember the animal-skin handle. It was pointing at him. Then—"

"Jennifer, don't *do* this to yourself!"

"I'm all right, mother. Then he moved toward me. My hand with the knife wouldn't budge. It stayed there, pointing right at his chest. He must have thought I was shielding *you*, that I'd kill him if I had to."

I paused, gulped, and went on: "He raised his hand like he

was going to zap me and he called me a dirty little bitch. That and the way he looked—I'd never seen him like that before—made me jump. My hand, the knife, jabbed forward and he ran right into it. I saw it go in, just below his bottom rib. Then all I remember is how surprised he looked, and the blood, and John standing in the door."

Mother's face was clutched in her hands. "What made you remember?"

"A lot of disconnected things that suddenly all came together. Intuition, too, I suppose. Then when I thought about how eager you were to confess—and your private rap sessions with the judge—well, you *had* to have been protecting me. I was only ten and I guess you thought that if I knew the truth, I'd end up in the giggle factory. John must have felt the same way."

Mother raised her eyes. They were dry but tortured. "There were also other things I didn't want known. Your father—" She shook her head. "Some other time."

"Forget it," I said. "When some of his buddies bad-mouthed him, I figured it was because you swung a lot of weight with the company and they were afraid of the shaft. But they were really leveling. Apparently when the great Frederick Ridgway was smashed, he could be the world's worst s.o.b."

She looked puzzled. "It doesn't bother you?"

"Then, I'd have flipped out. Now, yes, it bothers me, but it's not that big a deal. I don't belong to him anymore."

Relief flooded her face. "You belong to yourself."

Not quite, I thought, but close. I said, "Now I know why you really didn't want Elga caught. You were afraid an investigation would shake out what I did to father."

She drew me down beside her. "It doesn't matter now. We're together, the way we always should have been."

"To think of all the years I blamed you, hated you. All the bad times I've given you. You should have slit my throat."

"I may have deserved some of that. I wasn't the world's best mother."

Her arms tightened around me. For the first time in ten years I didn't feel famished for love.

"Jennifer, I suggest you don't say anything about this to Paul. He's had enough shocks for one weekend."

I agreed. But eventually I'd have to tell him.

We sat in silence until there was a knock on the door. Mother opened it and Paul stood there.

Becoming impatient, he had phoned the police, just when they were about to call us. They had located the T-Bird.

TWENTY

THE CAR HAD BEEN SPOTTED in the parking lot outside the heliport in Sausalito. Mother and I knew the place. It was at the edge of the bay and provided overwater helicopter service to and from San Francisco airport; about ten minutes instead of almost an hour by car.

"So by now she's probably out of the country," Paul said.

I said I'd drive him to get the T-Bird.

"It's not that easy. First I have to go to the main police station in San Rafael to prove ownership. There'll be papers to fill out, releases to sign."

Mother sighed and gave an eye-roll. "Then I guess I'll have to go too. The car's in my name."

"The police said I could handle it for you. In fact, they'll drive me to pick up the T-Bird. Jennifer can drop me off at Civic Center and come right back. You shouldn't be alone for long."

At least forty minutes, I thought. I considered where the car had been left and began to get uneasy. "I don't like you staying here by yourself, mother."

"Come along," Paul said. "Keep Jennifer company on the ride back."

"If it's really not necessary, I'd rather stay. I'll get something together for dinner."

"Do you good to get out of the house. Tell you what. After I get the car, we'll meet someplace for a drink."

She smiled gratefully. "Thanks, Paul, but I'm not up to it. I'll take a rain check."

I knew she wanted to be by herself to adjust to the latest bombshell, so I didn't press it. She got a duplicate ignition key from a drawer and we went down to the library for the owner's pink slip that she kept in the safe. When she opened it, my uneasiness edged toward fear. I hung back while Paul went to the garage for the Volks.

"I wish you'd come with us, mother."

Her smile interpreted my insistence as simply a spin-off of our reunion. "I like being wanted. But I need a little time to calm down. Hurry back, though."

I dropped it; what I was really thinking might scare her out of her socks. Anyway, I was probably hallucinating. I gave her a hard squeeze and kissed her cheek.

Maybe she got the message then because as I left she was staring speculatively at the safe.

"You seemed worried about your mother," Paul said as we rolled down the driveway. He was behind the wheel. Darkness was gathering and mixing with a thin layer of ground fog. He switched on the lights.

"I can't help thinking Elga hasn't given up on the bonds."

"Oh hell, she's probably in Mexico. Look where they found the car."

"That's just it. She could have left it at the heliport to make us believe she'd flown out. Meantime she's lying in the weeds ready to pounce."

He said with less certainty, "But she couldn't get into the safe."

"Maybe an accomplice could—Chris's connection. He, or a buddy of his, might be an expert safecracker."

Or Elga herself could point that black Luger at mother's head and . . . An inner twitch snapped off the image.

I glanced at him. His face was grim.

"Okay," I said, "I guess it's pretty far out."

"It is. But, my God, so is everything else that's happened."

We brooded in silence until we were a few miles up the highway, nearing Civic Center. Suddenly I had a thought and something icy climbed my back. "Paul, maybe we'd better go back. We can get the car tomorrow."

He slowed down and gave me an anxious look.

"It just hit me," I said. "After what's happened, Elga must realize that those bonds will go to the bank first thing tomorrow morning. If she wants a shot at them, it'll have to be tonight."

He groaned. "I hadn't thought of that."

Ahead we could see the blue-tiled roof of the Civic Center building showered with lights.

"We're practically there," he said, pointing. "Let's do this. As soon as I'm inside I'll call her. Then we'll decide whether or not to get the T-Bird."

"Good. And if anything seems wrong, we'll whistle to the cops."

We took the next exit, whipped along a straightaway, then crossed over and started up the long driveway. The Civic Center building, designed by Frank Lloyd Wright, was a low, rambling, pink structure spread out on a gently rising hill. It was the pride of the county, a pride insulted a few years ago when prisoners with smuggled guns had taken over a courtroom and moved outside with several hostages, including the judge. The attempted escape had turned into a shootout and the judge was killed. Ever since, anyone entering was electronically searched for weapons.

Now, under the glare of lights and with two pistol-packing policemen strolling toward the plate-glass front doors, it looked like the safest place in the world. Paul pulled in behind half a dozen cars parked next to the narrow sidewalk. We were about twenty yards from the entrance.

"I'll make the call," I said and hopped out before he could say anything. I had this thing about hearing her voice, not only for reassurance, but also because it now had a warmth that my ear never before had tuned in.

Paul handed me the keys to the Volks as we hurried up the curving sidewalk. Inside, a policewoman sitting on a stool passed us through the electronic gear and pointed out a public phone booth down the corridor. Paul went to check on where he was to appear while I headed for the booth.

My call was picked up on the first ring. Mother's hello sounded natural. I almost collapsed in relief.

"Hi, mother. I'm at Civic Center. Just thought I'd call and see if I could get you anything on the way back."

"Thanks, but everything's here for dinner."

"Where are you now?"

"Lying on my bed reading a book. I'm used to being alone, so don't be concerned."

"I will be until those bonds are in the bank."

There was a pause. "Try not to think of it. Are you leaving there soon?"

"As soon as I hang up. Like now."

But I was held up a few minutes by Paul. He came scowling down the corridor to me saying, "I'll be longer than I expected.

The sergeant I've got to see isn't here. But he should be back any . . . Oh, how's Diane?"

"Alive and well and living in her bedroom, right next to the phone. We got all uptight for nothing."

"Fine. If anything was going to happen, it would have started right after we took off. We've been gone half an hour. I'd about decided to go back with you, but now I'll wade through the red tape and get the car."

He walked me to the door and I left him.

When I got to the Volks I saw that a number of cars were now parked behind it. The one directly back of me was practically touching my rear bumper. In front, there was less than a yard of open space. I slid in, wishing for power steering but glad I was driving a bug. Starting up, I yanked the wheel full left and started to ease out. I stopped before I bent the front car's fender, backed up, and did it again. This time I barely cleared. I was looking out the window for oncoming cars, my head twisted almost backwards, when I heard the passenger door click open, a body thump down, and a low, harsh voice say, *"Drive!"*

My head snapped around, but I didn't need eyes to know it was Elga. And I didn't have to touch the thing poking into my ribs to know it was a gun.

Funny, I didn't feel my expression change. I just looked at her like I'd been expecting her all the time, which I guess was true. I didn't even blink at the way she was dressed—dark, wide-brimmed hat over tucked-up hair, dark suede jacket with the collar framing her white face, dark shades that blanked out her eyes. Real cool, that was me. Except my hands stuck to the wheel like a factory weld job; ditto my foot on the brake.

"You now have room," she said. "Turn around. Go to the highway."

I couldn't move a muscle. My mind was a weird conglomerate of mother alone, Paul sweating out a cop, bonds in a safe, a gun in my ribs. The last item jabbed into me and a reflex jerked my foot to the gas pedal. The car bucked forward and I swung it around to the downhill side of the driveway. I coasted to the bottom, halted at the Stop sign, looked left, then glanced up at the rearview mirror. Bright lights reflected, blinding me for a second. They dimmed, then flashed back to bright. As I made the turn, the twin beams swooped around me to the far lane.

But not before I'd caught a blurred glimpse of the driver. He was hunched low over the wheel and wore a gray felt hat pulled low on his forehead. My memory described him further—fat, swarthy, and dummy faced—the man Chris had met at the airport. Apparently the lights had been a signal to Elga that he knew she was in charge.

His car gunned ahead about a hundred yards. The street lights showed it to be a beat-up Ford sedan—rusting fenders, dented trunk, sagging rear end. Bought that day, no doubt, for this one big caper. It paused at the highway Stop sign, then sped on through. By the time I had reached the sign, the Ford had disappeared.

"Go south," Elga said. Her voice was now cool and confident. Arrogant. I looked at her, defiantly I guess because she said, "I shall not hesitate to shoot you, Miss Ridgway." Her mouth turned nasty. "Any more than you hesitated to shoot Colonel Warren."

She drew back the gun, tilted it to point at my throat, and I saw that it was a short-barreled pistol. So apparently the Luger had been dumped, probably to prevent any chance of it being matched to the slugs in Chris, which could hang the killing on Elga. The pistol, I was sure, had been furnished by the man in the Ford. No problem for him; he'd probably brought home a small arsenal from his hitch in TUSLOG.

I crossed the intersection, wound over a hilly road, and came back on 101 South. The Sunday night traffic was fairly heavy with weekenders returning from Lake Tahoe, Russian River, Clear Lake, and my speedometer stayed at about forty. Elga was as stiff and silent as an armed sentry. I was too busy thinking to speak.

I tried to put it together. Elga must have enlisted Chris's confederate to steal the bonds, maybe offering him the big end of the split. The T-Bird had been left at the heliport for a double purpose: It was evidence that she'd caught an outbound flight, making us drop our guard, and, more crucial, it was also a ploy to draw us away from the house.

Probably they'd hoped all three of us would go, but they could at least count on two, one to drive the Volks, the other to drive the T-Bird. Most likely, they'd figured on mother, because she was the T-Bird's owner, and Paul, simply because accompanying her would seem to them like a man's job. In that case, they'd have tied and gagged me (Elga maybe clouting me over the head in memory of her dead lover) and the man would simply open the safe with burglar tools or nitro. Or maybe he could do it by touch and by ear. That way, if I'd been upstairs, I might not even know they'd been and gone.

But then they saw me instead of mother with Paul and must have quickly decided to change strategy. Why not have Elga snatch me as hostage? Then the man could simply stroll into the house, break the news to mother, and she'd instantly open the safe herself and surrender the bonds. It was even neater than the first plan, except that a charge of kidnapping would be added to armed robbery. But, of course, they were sure they'd get away with it. So was I.

Right now the man could be wheeling toward the house where mother lay on her bed calmly reading a book. I started to feel sick. Suppose she heard a noise downstairs and somehow knew it wasn't Paul or me. Would she grab the bedside phone, call the police, and holler bloody murder? If she did, the bastard might pulp her after he'd dragged her down to get the bonds.

"Pay attention to your driving, Miss Ridgway."

The Volks had swerved across the white line. I gripped the wheel hard, leaned forward, and tried to concentrate on the road. But my thoughts were now with the tall blond guy I'd left, and my mind kept repeating to the rhythm of the tires, *Paul, Paul, please hurry home!*

We passed the turnoff to Belvedere, crossed Richardson Bay, and began climbing the grade that descended to the Golden Gate Bridge. Nearing the crest, Elga ordered me to take the next off-ramp, then directed me along narrow blacktop roads that circled and rose through dense woods.

"There is a driveway just ahead. Turn in there."

The headlights picked out a white concrete strip next to a sign marked PRIVATE PROPERTY. I drove up in low gear, hearing tree limbs brush the top of the car. We reached a flat area where the concrete was cracked and darkly stained. Off to the right, almost hidden in a grove of redwoods, stood a small cottage. The glow of a lamp showed through a curtained window.

"Stop. Turn off the engine and the lights and get out."

She was standing beside the hood pointing the gun when I stepped out. My legs buckled, then straightened. As she marched me ahead of her to the front door, I heard only the blood drumming in my ears. By now, the man in the Ford could be at the Belvedere house, might even have entered.

Elga had me stand aside while she unlocked the door. It opened on a small living room furnished in cushioned maple, a couple of worn hooked rugs, and a few dusty prints on the wood walls. Beyond were a small kitchen and a bedroom, their doors half open. She took my keys to the Volks, pocketed them, and sat me under a lit floor lamp. Pulling up a rung-backed chair, she placed it between me and the front door and perched on the edge. Her dark glasses had been removed and the blue pupils of her eyes looked as big as poker chips. She kept on the funky hat and the suede jacket. The pistol was aimed at my navel.

I looked around the room, my eyes stopping on a long-corded telephone sitting on the floor just back of Elga. She followed my gaze. Her lips curled in a smile.

"I hope you are not so stupid as to think you can be rescued. You are quite helpless."

"Where are we?"

She shook her head, then shrugged. "I will tell you this. We are in a guest cottage. The main house no longer exists. It was destroyed by fire many months ago. The owners are abroad. We are quite isolated. So you see, it would be useless to hope that anyone will come here."

Chris had probably rented it even before coming to the Belvedere house. "Then this is where you shacked up with the Colonel, where you planned it all."

Her eyes bulged and her cheeks whitened.

"But now you've got a new partner."

She stared at me.

"I saw him tonight, driving that Ford heap. He was headed for my mother's house. I saw him once before, at the airport, meeting your Colonel."

She exploded a shrill laugh, quickly cut off. "Why do you tell me this? You think it will make a difference? The result will be the same as if the Colonel had lived."

"The creep you've got now looks like a real con artist. How do you know you can trust him? Why should he deal you in? He'll get the bonds and fly away while you're still sitting here."

She looked past me toward the bedroom. I turned my head quickly and saw through the half-open door two big suitcases lying flat on the bed. When I turned back, Elga was standing.

"Your tactic is a very old one, Miss Ridgway. Still . . ." She waved her gun toward the bedroom. "Go and stand outside that door."

I obeyed. She circled around me and entered the bedroom. Her eyes and the gun were on me as she unsnapped one of the suitcases. She lifted the lid a few inches, darted a glance inside, then closed it. The opening was facing away from me, so I saw nothing. She unsnapped the second suitcase, which was at a slight angle to the other. As she opened and closed the lid, my eye caught a flash of green.

A riot started inside my head. I stopped it long enough to say, "What happens next?"

"We wait." She came forward, wearing a smug little smile. "For the telephone to ring."

Diane

TWENTY-ONE

JENNIFER'S CALL had obviously been incited by alarm for my safety. The implied reason for it—that Elga might try again for the bonds—seemed preposterous. After a failure marked by an inconceivable death and a ghastly aftermath, any rational thief should have considered herself spooked and given it up.

Still, it would be stupid to ignore Jennifer's theory—that Elga might persuade Chris's accomplice to join her in another attempt, presumably with him making a direct assault on the safe. I slid my feet off the bed, sat on the edge, and thought about it.

Surely anyone who believed himself capable of opening the safe would prefer stealth to confrontation, if only to avoid being identified later. If I remained upstairs, chances were he'd think I was either asleep or had left the house with Jennifer and Paul. He would then go about his business with a feeling of relative security, especially if Elga was posted outside as lookout.

What if he should open the safe and find it empty? His next

move would either be to call it quits or start ransacking the house. But before that, I would have had time to pick up my bedroom phone and quietly notify the police.

Ridiculous, of course, every bit of it. The only arrivals would be Jennifer and Paul, the only sound the familiar one of a casually opened door. Nevertheless, the back of my mind was rummaging about for a good place to transfer the bonds.

The study, I decided. In the lower drawer of the desk was a bolted-in strongbox made of thick steel. It would take the right tool and a lot of time to force it open, more time than I would need.

I got the key from the night table, went downstairs, and made the switch.

Back in my room, I changed to a nightgown and a white silk robe. I was putting on slippers when I thought I heard a noise downstairs. Like a door softly opening and closing. My heart gave a pump. Quickly I glanced at my watch, and felt a flood of relief. Jennifer, of course; it was just about the time I had expected her.

I half ran to the stair landing, then stopped. Odd that I hadn't heard her Volks come in; usually its cough and rattle echoed through the walls of the garage. But perhaps after cresting the driveway, she had turned off the engine and coasted in, thinking I might be asleep. Yes, it must be Jennifer. All that foolishness with the bonds had made me paranoid.

I started down the stairs, but stopped again where they curved and faced the entrance hall. Jennifer was not in sight. Probably in the kitchen for a cup of coffee while she waited for Paul.

I continued down, walked toward the rear of the house, and opened the kitchen door. Darkness. I clutched the collar of my robe and flipped the light switch. The fluorescent glare was blinding after the dimly lit entrance hall and the darkness of the corridor. But it illuminated nobody.

Of course, nobody. The noise I had heard must have come from outside—a squirrel skittering up a tree, or a breeze playing tricks in the pine branches; sounds so commonplace they usually went unnoticed.

I snapped off the lights and went back to the entrance hall. Both the library and living room doors were closed, as they had been when I first went upstairs. I peeked into the library and saw only the goggling fish. The living room, too, revealed nothing unusual. But a mental picture of the horror that had exploded there sent me bounding up to my bedroom.

I stood by the phone, staring down at it, feeling a quaking unease. What was keeping Jennifer? Was it or was it not an opening door I had heard? Suddenly my whole body stiffened.

A door. Certainly it could have been a door. None of us had thought to take back Elga's house key!

I flopped to the bed, struggling for control, telling myself that I was yielding to a neurotic, childish fear. It did no good. I must call the police. I would simply say I had heard a prowler. If I was wrong, I would suffer nothing more than embarrassment.

My personal address book was in the night table, but not the county directory. I eased up the phone, poised my finger to dial the operator for the number, and heard a slightly accented voice say in my ear, "Miss Ridgway claims she does not know where they are. Naturally, she is lying. Perhaps because they are hidden in her mother's bedroom."

The phone seemed to jump from my hand. I fumbled with it, got it back to my ear. The line was dead. Then the dial tone, like an eerie signal from another planet.

Elga's voice.

From somewhere outside the house. Talking to someone *inside* the house.

Elga was holding Jennifer captive.

The police. Call them *now!*

I had spun the dial halfway when my finger froze. No! If I involved the police, Jennifer might be harmed.

I hung up the phone.

". . . hidden in her mother's bedroom."

Oh, my God!

I crept to the door, glanced down the hall, hesitated, then dashed to the end: Jennifer's old room, not occupied in the two years she had been away. I darted in, gently closed the door, and stood in the pitch dark, trembling, listening. And thinking.

If I gave myself up, handed over the bonds, would they free Jennifer? Something told me no. The man downstairs was a hardened criminal, presumably vicious and ruthless. (I recalled Jennifer's description of him.) He probably had a record. If he knew I could identify him, he'd kill me without thinking twice.

My only hope was escape. Then I could somehow arrange with Elga to ransom Jennifer. Elga might trust me not to inform the police because that would involve Jennifer with the shooting of Chris.

And Paul! He should soon be home. If I could hold out until then, he might overpower the intruder, force him to order Jennifer's release.

What phone had the man called from? Surely not from the one in the room Jennifer now used. That left the living room, the library, the den, the kitchen. Logic said the library; he could have concealed himself when I opened the door. Apparently he had got into the safe, seen that the bonds were missing, perhaps searched the bookshelves, then phoned Elga.

I opened the door a crack. Footsteps whispered on the stairs, ascended, then stopped abruptly. He had reached the carpeted hall. A long, quivering silence. My mind counted out the seconds. He must be at the open door to my bedroom, staring at the bed. The lamps were on and he would know instantly that I was not there. More seconds. Now the bathroom. My hand was pressed to my cheek and I could hear the ticking of my watch. It seemed to tick for an eternity. He must be searching the room.

Then I heard the slither of his feet on the hall carpet. Coming my way. I shut the door, turning the knob slowly to prevent the click. Heart beating wildly, I crossed to the front window, gazed down, measured the distance, and recoiled. A broad flagstone walkway reached from the house to the macadam driveway. It could be a death leap. I crept back to the door and braced my shoulder against it, aware of the futility of the gesture.

The footsteps had stopped. I guessed he had entered Paul's or Jennifer's room. A quick snapping noise told me it was the latter. I threw a hand over my nose and mouth to hush my breathing. Ear pressed to the door, I heard the floor creak as he reentered the hall. Then the brush of leather soles as he descended the stairs.

I opened the door, peeked down the hall, and scurried to Jennifer's room. Behind the night table, I found what I had expected: the phone cord had been yanked from the wall.

I practically shook myself to my own room. Drawing the phone cord from behind the table, I eyed the splayed, unattached end as if it were a dead snake. The upper floor was cut off from the world outside.

Right now he was making the rounds, ripping wires from the walls. I stepped into the hall—and was staggered by the shriek of a solitary phone downstairs.

Apparently he had saved one for his own use. He would need it to communicate with Elga. But why would *she* be calling him? Jennifer couldn't have revealed the whereabouts of the bonds because she didn't know. A wrong number? Too coincidental.

Suddenly I gasped and felt myself sway.

It could only have been Paul. Probably calling to say he had been delayed. (He would have shared Jennifer's anxiety.) Elga's accomplice would not have spoken first. I imagined Paul repeating his hello, voice rising in frustration, demanding to know if something was wrong. Getting no reply, hearing a click, calling back . . . but getting a busy signal because the phone would have been left off the hook!

Now the thief would know that Paul suspected his presence and would rush to the house, perhaps first phoning the police. Time had run out for him. And so had caution. If he was to get the bonds, he must quickly get *me*. No matter that his face would be etched on my mind. The image could be destroyed by a bullet.

My bones seemed to rattle against the wall as my eyes rolled frantically about for some means of escape. They focused on the door to a linen closet a few paces away and opposite me. I hesitated, terrified at the thought of becoming a mouse in a trap.

I heard him start up the stairs.

A reflex sent me leaping to the closet. Every muscle tensed, I willed myself to turn the knob slowly, slide in like a shadow, close the door as if it might explode. Blackness, as though I stood at the center of the earth. I took an enormous breath, held it, and pasted my ear to the door.

In a moment, his feet glided warily by. He was again in my bedroom. I had to take a chance, *had* to; not for another second could I stay in this claustrophobic prison. I turned the knob and admitted a splinter of light. Squinting through the crack, I could see a fraction of my open bedroom door. The back of one shoulder came into view. It moved away, toward my walk-in closet. I slipped out and scurried silently to the stairs.

I reached the curve overlooking the entrance hall, and beyond it, the front door. If I could get through that door without being heard, if I could run down the driveway to the road, if I could hail a passing car . . .

I virtually slid down the remaining stairs, whisked across the entrance hall, grasped the brass knob, turned it, pulled. The door sprang open a foot, erupting a ratcheting sound that tore through my ears. *What . . .*

The chain lock! Probably fastened the moment he was inside. I slammed the door, fumbled with the chain, then left it as I heard the race and pound of feet.

Instinctively I flung out a hand and switched off the lights, thinking to elude him in the dark. For an instant the blackness was as absolute as in the closet. Then it thinned as my eyes absorbed the light filtering down from above the stairs. By then, I was dashing toward the rear of the house, pursued by a man who had abandoned all stealth.

The lanai! The door to the terrace! And off to the side, the thick dark woods! If I could reach them, I could hide, eventually make my way to the road. Behind me, I heard him sprint across the entrance hall.

Through the lanai to the glass wall. I snapped a lever, rolled back the door—and knew I couldn't make it. He would catch me before I reached the first tree. I left the door open—a diversion—and veered off to the right and through an archway that led to the hall running past the kitchen and the den.

The den! The phone that had rung! The door was open and I skipped inside. I heard a staccato buzzing sound and even in the darkness could see the receiver lying on the desk.

I seized it with one hand and with the other pressed down the crossbar. Releasing it, I got a dial tone. But overwhelming it was the hammering of approaching feet. The open lanai door had diverted him for only a few moments. The den with its functioning phone would be the next place he'd look. I cradled the receiver, ran out, and sped back to the entrance hall. Perhaps the library. The door could be locked from inside and I could break out through a side window.

I got to the door, opened it, whirled to slam it shut, and the huge slab of solid oak crashed into me. I reeled back, spun around, caught a flashing glimpse of an upraised hand, and thudded to the floor.

I lay face down, gasping for air, smelling the dusty wool of the carpet. A whimper broke from my throat. I gulped it down. Painfully I rose to my feet, to surrender at last to the dark figure behind me.

"I'd hoped to avoid this," he said.

My body gave a convulsive shake. Stupefied, I turned around. I knew then why he had hoped to remain invisible, and why he had planned to confront me with Jennifer's kidnapping only as a last resort.

All life seemed to drain away as I stared transfixed into the sardonic face of the man I had married.

"Colonel Christopher Warren," he said. "Come to claim what I so carelessly left behind."

I fainted.

Jennifer

TWENTY-TWO

THERE WAS NO DOUBT about it. What I had glimpsed in that suitcase was cash. Getaway money? A few thousand dollars, say? If that was all, why had Elga been so anxious to check the suitcases—*both* of them?

That's when the phone rang and I nearly left my skin.

"Yes?" Elga said. She held the receiver in her left hand; the other pointed the pistol. A double line formed between her eyes as she listened. "Perhaps we should be content," she said. Her tone was cautious, as though she was afraid of a hassle.

Apparently that's what she got. The voice that growled back spoke only a few words (unclear to me) but they made the receiver jump from her ear. "Yes, yes," she said (humbly, I thought). "Hold on one moment."

She lowered the phone and glared at me. "Where are the bonds?"

It seemed like a dumb question. "I don't know."

Her mouth tightened. "The safe has been opened. The bonds are not there. Now you will tell me."

So mother must have finally worried about a break-in and moved them. "I don't *know!*" I said, this time hitting it hard.

She said into the mouthpiece, "Miss Ridgway claims she does not know where they are. Naturally, she is lying. Perhaps because they are hidden in her mother's bedroom."

There was a short answer and a click. Elga hung up.

My heart flipped. So now he would go up to her bedroom. I cringed from the thought of mother at the mercy of that cold-fish character I'd seen with Chris. But force, I kept telling myself, wouldn't be necessary. Once mother knew I'd been kidnapped, she'd surrender the bonds and that would be that. Costly but not fatal.

But would they stop there? Would they risk being tracked down, caught, and identified? Why not silence us for keeps? Jesus!

Our only hope was Paul. Where was he now? On his way to the T-Bird? Still waiting for that sergeant? Dammit, why hadn't we turned back before reaching the police station? But maybe he'd get to the house in time. He would. He must. Not seeing the Volks, he'd instantly recall our fears about Elga and prepare for the worst. He'd enter the house like the burglar before him and take the bastard before he could turn around.

Feeling a spark of optimism, I sank back in the chair.

I tried to concentrate again on the suitcases, but Elga's voice kept nagging at my mind. I started to replay her end of the conversation, not getting beyond her first words. "Perhaps we should be content," she had said. Content with what? The only possible answer was money.

Now I was sure of it—the two suitcases were stacked with the stuff. But the money could only have come from cashing in the bond certificates. And those were still in the house.

Fakes! The word popped on my brain like a movie title. And suddenly I knew what Elga's new partner had brought Chris that day at the airport. Not forged passports, visas, etc., but duplicates of mother's bond certificates. Those, the phonies, were the ones that had been locked in her safe, making her feel secure, while the others, the real certificates, had been cashed in by Chris.

So he must have known the safe combination all along (easy; he just had to look over her shoulder a few times) and had probably made color photos of the originals.

But why would the counterfeiter want the phony certificates back? To avoid being incriminated later? I sat up.

Those weren't what he wanted. He was after the *genuine* certificates mother had hidden in the coat, the ones she'd gotten from Paul the night before the shooting. A quarter of a million dollars worth. They'd have been faked too if Paul hadn't gotten the scoop on Chris from his New York contacts. Probably Elga and company hoped to cash them before word got out they were hot, or at least fence them.

I looked at Elga. Her legs were crossed and the hand with the pistol rested on her thigh. Her eyes were on me but seemed unfocused, and her head was slightly tilted. She was waiting for the phone to ring again, for her partner to announce mission accomplished. I prayed that Paul had already cancelled that call.

Suddenly it seemed incredible that Elga, with three-quarters of a million dollars stashed safely in the bedroom, could be so greedy as to risk everything in order to get it all. In fact, it was just plain crazy, because she wouldn't get it all. She'd have to split with her accomplice. For God sake, she'd get a lot less than what she already had! Then *why?*

Had she been forced into it?

Only one man could have done that. Only one with the greed

and the pride and the arrogance and the recklessness: *"The objective was one million dollars, Elga. I wasn't trained to accept partial victories."*

But that man was buried under a load of sand.

I closed my eyes and saw Paul digging. I saw him drop the drape-wrapped body into the grave. I saw him on his knees pushing back the sand. I saw Elga grab the shovel and bash his head.

She'd *had* to knock him out! Not just to give her more time to escape, but to keep Chris from *suffocating!*

And the resurrected Chris had filled in the grave so that Paul—and mother and I—would never question his death.

A hoax, every bit of it. The bullets I'd shot had been blanks. Nothing else explained why Elga was here in this room instead of far away with a fortune she wouldn't have to share with anybody.

I felt like Madame Curie discovering radium. But I knew that the whole theory would fall apart if those suitcases weren't loaded with cash. I hitched forward on the cushion.

Elga raised the gun from her thigh and her eyes sharpened on me.

"Elga, I know what's in those suitcases."

She blinked and the gun wavered slightly. "How brilliant of you. No doubt you can describe each piece of clothing."

"All green. But not clothing. Money. Three-quarters of a million dollars."

She licked her lips. A film seemed to slide across her eyes. "You are talking nonsense."

"I know about the fake certificates."

She twitched and her face turned pinker.

"And that man in the Ford—your partner—I was wrong about him. It was Colonel Warren."

Her mouth worked, then settled into a disdainful smile. "It does not matter now *what* you know."

But it did, I suddenly thought. What I knew, and what mother was probably finding out, would get us killed.

Diane

TWENTY-THREE

MY EYELIDS FLUTTERED. A hand seemed to be pulling on my head. I heard a clicking noise. Fumes rose to my nose. A glass was being forced between my teeth. I must have . . .

I looked up from where I lay on the carpet and nearly fainted again. The tip of a long nose was only a foot from my face. I gulped the brandy. The glass went away.

In a moment, lamps went on. My eyes listed from side to side. It was all a bizarre dream: I was lying on the operating table in a large amphitheater; the student observers, rigidly attentive, were staring at me with the bulging eyes of fish. The operation must be over because I felt weak and drugged.

I sat up and peered at the surgeon, now towering over me. The dream collapsed. Chris Warren was real. I started to shake.

"I assume you expected someone else," he said.

I opened my mouth to speak, couldn't, managed to nod.

"Get up."

I drew up my legs, pushed on the floor, and lurched to my feet. He made no move to help.

"Another brandy?"

Again I nodded.

The bottle was in his hand. He splashed amber liquid into the glass and handed it to me. I downed it, feeling no burning in my throat. He took the glass and set it with the bottle on an end table.

The brandy loosened my voice. "You and Elga—"

"Yes. A winning combination, although it was she who was supposed to fire the shots. Hitting me accidentally, of course. But Jennifer doing it made it even better. Your concern for her welfare gave Elga immunity from pursuit."

"Jennifer! Where is she?"

"She's with Elga. You don't really expect me to tell you where."

"Is she all right?"

"The last I heard, yes. Whether she continues to be all right depends on you." He stepped closer. "Where are the bonds?"

Somehow I had to stall him. Paul should be arriving any second. Or the police, if he had called them. But my mind was empty.

"Why not avoid violence, Diane? As for me, I'm not entirely averse to it. Both you and your daughter are badly in need of discipline." He reached out and grabbed my shoulders.

I had a sudden thought. "The bonds aren't here. I mailed them to the bank."

He scowled, removed his hands, stroked his chin. His face cleared. He said casually, "About a million dollars in negotiable securities. I'm sure you wouldn't trust them to our postal service without taking some precaution. I assume you sent them by registered mail."

I hesitated. "Yes."

"Then you have a receipt. Get it."

I shut my eyes to cover a trapped look. "I . . . I can't recall where . . ."

His hand slipped into his jacket pocket and reappeared holding a black gun. The German Luger. I saw it jerk in Jennifer's hand, saw Chris claw at his chest, blood spurting through his fingers. A lump of anger formed inside me at the brazenness of the hoax.

"I'm sure I don't need this," he said. "But the sight of it should refresh your memory."

Anger burst through me, producing an adrenal strength. Defiantly I said, "I threw the receipt out. I knew I'd get a card that the certificates had been delivered."

"Give it up, Diane. The post office is closed on Sunday." He waved the gun in a resigned gesture. "I've wasted enough time. Go into the den. There, I'm sure, we'll cure your amnesia."

I waited until he prodded me with the gun. Then, like a sleepwalker, I floated across the entrance hall, down the corridor and into the den. He snapped on the lamp. My eyes went instantly to the telephone. He took a stride to the desk, turned his back to the window and faced me.

"At the moment, Diane, I'd rather not hurt you." He placed a hand on the phone. "But I've no such compunctions about your daughter."

My lips closed on my teeth. I *wanted* him to call. I must know if Jennifer was safe.

Quickly he dialed a number. Even more quickly the call was answered.

"Elga? Unfortunately, I had to reveal myself. But it seems that my dear wife is reluctant to confide in me. I suggest you make things uncomfortable for Jennifer."

"You're bluffing," I said. "Jennifer's not there."

"Hold on, Elga." He said to me, "Perhaps you'd like to speak to her."

I nodded.

"Put Jennifer on, Elga. But if she starts to say one word of your whereabouts, break her jaw." He handed me the receiver.

I gripped it like the lifeline I felt it to be. There was a pause. Then:

"Mother?"

"Are you all right, Jennifer?"

"Yes. What about you?"

"He hasn't harmed me."

She burst out: *"They're going to kill us! After they get the bonds, they'll kill us!"*

Chris wrenched away the receiver. Apparently Elga had done the same: "That's enough. Elga, I'll call you back." He hung up.

I backed off, eyeing him as if he were a rattler poised to strike. "You . . . you *wouldn't!*"

He regarded me placidly. "Jennifer's a bit mixed up. There won't be any killing unless you refuse to give me the bonds. In that case, of course, Jennifer goes first."

He meant it; I knew it clear through to my marrow.

"They're in that desk. In the strongbox. I'm sure you have the key."

He smiled at me. "Thoughtful of you to make it so convenient." He dug into his pocket, brought out a ring of keys, and studied them. I glanced at the gun. It pointed straight and steady at the pulsing hollow in my throat.

He selected a key, opened the lower drawer, and unlocked the green steel box. His eyes glittered as he took out the bonds. The latest certificates were still in the manila envelope that had once been hidden in my coat. Ignoring the others, he opened the envelope. He drew out the bonds, unfolded them, and smoothed them out on the desk blotter. A quarter of a million dollars.

"Yes, I'd say they're all here."

He returned them to the envelope and pocketed it. The rest of the certificates—representing three times as much as the others—remained on the desk. He considered them for a moment, then gave a little shrug. Without bothering to check the amounts, he folded them and jammed them in next to the envelope.

I looked at him, puzzled and uncertain. "You've got what you want. Now tell Elga to release Jennifer."

He sneered at me as if I'd said something foolish. "And have her running to the police? You surprise me, Diane."

"She wouldn't. You could keep me here until she's brought home. Then you could tie us up. You'd have plenty of time to get away."

"And after you got *un*tied?"

I was silent. Even an idiot would know I'd summon the police.

"No, Diane, I'm afraid your daughter won't be coming to you. Instead, you'll go to *her*."

Now it was all too clear. We would be murdered, our bodies buried, perhaps never to be found. How often I had read in the papers of campers stumbling upon the skeletal remains of someone killed years before, sometimes even the teeth defying identification. Was it better to risk death by fighting it, or wait for it to come?

"I'll notify Elga to expect us," he said. "As well as the bonds."

With his left hand, he adjusted the certificates in his pocket. With his right, the gun hand, he started to dial. He used his forefinger . . . his *trigger* finger . . .

I sprang at him as he made the next spin of the dial. My hands were on the Luger, twisting it from his fingers. It broke loose, flipped to the floor between us. I pounced on it before he could move. My hand clutched the grip, my fingers found the trigger. A heavy foot stomped down on my knuckles. I heard the crunch.

Pain screamed up my arm. I lurched up and back, flinging out my crushed hand. It struck something—the lamp. I heard it crash to the floor. I gazed dazedly at the lopsided lampshade covering the still-burning bulb. We were in semidarkness. I tucked my throbbing hand under my arm and turned to him.

He had slammed down the receiver. His face was calm but his eyes were maniacal. The gun no longer pointed at me. He held it now by the barrel and was slowly raising it.

"I think I'd better put you to sleep," he said.

The gun started down, the butt streaking for my head. My eyes closed, then flashed open. He had stopped in midswing. His mouth fell wide open, emitting a tortured growl. His eyes crowded their sockets as if transfixed by a ghost. His body gave a grotesque heave and flopped forward.

A heart attack!

His chest had not hit the floor before I saw the thing sticking from his back. And as he hit, I glimpsed the shadowed figure behind him, arm outstretched and shaking.

Paul! He must have come in through the lanai, stopped in the kitchen for a knife . . .

"You dirty bastard," a familiar voice said.

Never before had I heard that voice speak in anger. Not Paul's. It was . . .

"John! Oh my God, *John!*"

I rushed to him, whimpering wildly, and buried my head against his shoulder. I felt his arm go around me, quivering across my back.

"It's all right now," he said softly. "It's all right."

I was unable to move. "How . . . what . . ."

"You gave me a key, remember? I said I'd be here to make breakfast. I decided to come tonight."

"Oh, thank God."

"I called from the bus station. The phone was picked up but no one answered. I dialed again and the operator reported it out of order. I took a taxi. Your cars were gone, so I just came in."

He pushed me gently aside and gazed with revulsion at the stricken figure on the floor. Chris was alive, chewing for air, legs thrashing against the desk. Blood oozed from around the hilt of the knife.

John went to him, bent down, and carefully withdrew the dripping blade. Only after he had righted the lamp did I really see it.

It was the short Japanese ceremonial sword that, together with the German Luger, I had been shown in Mendocino. A souvenir. Used for hara-kiri, Chris had said.

"It was there in the closet," John said. "I was outside the library when he ordered you into the den. It's fortunate I got in here first."

Chris now lay on his right side. His breath came in panting gasps. John stepped over to him and pointed the sword at his throat.

"John! No!"

"It won't be necessary. The one wound is enough. The brute will die if he's not attended to." He kneeled, grasped Chris's chin, turned it, and looked into his terrified eyes. "Tell us where Jennifer is. The address."

Chris licked his lips. He didn't speak.

"If you tell us, I'll call an ambulance. If you refuse, I'll let you lie there and bleed to death."

I cringed. The blood was soaking his jacket. The puncture

point appeared to be just to the inner side of his left shoulder blade.

We waited.

Chris moaned. His features in the lamplight were turning waxen. "Call the . . . ambulance."

"First tell us the address."

He told us, haltingly, in a thin, reedy voice.

John phoned the police. Just as he had done on that night so long ago. They said they would send an ambulance.

John had no sooner hung up than the phone rang.

"You answer it," he said. "If it's Jennifer's kidnaper, I'll put Colonel Warren on. I'm sure I can convince him to say the right things."

But it was Paul, calling from the heliport, where he'd finally reclaimed the T-Bird. He, too, had phoned earlier but had got a busy signal. Ironically, he had placed that call from the police station, where he'd been delayed.

After I had dumfounded him with the news and rung off, I heard a distant siren.

Jennifer

TWENTY-FOUR

It wasn't like any of those shootouts in the movies. As soon as the spotlights hit the cottage and the God-voice blasted through the bullhorn, Elga did exactly what she was told.

Without batting an eye, she got up, opened the door, threw out the pistol, and walked into the glare with her hands up. She didn't even glance back at me.

After she was driven away, the cops spent some time rapping with me, then wasted some more making a rough count of the money in the suitcases. By the time I got home, Paul and mother and John had only a couple of minutes to fuss over me before I was taken into the library to be interviewed by the boss detective. They'd already been through the drill.

Inspector George Jamison looked more like an accountant than a cop—bald head with a fringe of gray hair, tortoise-shell glasses that magnified sharp, inquisitive eyes, thin face, a gentle way of speaking. He pulled his chair up close to mine beside the fireplace, quickly told me all that he already knew, then gave me the floor. We were interrupted only twice, once when he got up to send a cop on an errand, and once when the cop came back.

Half an hour later, totally strung out, I went into the kitchen. Mother and Paul were alone at the dining table, John having gone someplace to unpack his bag. Paul got up and put his arms around me.

"There's nothing more to worry about, darling," he said.

My legs came unhinged and he helped me to the table, where I sat beside mother. She touched my hand, my shoulder, my knee, as if to make sure I was alive. Paul suggested brandy in my coffee and I nodded. After giving me a lot of affection, mother got up, saying, "I'm sure you two would like to be by yourselves. Anyway, I've got to get some sleep."

Paul gave me his small smile and I gave him back a big one. I had the feeling that we really hadn't been alone together since Hawaii.

Mother stopped at the door. "By the way," she said, trying to sound casual. "There's no reason at all why you two should continue to have separate rooms."

I said, "That's the only happy thing I've heard in days." I felt Paul's hand on my thigh. The brandy was beginning to work. I heard police cars driving away as mother walked out. "Let's have one more," I said to Paul. "This time in a brandy glass. We can take them up to my room."

"*Our* room."

"Yes, our room. You wait here, though, until I get into something indecent."

When I opened the bedroom door for him, I was in a shorty black nightgown. He picked me up, took me to a silk-covered armchair, and sat me on his lap, holding me close. We sipped our brandies.

"I can't stop thinking about it," I said.

"Something in particular?"

"The whole thing, right from the beginning. It's so damned far out. Here's a guy who spends weeks, maybe months, researching a woman. He sets up a terrific romantic meeting. He plays a little hard to get, which really breaks her down. They make it big together and he convinces her he doesn't want a penny of her money."

He kissed my cheek. "Let's forget it, at least for tonight."

I stroked his blond hair, feeling the slick Band-Aid. "Maybe it's better if I get it all out." I stood up. "Then he gets her to transfer a million bucks in stock to Harrison and Weeks—my father's old brokerage—where he's in a position to control it. And he gets her into bonds, nothing but bonds. Why? Because they're negotiable, just like dollars. Meanwhile he's fixed it with some counterfeiter from his old gang of thieves—in TUSLOG—"

"That's what we think anyway."

"Okay. Our evil genius then gets the phony certificates and lays them off on mother. That makes her believe everything's just dandy. Who'd ever think he was turning the realies into cash? Three-quarters of a million dollars worth. It was all in those suitcases the cops hauled away."

Paul smiled sympathetically. Let her rave, I guess he was thinking.

"They almost made it," I said. "That trumped-up shooting, the movie blood, Elga bargaining the bonds and the body for her freedom. God, I believed the whole schmeer. For the rest of their lives they'd never even have to look over their shoulders, they'd feel so safe."

"Eventually your mother would discover the certificates were counterfeit. In about six months, when she didn't get any interest."

"Sure, but she wouldn't do anything about it. She'd still think

I'd killed her husband. She'd shut up and take the loss, figuring she could afford it."

Paul got up, stretched, and sat down again. "All right, you've got it all out. Enough of the Machiavellian Colonel Warren for now."

"Colonel Warren? Yes, all the things I've said fit him perfectly, don't they?"

He looked at me curiously and set his glass on the floor.

"But they also fit *you*, Paul."

His face seemed to freeze.

I took a big gulp of brandy. "And it's *you* I've been talking about. You and me."

He wet his lips. "Jennifer, what in hell is going on in that mind of yours?"

So many things. Things I'd tried so hard not to believe when I was under the gun at the cottage . . .

Paul trailing me around Waikiki until he found a dramatic opportunity for a pickup. Renting a houseboat he knew was condemned, as a set-up for the move to mother's. Chris hiring him on the day they met, then creating some heroic references. My sudden thought that the bond certificates could so easily be counterfeited *before* Paul brought them home. The scene in the living room when Chris was still in charge; saying to me, "If it hadn't been for you, none of you would be in this position." Me thinking instantly that he knew I'd found out about his made-up job and that I'd seen him at the airport. How could he have known if Paul hadn't told him?

As for the shooting and the burial, I'd had to make a huge effort to shut that out of my mind. It was too much to think that Paul could have been part of that act. The other things, they'd just drifted through my head like dark, cloudy shapes that threatened me but never really struck.

But they joined together and struck like the whole sky had

fallen when I talked to Inspector Jamison. I didn't tell him my suspicions, except that the bond certificates had to be fakes, or how else account for all the cash in the suitcases? He hadn't gotten around to considering that, but when he did, it was like an earthquake hit him. After tugging at his chin and whipping off his glasses to stare into the fireplace, he went to the door and talked to a cop, who took off down the hall. When the cop came back and shook his head, it was all over for Paul.

No, not quite over. I still had to get him to admit it.

"*You* were the one who was assigned to shoot Chris," I said. "Then somehow you'd have lost the gun to Elga."

He reached down, picked up his brandy, and took a slug. I saw the same look in his eyes as when he was bargaining with Elga. "You've been through a shattering experience, Jennifer. You're not thinking straight. If I was tied into this, why wouldn't I just let Elga do the shooting?"

"Because your doing it would be more convincing. And it would keep you on the side of the angels. God knows, you'd worked hard to get there—telling me you suspected Chris, inventing those contacts in New York. The only time you leveled was when you came up with the results of that planted phone call." (The source of that had thrown me. Simple, the Inspector had told me. He could dial the operator and ask her to ring back, to check if the phone was working.) "I figure all that stuff about Colonel Warren and TUSLOG has to be true because you were *there*, like that counterfeiter was there—both of you top bananas in the Colonel's black-market ring."

His eyes flickered just enough to tell me I'd scored. But he shook his head as though enduring the rantings of a madwoman. Finally he said, "How in the name of God could anyone put together a story like this?"

"The T-Bird helped," I said.

"What does that mean?"

"You never reported it to the police."

"Oh, for God sake!" He said it as though he wanted only to hold me off, give himself time to think.

I gave him the time. "You *told* us you'd reported it. That was when mother and I were still upstairs sleeping. Then, in the late afternoon, you said you called the police and they said it was found. They were about to call, you said. That time, mother and I were out by the pool. Very convenient."

"You don't really believe that. Hell, you drove me up there. I signed the release."

(Jamison had said, "Only the owner can sign the release. That's regulations." But I couldn't let Paul know the Inspector was on to him.)

"That was to get me out of the house. You wanted mother too, but not inside the station. So you assured her that you could handle it. You were setting it up so that Chris could go for the bonds he'd missed and not be seen."

"You're out of your head!"

"But if one of us stayed home, you and your partners were ready. Elga would kidnap—but I don't have to go into that."

"Nor anything else."

"One last thing, Paul."

"What?"

"That zap on the head with the shovel."

His body seemed to tighten. "You're not insane enough to think *that* was a put-up job! Do you think I'd risk a skull fracture simply to go along with the Colonel?"

"There wasn't any risk."

"What do you mean? Good Christ, you saw the blood!"

"The same kind of blood you so eagerly scrubbed from the living room carpet. *Manufactured* blood."

"That's enough! Goddamn it—"

"It's easy to prove."

He looked at me.

"Take off the Band-Aid and let me see your scalp."

"The hell I will!"

"If you don't, I'll have to ask the Inspector to do it."

He raised his glass to his lips, and gave me a long thoughtful look over the rim.

"He's still got a couple of men downstairs," I said. "They're going over the den for exhibits."

Suddenly his shoulders sagged and he lowered the glass without drinking. He said quietly, "Did you tell the Inspector your suspicions about the T-Bird?"

I'd been waiting for the question. "It didn't hit me until I'd left you downstairs. Then *pow*. But he'll learn it soon enough."

He eased out a breath. "And the other things?"

"Same thing. I was coming up here when it started flying at me all at once."

He took a step forward. "Why not keep this between the two of us, Jennifer?" Now his tone was almost plaintive.

I didn't move. "Then you admit it?"

He nodded sadly. "Yes, I admit it, all of it." He reached out a hand, then let it drop to his side. "But there are a few things you should understand."

"I'm listening."

He retreated to the chair and sat down. "For one thing, I was vulnerable as hell when the Colonel made me his proposition. There'd been a woman, a married woman, one of my clients in New York. The details aren't important. But her husband, a very influential man, got on to us. He threatened to have me blacklisted by every brokerage house in New York unless I got out of town. I was pretty desperate. As desperate as the Colonel. He was practically broke and couldn't land a decent job because of what had happened in Turkey. That talk about the money he'd made in the market was only talk. All he had invested with me out here was a few thousand. Enough to get him on the books." He gave me a direct, honest look. "But I don't want you to compare me with him. He's a cold-blooded, almost pathological crook, while I'm"—that wisp of a smile—"simply an opportunist."

"What about the short, fat guy. Who is he?"

"I won't give you his name. But it doesn't matter. He's nothing more than a small-time forger. The Colonel took him on in Turkey when he was making funny money. His payoff was five thousand dollars." He paused and gazed at his brandy, now almost gone, then went on:

"The second thing is something I'm sure you won't believe, but I've got to say it. Granted I got on to you in Hawaii for purely mercenary reasons. A pincer movement, the Colonel called it—one thrown in against the mother, the other against the daughter. Everything went according to plan. Then something happened that neither of us anticipated." He looked at me and waited.

"Which was?"

"The second pincer fell in love with the daughter."

My heart didn't skip a beat. "You were right. I don't believe you."

He shrugged. "I don't blame you. Anyway, I did make a practical gesture in that direction. Those bonds—the good ones worth a quarter of a million—I could have given those directly to Chris. I didn't. I gave them to your mother."

"Why not? You thought she'd put them right in the safe where Chris could pick them up before he was, as we say, killed. The way I see it, Elga was to take those and leave the phonies as part of the bargain for ditching the body. But they were in mother's coat."

He looked disconcerted. "You'll remember I backed up your mother when she denied having them."

"You had to. If you hadn't, we'd have known you were on their side."

He waved a hand helplessly. "You're too much, Jennifer. But my God, if you could have heard how I argued with the Colonel against coming back for those bonds. But no, this was his only chance, he said, the bonds would be banked come Monday morning, and what's more there'd be a private detective snooping around. The man, I think, is crazy."

"It makes no difference now." I started for the door.

"Doesn't it?" He got up and moved toward me. "Jennifer, why hook me into this? Damn it, I love you. We can go away together. Tomorrow."

"You mean before your friends start talking? Now *you* sound crazy."

He looked at me appealingly and I was struck again by what a beautiful man he was. "Jennifer, why should you care about this thing happening to your mother? You don't really give a damn about her. In fact, you said you hated her. All right, I helped you even things up."

I would never have gone with him. But I wondered for a moment if I would have kept my mouth shut to the Inspector if I hadn't been drawn close to mother by the truth of my father's death. Paul would then have had time to escape. It was a question I couldn't answer.

I opened the door. Inspector Jamison stood there, mother behind him.

"We taped it all," Jamison said. He moved from the door and was replaced by a uniformed policeman. At the bed, Jamison kneeled and reached for the bug planted when Paul and I had been in the kitchen.

I looked at Paul. His expression changed slowly from consternation to loathing. Suddenly I had the feeling that submerged inside him was a hatred of all women, festering since his childhood in that household of witches.

He finished off his brandy and said to me, "Well, I tried."

I turned my back on him and went to my mother.